Annie Shaw bursts from the cedars, eyes blood-red and popping, her mouth open impossibly and hideously wide. She howls like a banshee, her legs wobbly, her arms flung outward as she skids down the knoll. Her hair is wild, crusted with leaves and sticks and dried mucus that glints in the sunlight.

Kathy screams, scrambles backward, trips over a large stone, and falls into the creek. She lands hard, falls, striking her head on a submerged log. She bites the inside of her cheek, tearing out a chunk of flesh in a bright flash of pain. Stars shatter her vision, and it draws in on itself, dark as midnight. She gasps, comes up choking on the gritty water she's sucked in, spitting blood. Her vision opens again to reveal her mother, Annie, clambering into the creek, head wobbling, tongue lolling, hands opening and closing like claws.

"Mom!" Kathy scoots back in the water, her hands up, waving her mother away. "Oh, my God! Dad!"

DESPER HOLLOW

ELIZABETH MASSIE

1
Granny Mustard

There is a thick, putrid stench surrounding her, a rancid mixture of decay, charred pinewood, soaked dirt, and alcohol. She can't turn her head to find the source of the smells because something heavy and jagged is on top of her, pressing her down, pinning her in place, forcing her eyes to remain closed. Not that she really gives a shit one way or other. Her thoughts aren't so much thoughts anymore but foggy, vague images that bleed in and out of her brain like custard out a cracked pot, dotted with sparks of light that hurt like nails driven into the back of her eyes.

If she were as she once was, her synapses would have connected those smells to her daily life. Granny Mustard always burned pinewood in her fireplace for heat and light, never having had electricity in her cabin. And the stink of decay was an ever-present companion in the mountains. Raccoons, possums, squirrels, chipmunks, voles, and all other form of wild critter often crawled up under her cabin porch to die, and one dead carcass stunk as bad as another. And then the odor of wet earth, of course—it rains hard as a miner's jackhammer in the Appalachian Mountains when the sky gets a wild hair and decides to cut loose on those below.

The scent of alcohol, now that would have been a good smell. Granny is—was—the best moonshiner in the area spanning the town of Beaver Dam up to Black Rock Ridge and clear over to Desper Hollow, a near fifteen-square-mile area. She has been for the last seventy-some years.

Raising corn and barley, or stealing corn and barley, then

adding her own special ingredients—sometimes a few drops of apple or pear squeezings, sometimes a bit of squirrel blood or deer urine. Nobody could beat Granny's shine, and folks didn't dare try to undersell in her territory, or her grandsons would beat the life out of them. Just the way it was. Suck it up, if you don't like it. Or move. Either one.

But right now, in this strange and shadowed moment, the smells that are independently familiar and benign are woven together into something disturbing and desperate. Pressing down on top of her, closing in beside her and beneath her.

But the anxiety is not only around her, it is within her, too. Granny's own physical desperation is acute. She is hungry.

Intensely, insatiably hungry.

Her shoulders twitch and hunch; her hips twist and writhe. But she can't move whatever it is that has her trapped.

Hungry.

So hungry it feels as if her stomach is coming out through her chest in search of food. With effort she slides one hand up from her hip toward her abdomen, and her pattering fingers discover that her stomach is, indeed, coming up through her chest. It is wet, sloppy, slippery, and gritty with soot.

But that doesn't matter. What does matter is the hunger. It's hot and demanding. She has to eat.

She must eat now.

NOW.

She tries again to get up. No luck. She attempts to roll, to wriggle, to drag herself out from under the heavy pile; her heels drive into the earth but can't get enough purchase to do any good.

Her mouth flops open to scream; all that comes out is a strangled, hissing sound. She struggles again, her shoulders bucking against the weight of the pile on top of her. The ball in the left shoulder socket pops and goes loose. Doesn't hurt, though.

What hurts is the hunger.

What chews her up is the craving.

She has to get out to eat.

And when she does, she's going to eat whatever she finds. She's going to devour the first warm, living thing she encounters.

2
Bobby Boo Anderson

B obby doesn't like to be told what to do. You tell him not to do something, he will. You tell him to do something, he won't. He's his own man, he tells everybody, even though he has never held a job (never tried to, never wanted to, never really needed to) and lives with his Great Aunt Dottie who pays all the bills with her Social Security check and with money she makes selling quilts down at the antique store in Beaver Dam.

Though now the homemade quilt cash cow is out the window with the town gone, Bobby thinks sourly.

At thirty-four, Bobby has his routine pretty much down pat—waking up, scratching himself, rolling into the kitchen to eat whatever catches his fancy (usually Aunt Dottie's biscuits and crabapple jelly), pumping his weights for a few minutes, then sitting on the ratty sofa on the porch and looking out at the dirt road in front of the cabin, yelling at whoever happens to pass by, telling them to slow down, speed up, quit looking at him, or to look at him when he's talking to them.

He imagines himself the star of a movie, a story about a heroic loner who lives on the mountaintop and who has supernatural powers that he keeps under wraps until he is needed. To rescue the half-naked girl who was chased up a tree by a two-ton black bear. To pick up the derailed coal train and put it back on its tracks and then assist the half-naked girl who was thrown off the train, out of her clothes, and into the briars below. To fight an inbred, meth-making family—nine burly brothers and a dad and a goat-shit crazy grandpa tossed in for good measure—to stop them from trying to take over the forested land around them, land where a poor crippled farmer lives with his deaf dog and his beautiful blind daughter who, because she can't see, never dresses herself properly or completely.

Bobby loves his daydreams. Maybe, he thinks, he should go to Hollywood and tell them his movie ideas and they can make them and let him star in them. How great would that be? The folks back home would be so jealous they'd spit nails.

Today, however, it's about all he can accomplish to sit on the porch in the chair and throw pebbles and insults at the occasional passersby. The radio batteries have died, so there isn't any music or preachers to listen to.

The TV in the cabin can't pick up anything worth shit until nighttime.

Bobby Boo reaches inside the front of his pants, digs around against an itch, and then lets out a loud, rubbery breath. He glances up at the puffs of white clouds against the pale blue sky. There are some pockets of soot still drifting about on the breeze.

The air stinks of the recent fire.

And he starts thinking.

Two nights ago, Beaver Dam burned to the ground. Beaver Dam was a small, unincorporated mining town until 14-year-old Suze Mustard took a pack of matches and can of gasoline and lit every one of the ten businesses along Main Street, sending them up to heaven in a ball of fiery glory. Everybody in the Beaver Dam Motel burned to death—the owner Paul Via, his wife Mindy, and all six customers, two from town and the rest tourists from somewhere in Pennsylvania (their car's license plate was still readable in spite of the damage to the vehicle.) Since Suze set the fire at night, no one died in the town's other businesses. However, some flames leapt back from Main Street and onto the trailers and cabins one block over, the section jokingly called Beaver Dam's "residential section." Thirteen more people died there, sixteen homes destroyed. In a matter of five hours Beaver Dam went from mining town to ghost town.

The sheriff's department has the town cordoned off since it's considered a crime scene even though they know Suze Mustard did it. Several whose homes didn't burn or were left standing but fouled by smoke have moved out and in with cousins a little farther north or south to get away from the stink. Others packed their trucks with their belongings and hauled them off to the tiny town called Tiptop, while some took their stuff all the way down to the county seat of Tazewell.

Deputy Sheriff Buddy Floyd caught Suze, who was crazy and wild-eyed and hiding in a tree beside the gate to the Beaver Dam Mines on the south side of town. She was pretty well scorched herself, hair singed off one side of her head and her face and arms a bright, blistery red. Then somehow and for some reason she'd gone and lopped off her left hand, a ragged poor job, Floyd had said. Suze died on the way to the hospital in Tazewell, a trip of nineteen miles, bleeding and thrashing and screaming about Granny Mustard and about setting the town on fire and about severed chicken heads crawling around on a kitchen floor.

Word of the inferno spread from Beaver Dam as fast as the smoke did, up to the isolated cabins and trailers and houses along Black Rock Ridge. Surely a young girl wouldn't have decided to burn down a town all on her own. What reason would she have had? Some wondered if the owners of the Beaver Dam Mines had put her up to it, hoping to scare the town's miners who had been reporting safety shortcuts to the authorities.

Others suspected that the owners of the financially wobbly Waffle House gave Suze Mustard a pocket full of cash to get rid of the restaurant so they could collect insurance, though that seemed far-fetched. Suze burned the whole town, not just the restaurant. And why pay a kid when there were certainly needy adults who would have been more careful with their target.

Still others just thought that for some reason, Suze had simply lost her mind. That made the most sense, really. The Mustard family was a big family. They lived in a compound of trailers and cabins on Black Rock Ridge, fiercely protective of their own, especially Granny Mustard, the ancient family matriarch who had a profitable and illegal moonshine business. The Mustards were suspicious and vicious, rarely having anything to do with outsiders except when they came into Beaver Dam for batteries or sugar or blue jeans at the Dollar General, or, in the case of Suze's mama, Penny, making a little money on the side peddling her personal, intimate wares to miners at the Beaver Dam Motel.

So it wouldn't be beyond imagination to think Suze Mustard just lost it and decided it would be fun to set the whole damn place on fire just to see it go and then cut her hand off just to see that go, too. Crazy was crazy.

Bobby Boo Anderson sits on the porch of his aunt's house and thinks about all these things. He thinks of it as the beginning of a movie—insane teenager torches an Appalachian mining town, killing dozens. He rewinds the scenario in his mind to this: insane teenager torches an Appalachian mining town, but before anyone dies, the heroic loner with superpowers races to the rescue. With one gigantic breath he blows out the flaming buildings like a giant blowing out candles on a birthday cake. He ties up the scratching, screaming teen so the sheriff can arrest her and then he checks all the motel rooms to make sure everyone is safe. He finds a half-naked young woman in the bathroom of room 6, hiding in the tub, shaking and terrified. He comforts her as only the heroic loner can.

Oh, yeah.

He licks his dust-chapped lips at the thought and reaches into his trousers.

When he is done with that, he gets up off the porch and huffs across the yard to the dirt road. Aunt Dottie, who is boiling jelly in the kitchen, calls from inside, "Bobby Boo! Where you off to?"

He waggles his head to let her know he's heard and marches down the road toward the remains of Beaver Dam. It's just over a mile away, pretty much straight down, past occasional houses tucked up beneath locust trees and cone-heavy pines. People don't yell at him when he's on the road. Granted, he's rarely on the road, but they also know if they opened their dumb-ass mouths to give him grief he'd haul them off their porches or out of their houses and knock their heads against a tree. At six-four, Bobby Boo isn't one you'd be teasing.

It's late afternoon, and the sun sends long, wavering shadows across the road in front of him. He kicks at them, practicing his karate. He swings his arms, feeling the wonder of his muscles.

Next week, he thinks. *No more puttin' it off. I'm leaving this place and goin' to California. Hop me a coal train then some*

*Amtrak train and ride across the country and show 'em my stuff.
I seen movies on TV and DVDs. I know what they's lookin' for. I
got it, oh yeah, I got what they want and what they need.*

He has no money but knows how to catch a train. When he
was little, he lived in Beaver Dam with his dad. He hopped a few
trains for short stints, a couple miles down a ways, hiking back
home. When he was ten, though, he rode a coal-filled car all the
way to Roanoke before he was caught, dusted off, and driven by
social services the 126 miles back to Beaver Dam. That's when
he was taken from his dad and given to his aunt. His dad had
cried, and that was the strangest thing Bobby Boo had ever
seen. His dad, a big burly man much like Bobby is now, leaning
over his mining boots and weeping. Several months later, his
dad left town, and nobody knew where he went.

Down Bobby walks, bits of the road scooting out from
under his feet, chipmunks skittering across in front of him.
The smell of the charred town is heavier now, and he can see
white ash clinging to roadside trees and brush. Bobby pulls at
his nose. His calf muscles begin to sting; he's not much of a
walker. Around a bend, past the Ricketts' cornfield, up a slight
rise, down again, there's the lopsided Shewsbury house with its
screen porch, eternally shuttered windows, its outbuildings and
countless doghouses. The road widens then and joins the "real"
road, Route 687, a paved stretch that connects Beaver Dam to the
rest of the world.

He hits the pavement and turns toward town, or toward
what used to be town, and hikes on, sweating profusely. His
T-shirt sucks his chest.

Around another bend then, past the New Light Church
of the Creator with its little weedy graveyard out back and its
big, plastic sign: "Worship With Us. 10:30 Sunday Mornings.
7:00 Wednesday Evenings. All Welcome. Minister Hank
Shaw." Down another incline now. Some trees link their hands
overhead to create a canopy while others stand back from the
road to let the chicory and Queen Anne's lace have some room.
Shattered beer bottles sparkle at roadside; plastic grocery bags
wave from low tree branches like cheap-ass Christmas tinsel.
Every so often, the railroad track can be seen on its slightly

raised rail-bed behind the tangle of trees, vines, and shrubs to the left.

One last curve and there is the town sign for "Beaver Dam, Unincorporated." Beyond the sign, straight out, he can see the charred remains of Main Street. Tangles of yellow "crime scene" ribbons run here and there, back and forth across the street, tied to the remaining nubs of light poles and the blackened bits of store walls that still stand. The sheriff's car is parked in front of what was the Waffle House along with another car, a brown sedan. The cars look empty, though it's hard to tell in the fading sunlight.

Bobby Boo feels a lurch of excitement. He picks up the pace, reaches the first yellow ribbon strung from a light pole across the street to a bit of porch that used to be Angie's Antiques, steps over.

The smell is wet, heavy, and acrid. The Tazewell County fire department did the best they could once they reached Beaver Dam, but there wasn't much left for them to do once they got the call and wrangled their trucks up into the mountains. It was always assumed the Beaver Dam Mining Company would come to the rescue if the town were ever in need, but someone was asleep or someone was drunk but however it went, they didn't get their equipment to town until twenty minutes after the first call came in from a sleepy miner who lived in town. Together, the county department and the coal mine firefighters saved three light poles, the west wall of the Waffle House and the back wall of the Dollar General. The steeple of the Baptist Church is still pretty much intact, though lying on its side beside the demolished house of worship. The Exxon station is a blackened and fragile shell (Shell, thinks Bobby. Wouldn't it have been funny if it had been a shell of a Shell station? Ha ha!); a stiff wind would likely topple it, though the pumps still stand. Trees behind the businesses on either side of Main Street are burned bad—some down to nubs. The railroad, paralleling Main Street on its way to the mines, is covered in hunks of wind-blown, charred rubbish that will have to be cleared off with a backhoe.

Bobby Boo strolls up the middle of Main Street, stepping over wood and broken glass. He reaches the two cars. Nope, nobody in them. The brown sedan has a small magnetic sign on the side, "Green Vista Insurance Company."

The sun dips behind the towering western slope, turning everything a washed-out pewter grey. The few remaining light poles don't light up. No glows appear in the windows of the remaining trailers and cabins. Everyone is gone. Yep, big-time ghost town now.

Here is the movie in Bobby Boo's mind: The town has burned to nothing. Only a few scraps, bricks, blocks, and half-walls are left. The sheriff and the insurance adjuster are trapped in the rubble of the Exxon Station. Bobby Boo Anderson, lone hero with superpowers, hears their muffled whimpering. Bobby races to their aid, and as he tosses aside several hundred pounds of wood, the bleeding sheriff whispers, "But my daughter! She was in the motel! Save her first!"

Of course, Bobby Boo leaves the sheriff for the motel, which is little more now than its cracked sign and collapsed walls, burned dime-store paintings, and blackened bathtubs and toilets. He hears sobbing and throws aside a melted plastic shower curtain to find a half-naked young red-haired woman, bruised but otherwise unharmed, cowering with her hands over her eyes, her breasts trembling. Bobby Boo says, "Don't be scared no more. I'm here, okay?" Her beautiful eyes open—dark green, large, wet with tears—and she says, "Are you an angel from heaven here to save me?" He answers, "I'm whatever you want, sweetheart."

"Hey there, Bobby Boo!" The voice is deep, loud, pissed-off.

Bobby looks around from the pile of crap that was once the Exxon station. In the middle of the road stand Sheriff Joe Mullins and what is likely the insurance man. The sheriff is very round, with pinked cheeks and big round wet circles beneath his pits. The insurance man is thin, wearing a white shirt and skinny black tie that looks like a snake flattened by a tractor. He is holding a wilted legal pad and there is a pen behind his ear. Neither is happy.

"You know what that yellow tape's for?" says Sheriff Mullins.

"Yeah."

"And?"

"And?"

"What's it mean?"

"Don't go in."

Sheriff Mullins nods; his neck squeaks a little. "Right. I should arrest you right here and now. I been chasing kids out of here ever since the fire, and now you come down here like you own the place, messing up evidence and such?"

"How much more can it get messed up?" asks Bobby.

Sheriff Mullins makes a face, says, "Get the hell out, Bobby Boo. Go home to your Aunt Dottie. You hear me?"

Bobby Boo shrugs.

"And don't come back until all this is cleared away and we give the green light for folks to start rebuilding."

Bobby chuckles. "Rebuild?"

"Demolition folks are bringing their equipment up here tomorrow. Gonna break down what ain't broke down, scrape it all up, haul it all off. Maybe rebuild. Maybe not. Time'll tell. But 'til the diggin' and scrapin's all done, you keep your sorry ass out of Beaver Dam."

"Okay, okay." Bobby Boo looks back in the direction he came from, and then looks over at the Exxon mess and slope up behind it where several burned, blackened trailers have caved in on themselves. "I'll just go out that way. Sit outside your prissy yellow ribbons. Can't arrest me for that, now can you?"

The insurance man grimaces. Sheriff Mullins says, "Get the hell out any way you want, Bobby Boo, just get out."

Bobby takes off and the insurance man calls after, "Don't knock anything down, now, you hear?"

"I hear your fat lips flappin'," Bobby mutters, and for spite he kicks a loose plank off a pile of toppled cinder block. He can hear the insurance man growl.

Bobby Boo hikes up the slope a short ways and sits between two fire-stripped pines in the yard of a scalded house trailer, his butt deep in humus and ash, waving gnats away, waiting. He doesn't have a watch, never did, so he has no idea how long the men are down there, studying the scene, waving their flashlights back and forth. It gets later, later.

Then, finally, he sees the cars' headlight circle around and leave town.

He doesn't know why he stayed. There's clearly nothing worth stealing in the town's ruins. Kids have probably picked it clean in spite of the deputy's stupid yellow tape. Maybe he stayed because he doesn't like being told what to do. He does what he wants to when he wants to.

"So there," he grumbles.

Everything is still now, except for an owl in a sycamore, the night bugs chirring to each other, and, to the distant southwest, the sound of the mines' night machinery running. Beaver Dam's dead. Empty, like a film set when all the movie stars have gone home to their mansions and swimming pools.

"Come'n listen to a story 'bout a man named Jed," Bobby Boo starts to sing, then laughs at himself for singing. He wonders if the town will rebuild. If so, he hopes they'll have a movie theater this time. Maybe they'll show X-rated films like the ones he orders through the mail. Aunt Dottie hates them, but he just tells her to get the hell out of the living room, go knit a scarf or something.

Bobby pushes himself to his feet, brushes off his ass, and lumbers back down into town, over a couple melted tires, around a scorched swing set and the remains of a doghouse. The ground crackles beneath his feet.

He wishes he brought a flashlight or even Aunt Dottie's rusty lantern, but the moon is three-quarters full and the silvered light washing the ground helps him find his footing.

Back to the Exxon Station; he stands and stares at it, and then glances over at the Beaver Dam Motel. The big, glass neon sign, which always had a couple burned out letters, is shattered and scattered, its shards catching the moonlight and throwing it back into the air like drunk fireflies.

All the bodies of the dead had been claimed within ten hours of the blaze, crispy or reddened or just choked dead from the smoke. Funerals started today, two up at the Baptist church and one over at Hank Shaw's Church of the Creator. This morning, while sitting on the porch and drinking some shine, Bobby'd watched as the Creator church mourners moved along the road past the cabin, dressed in their Sunday best, heads down, some crying, some just staring at their feet. He called to them, "I don't want to hear your snifflin'! Shut your fuckin' traps!" And they did because they knew Bobby Boo had a temper. Most of them were women, anyway, and a couple skinny teenagers. If the men had been with them, he might have hesitated to say anything. Usually the men would avoid him, what with his height and his muscles and the way he could make his eyes big and buggy. But a grieving man, now that's another story. A grieving man has no sense. A grieving man might charge a bull without thinking twice.

Bobby walks into the demolished motel, piecing his way across planks, plaster, and tubs, and sinks. He stops, puts his hands in his jeans' pockets, shakes his head. "Guess I'll never get my turn with Penny Mustard now. Damn, what a woman. Where the hell she gonna ply her trade now the motel's gone?"

A skinny dog trots past the motel, sniffing, nose to the ground. "Hey, can't you see that yellow tape?" Bobby yells at the dog. The dog just curls his lip and goes on.

Then he hears the sound.

A thumping, soft, muted grunting from the other side of the motel ruins. He cocks his head, listening. The sound stops, and then starts again. Bobby leans forward for balance and clambers over the debris to what had been the motel's rear delivery lot. The motel's two-wheeled, plastic trash barrels are melted into hardened, green, shiny globs that look like creatures out of a science fiction film.

Bobby rubs his nose against a heavy stench of decay and traces of alcohol. Gnats buzz around his lips and he draws his T-shirt collar up over his mouth.

Another dog, this one trapped, he thinks. But if it were a dog, wouldn't he have howled for someone to set him free? *Maybe his vocal cords are al burned to shit and he can only grunt.*

Bobby Boo grins for a second. Could be it's not a dog at all, but that beautiful half-naked girl he went to rescue in the bathtub, trying to call, "Bobby Boo, help me!"

There's another grunt from beneath the rubble, then a faint, raspy growl. The pile trembles slightly and a wave of hot stench hits him in the face again. He gags.

No, a beautiful, half-naked girl would never sound that mean or stink that bad. It has to be a dying, puss-filled dog. Or maybe a family of half-live, rotting possums.

Bobby Boo kicks at the pile. The grunting increases. The pile moves again, up-down-up-down, up and down. Something is under there, all right. No girl. No dog. Something damned huge.

Or damned strong.

Or both.

"You a fucked-up bear in there?" Bobby says. His voice surprises him, as high and squeaky as it sounds. He wishes he'd brought his shotgun.

Everybody needs a shotgun if they're going to be out after dark in these mountains.

"Hey!" He says. There's no answer. A chill cuts through his arms, down his spine. His heart picks up an uncomfortably fast rhythm. Where the hell are the deputy and insurance man when you need them?

"I ought to just leave it alone," he whispers into his shirt. "Sure ain't nobody in there. Everybody been found and 'counted for. Nobody gone missin'."

At least, nobody's been reported as missin'.

The pile continues to pulse up and down, up and down, scraping, creaking. Moonlight slides up and down along the edges of the wood and block, and the sight makes Bobby dizzy.

"Cut that out, you hear me!" He shouts, but again his voice sounds like a little baby-pants girl.

Hot wind blows across the motel debris, tossing bits of ash into Bobby's face. His eyes sting and water. He digs at them with his sleeve, blinks, and looks back at the pile. It's no longer moving.

"Huh," he says, swallowing down a bubble of nausea. "There you go.

You know you best do what I tell you!"

There is no movement, no sounds. Whatever is in there is dead, or almost dead. Good, good.

He sniffs, shakes the shirt down from his face, flexes his muscles. He feels strong again, he feels good. Screw the stink and the ash and the stinging eyes. He's going dig whatever is in there out and be a hero.

He picks up a cinderblock, tosses it aside. Weakened by the fire, it shatters.

Maybe there is someone missing that wasn't reported, he thinks, and he'll be the one to make the discovery. Like the hero in the movies of his mind, he'll be celebrated and cheered.

Another cinderblock, and another. One breaks into fragments, one doesn't. A bunch of bricks and some shards of glass, and warped sections of pine veneer.

Even if the person's dead, hell, at least he'll be the finder. The brave, heroic, lone finder, returning the body of the lost loved one to the doorstep of a confused, grief-stricken family.

More cinderblocks, glass, bricks, and a heavy piece of twisted pipe, thrown off the pile. The stench is worse now. Flies, excited by Bobby Boo's industry, hover around his fingers as if trying to help him. He flicks his hands and yells at them, but they don't give a shit, this is what flies do.

A large hunk of charred wallboard now, up, over, tossed as far as his arms can manage, which isn't very far. A hunk of wood next, which drives a nail into the palm of his hand, drawing blood immediately.

"Fuck!" He sucks the hole until the bright pain subsides.

More black and splintered boards now, and a chunk of more pine paneling. Up, off, away. He's sweating. Gnats fly up his nose and he blows them out.

Another bunch of cinderblocks dislodged, and Bobby is engulfed by the worst stench he's ever smelled. He gags, covers his nose with both hands. The flies go crazy, trying to get beneath the last piece of wallboard.

"Damn Sam!" Now he's not sure finding some lost person is worth all this. He buries his nose back into the collar of his T-shirt, glances around at the motel ruins and the silvered moonlight and the black shadows cutting savage patterns across it all.

"Fuck it, just get it done." Probably a dead dog after all. So a family discovers where their hound dog went off to. Not so dramatic as finding a human, but in some cases, real close. And maybe the owner of the disappeared dog is a beautiful, grateful mountain girl.

Bobby bends over, grabs the edge of the board and hoists it up and away.

And the dead woman sits up like a spring-loaded wolf trap, snarling, drooling, what is left of her jaws snapping.

Bobby squeaks and falls backward over cinderblocks and wood and glass, his eyes stretched to popping, "Oh shit oh shit!"

The dead woman pushes herself to her feet, tips what was left of her mangled, pulpy-raw head, and winks the only eye she has. It glows bright red like a hot coal on a cold hearth.

"Granny Mustard!" screeches Bobby Boo. He tries to stand up but his foot drops through weakened boards and plate glass, twisting and gouging his ankle and trapping him. "What you doin' under all that, Granny?" He pants, sweats, shakes like a wet dog after a bath. He grapples at his ankle, jerking on it, trying to get his foot out but it's caught tight in a flesh-shredding vise. His heart thunders like a runaway train. "What the hell happened to you?"

The old woman, shimmering with the putrid smell, clearly dead but moving just the same, steps over the broken blocks and wood—crunch, crunch—tottering, wheezing, her slug-like tongue slopping out of what was once her mouth but is now a raw hole in the front of her face.

Bobby's teeth clamp down on his lip, driving through the flap of flesh, and he screams again. He scoots back again, as far as he can with his foot caught, driving thick splinters through his pants and into his ass. He wriggles his leg, shakes his foot, but the wood and glass only dig deeper, slicing his ankle clear to the bone. The pain is beyond pain, bright and hot like the explosion of a star. "Oh God, oh God!" he screams.

Granny Mustard takes three more awkward, shuffling steps, her ghastly head tilting at an impossible angle as if trying to figure out who Bobby is.

Then she is right over him. Drooling, sniffing through the hole that had once been her nose, her teeth—the ones in her lower jaw, which is all she has now—chomping at the air.

"No, Granny, leave me alone! I'm Bobby Boo! You know me!

You know my Aunt Dottie! Go on, now! Get! Get out of here! You hear me? Go on!"

But Granny won't go on. Granny looks demented and deformed and hungry. She hovers for a moment then dives down on top of Bobby Boo, her jaw pumping, her body dead weight in more ways than one, and she bites him deep on his arm. She twists her head and rips away a great portion of muscle and skin.

Bobby squeals again in pain and horror. His fingers scrabble, scramble beside him, and make contact with a heavy bit of pipe, and even in his foot-trapped state he is able to swing the pipe up and around with so much force against Granny's head that bits of brain blow out the side of her skull. She flies backward, up off her feet for a moment, then crashes in a heap atop the wallboard that had been her prison. She shudders, grunts, kicks a couple times, then stops. Dead. This time.

Bobby, all alone with his foot stuck in a hole and a chunk of his upper arm gone and the smell of decay and burned wood all around him in the middle of the dark, moon-silvered night, folds over and weeps in big, whooping, soul-searing gulps. He fumbles, scrabbles with the glass and wood, at last freeing his foot, which hangs down, shattered, like the tongue of an old shoe. He feels his life draining out along with his blood. This is his movie, a small part of his mind tells him. This is his new role. There is no beautiful, half-naked girl. There is nobody to cheer him on. There is no prizes or rewards. But this is his role now, whatever that means.

And it's gonna suck big time.

3
Armistead

He is alone.

Though the mountains are filled with living creatures—owls, bats, rabbits, deer, foxes—he is alone.

And he is dead.

At one time the songs, the chirrings, and the rustlings would have calmed him, strengthened him, reminding him of his reason for coming to the mountains, reminding him that he is part of something bigger, something important, something beautiful and alive. But now the animal sounds only remind him that he is dead, and that he can't recall exactly who he is or what he is doing here. His memory is broken, fragmented, a mirror dashed against the floor, reflecting bits and pieces that he can't put back together.

He knows his first name but isn't sure why he does. He knows he has escaped from a dark, filthy trailer in Desper Hollow, but can't remember how he got away or remember coming here. He knows someone is hunting him. The One With No Eyes.

He has taken up in a dilapidated mountainside shack beside a creek.

The shack is but one room, with part of the roof gone and a stone fireplace that has worn down to gravel. The floor is warped and slimy. There is a hornet's nest hanging from a rafter—a large, papery ball, long evacuated. A large grey toad sits in the broken window and a sluggish snake lies along the floor against the wall, buried half-way beneath leaves that have blown in. Flies spin confused circles around Armistead's head. Armistead is painfully hungry. But he cannot eat flies or cold-blooded creatures. He needs warm food, living food.

He stands in the gaping hole that is the doorway, his tattered hands braced on the jambs, and stares out into the settling darkness of early evening. The Hunger gnaws at his mind and gut. He will feed soon or cease to exist. He will die again. He knows he ate foods before he became dead but cannot remember what foods sated him. He cannot remember where he once lived or what he did before the One With No Eyes took him captive with the others. It distresses him; it is a nagging emptiness deep inside his soul, but he is unable to take it out and look at it. It is too vague, a flittering inside him like a moth in a lightless cave.

He tests the air with his acute sense of smell, tipping back his head and picking up the acrid scents of juniper and dung and the rotting leaves that coat the forest floor. He waits, listening. He can feel the radiating heat of tiny bodies scurrying among the leaves and along the tree branches. He knows he has eaten such creatures before, but none of them are large enough to truly satisfy his raging appetite. If he could find something larger, something more like—

—like humans. Human blood and flesh. Human marrow, human brain.

He groans, and his muscles clench with that brief but brutal thought. He doesn't want to eat humans, yet even as his confused mind struggles against the idea, his tongue rolls and his teeth tap in delight at the prospect.

There are no humans in this wilderness, however, so he will make do with something else.

And now, there…

He breathes deeply, drawing in the odor of filthy hair and animal sweat on the autumn air. A deer. No, three deer, grazing in a small grassy clearing on the other side of the creek. They would not be afraid of him, because he no longer smells like a human, but more like a decaying carcass left behind by a black bear.

He moves as quietly as he can on sluggish legs and bare feet, through the underbrush to the creek. He thinks at one time he might have been very fast, so fleet and athletic his movements were almost like flying, but not anymore. Now he is dead.

Frogs along the edge of the creek shiver then leap away into the brush along the water's edge. A turtle trundles behind them, clawed feet dragging it forward and down into the frosty mud.

The deer are visible now through a thatch of oak saplings and briars, nibbling tall grasses. Their tails are down; no need to warn each other because they have no idea of the danger so close at hand. Two does and one fawn. The blood of the young deer runs hotter than that of its elders. Armistead will go for the largest doe, a muscular creature with delicate legs.

He drags numbed fingers through his hair; some of it comes out and drifts down like black feathers. It is still fairly thick, though. Not like the others who have lost it all. As far as he can tell, he looks much like he did back when—back when what? He can't remember a back then, though he knows there was one. His eyes are still grey, though rimmed with the tell-tale red. His face is still angular but covered with the inevitable splotches of rot.

The Hunger bites down on his insides, and he can wait no longer. As silently as he can, he creeps into the creek, wades across the slippery rocks and up the other side. His feet are nearly as numb as his fingers and don't register the chill of the water. Two of the deer look up, over, grasses hanging from their lips, but after a moment continue grazing.

He licks his lips, but his tongue is dry. He takes what feels like a deep breath, but it seems to run through his nostrils and out his chest. Another step closer, keeping balance, watching. A breeze rattles the husks of silkweeds at the edge of the clearing. He parts the saplings, and the deer, in unison, whip their heads about toward the sound.

He hurls himself forward just as the two does flash their white tails up and leap away. His hands clutch, fall short, and grab hold of the fawn's hind leg. It thrashes, kicks surprisingly powerful blows against his chest and face, but he doesn't feel them. His fist clenches around the leg bone, and he brings the fawn down on its face. It squeals, struggles. Armistead jerks the creature backward until he is over it, and he smashes the tiny skull with his fist then buries his teeth into flesh, bone, and brain. More struggling, more thrashing of the hooves, slower now.

Armistead swallows a chunk. Blood pours through his lips, no taste, but warm. He bites again, deeper into the soft brain, twists away a large portion and gulps it down. He is rewarded with an immediate surge through his cold body, a brief satisfaction that is hot and energetic and—alive. The fawn's movements abruptly cease. Its long, bumpy tongue slips out between its lips and drags the weeds. Armistead relaxes a little, digging the remnants of the brain from the skull bowl with his fingernails and cramming it into his mouth. The brain is what the Hunger most desires, the soft greyish matter filled with powerful currents that remain alert and bright a good many moments even as the victim dies, the energy that stirs his blood if just briefly.

When the last of the brain has been consumed, he eats a portion of the neck and then digs for the organs within the chest cavity. They are wet, and they are substantial, and for the moment he is filled. The pain of the Hunger is gone. He sits back and stares up at the moon. Sometimes he remembers it's the moon, sometimes he doesn't. Tonight, it's just a pearly bit of fascination in the sky. A lopsided silver ball dangling overhead.

After some amount of time has passed, Armistead stands and looks down at the mangled fawn. There is little left. A hoof. A portion of spine. Fur. He feels an odd sense of sadness for the butchered creature. He doesn't like to kill, but he must obey the Hunger. The other dreadful, captive dead ones back in Desper Hollow don't mind killing. They savor it. They kill then eat what live things are given them, growl, go quiet for a few moments, then get up to prowl and growl again. Back and forth and back and forth in the filthy, poorly lit room. They are fed from above by the One With No Eyes, though no doubt they would eat her if they had the chance.

Armistead wades back through the creek, up the bank, and into the shack. He pulls himself through the doorway, falls back against the slimy wall, and slides down into a crouching position, his knees up to his chest, his forehead furrowed. One more he tries to think... to think... about his current situation.

He puts his hands against either side of his head and pushes. A bit of skin on one palm sloughs off and hangs down in a fleshy ribbon. He bites the skin off and spits it out. Then he squeezes his head again; closes his eyes.

Think, he tells himself. THINK!

For a second something flitters in his memory, a pale blue flash, not water, not sky, but something else, something deep and comforting. He grits his teeth and tries to catch hold of this fragment, but it rips free like gossamer cloth and is gone.

"Damn it to hell!" he snarls. His voice is raspy and broken like old bones. He lets go of his head, clenches his fists, one within the other. Staring out through the doorway, he watches as bats stitch shadowed patterns among the trees. An opossum waddles by, its white pointed snout twitching in search of crickets. It peers through the doorway, shivers at something it doesn't understand and doesn't trust, then lumbers on.

Armistead believes that at one time, creatures did not fear him. At one time they even came to him willingly, with trust, and he did not harm them. He did not kill or eat them.

Long ago, he thinks he had peace.

Long ago, he suspects he knew love.

But he is no longer sure. He can no longer focus long enough or reach back far enough through the darkness to touch old feelings.

Because now he is dead.

And he really isn't surprised when, several hours later as a faint morning light begins to seep through the shack's doorway, he can smell the dogs and can hear the One With No Eyes calling, "You's in there, Stead! I know you is! Can't hide from me, you rotten, fucked up piece o' dead shit! Makin' me come way out here to find your ass! Come out now or I'll give you the charger!"

His teeth bare. He cranes his neck to look up at the rear window, a two-foot square hole with shards of broken glass rimming the frame. He senses a phantom, panicked rhythm in his heart, which no longer beats. He cannot go back and face the horrors in Desper Hollow. If he were fast enough, he would escape through the window. He is thin enough and wouldn't feel pain as the broken glass wedged in the sill tore at his arms, legs.

"Stead!" A sound now of crunching underbrush as the One With No Eyes gets closer. The hair on the back of Armistead's neck bristles.

He cannot go back. He'd rather die.

Though he is already dead. And what is dying to that?

A splash of shadow crosses the open doorway, and then a mangy, black-furred mongrel rushes through the doorway, its lip curled, its fangs glistening. Protruding from the top of its bushy head are two long metal screws, like silver demon horns. A wire is attached from one screw to the other. It is followed by the second dog, equally huge, equally bristled and adorned with the metal screws and wire. The dogs stop four feet in front of Armistead and stare at him with their ghastly, bulging red eyes. If Armistead could kill these dogs as he did the fawn, he would do so in a heartless beat. But though they are like him, dead and back again, they have a power of speed he lacks, and poisonous saliva that drips thick and heavy. If they bit him during a struggle he would not die but would further descend into the mindless, rotting abyss.

He stands up slowly. The mongrels' eyes don't blink. Their breath is cold and foul, and it doesn't steam the air as would the breath of living creatures. The nostrils quiver, leaking soured blood and toxic snot.

"Back off!" Armistead commands. His words slog over his defunct vocal cords, low and faint. "Back off!" he screams, but the scream is not a scream, it is muted, soft.

Another shadow at the shack's entrance now, and the One With No Eyes moves in to fill the space. She is a tall, lumpy woman, though not quite a woman yet, still in her teens with the acne and pouty lips to prove it. Her hair is a garish, artificial red, pulled up into a sticky ponytail. Her eyes are obscured by big, mirrored sunglasses that she wears all the time. Her face is puffed, sweaty, and she is breathing heavily. She wears zippered, hooded sweatshirt and grey sweatpants over green rubber boots. In one hand is a little box with a switch. The other is tucked inside her sweatshirt pouch. In that pouch, of course, is the charger.

The dogs take a step closer to Armistead. "Stay!" shouts the One With No Eyes, thumbing the switch on the little box in her hand. The dogs yelp, shake their silver horned heads, and stop in their tracks. She flips the switch again, turning the little box off.

"Fuck you, makin' me come all the way out here for you," the young woman says around a wad of gum. "You really, really think you can get away? You really think I'd let you get away? Let you ruin everything I've been doing? Let you run my chance for a show? For more money than I ever seen in my lifetime? Damn, I'd almost laugh if that weren't so stupid. Now, get your carcass out here. I got Bink on duty back at the trailer, but you know he ain't much for doin' what I tell him to do. Rather sit and watch them fuckin' Three Stooges."

Armistead leans back, his shoulders coming in contact with the wall.

"Get the hell out of here," he whispers.

The One With No Eyes steps into the shack. She sniffs, runs her arm under her nose. "You'll do what I say, or you'll wish you had. You know that. Don't be such a stubborn asshole." She pulls her hand from her sweatshirt pouch. In it is the dreaded charger.

"I should die than go back with you."

"Now that's kinda funny," says the One With No Eyes. She looks at her snarling dogs and snaps her fingers. "Don't you think that's funny, Doug?" Doug, the larger of the two dead dogs, flicks his rotting ears but continues to stare at Armistead. Dan, the other dog, who has lost the flesh on the side of his face as well as one of his eyes, growls low and long. His tail, shed of most of its flesh, does not wag but holds still against the cold.

The charger the woman holds is painted shiny purple. It is a little larger than a cigarette pack, rectangular with a trigger underneath. The One With No Eyes has never used it on Armistead, but he has seen her use it on the others. It shoots out barbs, attached to thin wires, and when they embed themselves into their scalps it makes them shriek and go to their knees. As long as the other is attached to the charger, the One With No Eyes can flick the trigger again and again, leaving the other unable to anything but twist on the floor like a grub in a frying pan.

The One With No Eyes waves the charger in one hand and the dog control in the other, like a gunslinger in the middle of an old-fashioned Texas town. "You comin', or am I gonna have to charge you?"

"I am not coming," says Armistead. With that, he turns as quickly as he can and thrusts his head part way through the window, stares down at the thick, jagged shards of glass protruding from the sill beneath him. The grey toad leaps from the window and out onto the ground.

"You ain't out-runnin' me," says the One With No Eyes.

Kill the brain...

"So here's how I got it figured, should you ever need to kill a hollow."

Armistead had been listening out the trailer window to the One With No Eyes and Bink talking outside yesterday, or last week, or sometime long ago. He isn't sure when but for some reason he remembers the conversation clearly. The two living ones were eating something out of a big, rattley yellow bag and chewing around their words. "Kill the brain," Bink had said. "Best way in a pinch to be rid of 'em fast if they ever get loose and come at you."

"How you know that?"

"Something in their central nervous system's still working. That's why they can move around and eat. So the brain's the clue. It's why the charger works, but only on the brain."

"I ain't never gonna let 'em get out. Ain't never gonna let 'em come at me."

"But you just mark my words," said Bink. "Kill the brain, kill the hollow."

"Whatever."

"Remember that. Kill the brain..."

Kill the brain...

"...kill the hollow."

The One With No Eyes laughs out loud and the dogs growl low in their tattered throats. "Don't be stupid, Stead. Don't bother tryin' whatever it is you got rollin' around in your little old mush-mind. You know I can make you hurt bad! Now you's comin' back with me to Desper Hollow."

Kill the brain…

Now!

Armistead drives his forehead down with as much force as he can conjure. Some of the glass gives way but the biggest piece pierces the flesh and some of the bone.

But only a fraction of an inch. Not enough.

He wriggles against the glass, trying to drive it in deeper, no pain, really, just a brief sense of light and a soft scraping sound.

The One With No Eyes chortles. "Oh, you a good one, you is! Think you can kill yourself? Idiot. Now get the hell out that window…"

Armistead clutches the sides of his head and pulls down. Die, please, die let me die! The glass squeals against bone but goes no farther.

There is a metallic click behind him, and then a sharp barb pierces the base of his skull, embedding in the flesh. Again, no pain.

Yet.

"Fine," says the One With No Eyes.

Armistead growls, lifts his head from the glass shard, shifts a fraction so the glass will go into his eye and deeper into his brain. He raises his head to slam it down.

"Have it your way."

And then, pain.

The world blows up inside his head, bright and orange and huge. Heat roars beneath his skull, blistering the synapses, driving his teeth against each other so hard that two molars shatter. His spine locks, his fingers spasm, his legs give out. He falls away from the window and onto the muddy floor, face down.

Then the heat is gone. The pain vanishes. He turns his head, squints upward.

The One With No Eyes stands over him now, her lips puckered. The dogs watch. She holds the charger, thumb poised over the trigger. "You want more of that? Huh? You want more of that? Plenty where that came from, you know. Bink don't mess around when he invents stuff."

Armistead just wants to die. But he can't.

She kicks him on the side of his face. A chunk of his left ear flies off.

Doug and Dan bark dead dogs' barks, sloppy and wet like they are barking under water. "Answer me!"

"Don't..." he manages, speaking into the mud.

"Then get up!"

He gets up, wobbling. He reaches for the barb at the back of his head, but she says, "You touch that, and I'll charge you again. Now walk!"

He walks.

It takes a long time to get back to Desper Hollow over the craggy rocks, through thick pines and briars and tangles of sycamore and mountain laurel, and up and down the ridges, because the One With No Eyes stops to rest a lot, smoke her cigarettes, squat to pee. She cusses the whole way, complaining about Bink, how careless he was to let Armistead escape, how she was going to kick major ass as soon as she gets back.

A long while later they stumble down the last slope and onto the uneven footpath that leads into the permanent shadows of Desper Hollow. Even from a good 150 yards, Armistead can hear the wailing and grunting of the hollows inside the old trailer there. He instinctively stops, tensing, clenching his fists.

He cannot go back.

"What's matter?" chuckles the One With No Eyes. "Don't wanna be in there with your kind?"

Armistead stares at the trailer, its dented sides seeming to pulse with the horrific non-life within.

"Want another charge? Don't cost me a cent. Bink buys the batteries."

Armistead backs up three steps. The dead dogs snap at his legs.

I can't go in there again! I will not go in there again!

No, no, please I can't go in there again!

"Fine by me."

Another charge, white-hot, supreme. He is slammed to his knees. She holds the trigger longer for good measure, and Stead feels something inside his body has begun to boil.

Then she stops and he manages to stand up.

"Gonna go now?" she sneers.

He cannot nod nor shake his head. He can barely move his feet beneath him. He trembles like a newborn colt.

Together, trailed by the corpse dogs and a swarm of late-season gnats that have picked up the stench of decay, they move on down to the trailer.

4
Kathy Shaw

She hauls her red canvas bag and yellow folding chair across the broad beach, leaning forward to get traction in the sand. It's early morning, early November, cold with a salty breeze. Sunlight sparkles on the frigid water. Only a few tourists are out on the beach with her—a father bundled in jacket, knit hat, and salt-crusted scarf, trying to herd his three young ones up and away from the water. The children, likewise in jackets and caps, are soaked and have rolled their jeans up to their knees. They shriek with delight and stamp on the incoming, outgoing waves. The father lights a cigar and complains but not enough to stop the kids. An old man shuffles along with a sweatshirt wrapped around his ears, the sleeves hanging down his back like thick black ponytails. He follows his metal detector, sweeping it back and forth along the sand, pausing only to hack a phlegmy wad out onto the ground. A young teenager, who Kathy imagines should be in school, chases his dog in and out among the wet-black supports of the nearby fishing pier. A middle-aged woman lies shivering on a chaise lounge in her blue two-piece bathing suit, goose bumps standing up on her arms and legs, a Cesarean scar visible where her suit bottom doesn't come up quite far enough. Kathy wonders if a late season tan is worth all that. A young couple stands against each other beneath a motel blanket, grinning, nudging each other, acting like every newlywed couple Kathy has ever seen on vacation to Virginia Beach.

Kathy doesn't come out to the beach for a tan, or to swim or seek lost quarters or stamp on the waves or to think, but to get away, to look at the ocean, and to do anything but think. She's worked as a waitress at Ocean Billy's restaurant on the fishing pier since May. It's a good enough job, the staff friendly enough and the tips okay. Much better than what she earned back at the Waffle House in Beaver Dam. The work hours are fair, 2 to 10, and she can get a 10% discount on the food, though the only fish she really likes is fried catfish, and Ocean Billy's doesn't serve catfish.

She plops the red bag beside her; already gulls are hovering overhead, screeching and watching for a snack. Unfolding her chair, she swings into it, twists her long brown hair into a knot, then pulls the hood of her ten-dollar "Virginia Beach is For Lovers" sweatshirt up over her head in case the gulls poop. She leans back, shoves her hands into the sweatshirt pouch, and stares at the churning, granite-blue sea. The sound of the surf eases her soul. Crashing, rushing forward, withdrawing, hissing, folding over, crashing, and rushing forward again. Powerful. Predictable. Reliable.

So much better to be here than back on Black Rock Ridge.

Kathy wasn't in the mountains when Suze Mustard went from ordinary weird to bat-shit-slap-your-mama-bald-headed weird. Kathy'd been here at the beach, settling in, making her new life as best she could, doing what Jack did in all those fairytales—seeking her fortune. But her father, Hank, had sent her a letter in late July, his usual steady block print a bit shaky this time.

Dearest Kathy,

I hope this finds you well and happy. We miss you, but know you are following your heart and doing what you need to do. And I am glad you were not here for the recent troubles.

You may have had some news about this but probably not, as far away as you are. A few days ago, Suze Mustard, for some reason known only to her and God, burned down the whole of Beaver Dam then killed herself. Twenty-one people died. All the businesses are gone, and most of the homes in town were destroyed. Those who survived are moving away from town.

Funerals for the dead are in progress. I have two to perform this afternoon. My heart is broken for these poor folks. They ask me why God let Suze do something so awful and all I can say it's one of God's Great Mysteries.

But there is more sad news for the Mustard family. Not only was Suze lost, but Granny Mustard, herself. She was found a day after the fire, behind the motel. She was scorched but it seems she died from a blow to the head. Seems a beam fell during the fire and struck her the fatal blow. Her grandson, Burley, wants me to perform the ceremony for the two of them, Suze and Granny, even though our two families have been on strained terms for years, and none of them attend my church. Yet I should probably do it. God might want me to do it. Maybe one of their hearts might be touched by the Spirit. Your mother says I should do what I feel moved to do, but she's so tired these days I don't think much matters to her one way or other.

Yet, and don't tell your mother this, I sense that the funerals, the razing of the ruins, and the talk of rebuilding a few stores won't put to rest what has turned bad here.

There is something terribly wrong, something dreadful in the air that burials and bulldozers and new bricks can't touch. I can smell it, not with my nostrils but with my soul. A foul stench is settling across the mountain, a stinking shroud that will tangle us up and suffocate us if we let it. I'm not sure what it is, but I know it is evil. I've faced evil before and know its means and goals. Pray for us, Kathy. Pray for me.

Kathy thought about calling back, but with only a landline she had no long-distance minutes and didn't have the money to spend on a call. So she wrote her father a short return note.

Dear Dad,

That's awful about Suze. I know her mama and Jenkie must be aching bad right now. So I guess I'm sorry for them in a way. But they're a dangerous lot, every one of those Mustards. 'Those who live by the sword, die by the sword.' Isn't that in the Bible somewhere? I know you hate me saying that. You'll think I'm

unkind. But it's true. And how could they not be like they are,
with their Granny Mustard in control? What a cruel old woman,
from all I've heard of her. Just thinking about her scared me. She
scared you, too, though you never actually said so.

And that's weird, isn't it, that Granny was in town when
Suze burned it down? When was the last time she left Moon
Peak, like, fifty years ago?

I dunno, Dad. That whole Mustard family is nutty as a bag
of pecan cookies.

Mostly I'm sad for the people who died in Beaver Dam. Think
anyone will take their anger out on the Mustards? Wouldn't blame
them. I know, that's not godly but neither are the Mustards.

I won't make it home until Christmas. I'm enclosing fifty
dollars. Not much but it could help with the electric bill. Wish I
were a millionaire. How do you even become a millionaire? One
of God's Great Mysteries, huh?

Make sure Mom takes it easy.

Love,

Kathy

The letters that followed from her father in August,
September, and October were less anxious and more newsy.
Nothing much about the fire or the deaths, thank goodness.
Nobody had taken a contract out on the Mustard family, and
the Mustard family had not offered any public apologies for the
actions of one of their own. Kathy's mother, Annie, was faring
pretty well considering her multiple sclerosis. She was moving
slowly but steadily with her cane. No need for a wheelchair yet,
for which Hank gave all credit to God. The vegetable garden
had produced more beans, cabbages, and pumpkins than last
year. There were three new piglets in the pen, and two new
members of Hank's congregation. Bobby Boo Anderson had
disappeared soon after the Beaver Dam fire, and then his Aunt
Dottie turned up dead and mostly eaten up on her front porch.
Everybody knew her death couldn't have anything to do with
Bobby Boo—he was a mean soul, but no human being could do

that to another person, the way it was all chewed up. Apparently a bear had got her, leaving nothing but her dentures, one hand, and part of her skull and a hank of her long grey hair.

Sheriff Mullins sent out a party and they found and killed a big black bear not a quarter mile from the Anderson home. They looked inside the bear's stomach to find nothing of interest and concluded the bear had pooped out all of Dottie that he hadn't digested. Then they nailed the bear hide to a roadside tree for a while to assure everyone in the area that ding-dong, the bear was dead. As to Bobby Boo, most folks figured he'd finally gone off to Hollywood like he always said he'd do. Most were relieved he'd gone.

In early August a lone hiker named Armistead Ciel had come through the area on his way from Florida to Canada and asked if he could camp in the churchyard for a few days. Hank had agreed, and Armistead had helped Hank paint the church's exterior and clean up brush, tall weeds, and downed branches in the churchyard, armed with a push mower, rakes, and a scythe. Armistead ended up staying more than a week, but then disappeared one afternoon when Hank had sent him up the road a half-mile to the Vias' house to borrow a ladder so they could get on the church roof to repair some loose shingles. Hank figured Armistead had just gotten bored and moved on, though he'd left his tent in the churchyard. Hank wished Kathy had had the chance to meet him. "He was a fine young man, bright, extremely strong, outgoing," Hank wrote. "Kind and thoughtful. I hope I didn't say or do anything to chase him away." The owners of Beaver Dam Mines got a new Exxon station in by mid-October, and a couple trailers for temporary businesses. Plans for some prefab company houses to be brought in before the end of the year looked to be iffy at best now, though there was a rumor that the mine bosses might finance a small restaurant/bar. Hank hoped not. He never liked what liquor did to men. He said he'd seen his share in his younger years and never touched the stuff, himself. As to the rest of the town, at this point there was no need for another motel, Waffle House, or antique store.

A gull lands beside Kathy's foot and she stares it down. "I

have nothing for you. I never do. Now get lost." It cocks its head then does as she said, fluttering off with its buddies to pester the shivering woman in the two-piece bathing suit.

Kathy doubts she will ever be truly at home here this busy foreign land a good seven-hour drive from the Appalachians of Virginia's southwest." . She loves the ocean, the smells, and the sounds. But she doesn't feel at ease with the people. They're a whole other breed. Tourists have too much money and buy stupid things they'll probably never use again—acrylic toilet seats with embedded sea shells, wind chimes made of dried out starfish and glittery plastics. Her co-workers are nice enough, but she has nothing in common with them except two legs and the ability to take accurate orders from customers. They talk about their dates and their fun-loving moms and their beer-binges and their on-again, off-again boyfriends. Kathy nods and smiles and keeps silent with nothing to offer in return. She has no boyfriend, fun or otherwise. She doesn't drink out of respect for her father, even though she's been tempted. She has a sweet, quiet, sick mom, not a fun one. But she'd needed to get away from the Waffle House and dust-covered miners and pig shit and the rutted roads and the dark, shadowy specter of the Mustard clan on the ridge just up from her own family's doublewide. She wanted out, she wanted free and fresh and new.

Her father knew it. He'd not argued the spring morning she packed her satchel in May and walked out onto the doublewide's deck, where he sat on one of the plastic chairs, Coke can balanced on the deck railing, Bible perched on one knee, scribbling madly on a bent yellow legal pad braced against the other knee. Kathy's mother was, of course, sleeping. She slept a lot.

Hank looked up from his writing, his brown eyes narrowed, his brows pinched. Women in Beaver Dam called him one of the best-looking men around, with strong features and thick grey hair. Even when he fell into one of the deep spiritual depressions that closed him down and shut him off from his parishioners and his family for weeks at a time, he was the kind of man whose appearance would catch you by surprise and make you stare, even if for a moment.

"Where goin', Kath?" His voice was roughened from the years he smoked, though he hadn't touched a cigarette since the Lord had touched him.

Kathy didn't want to lie. Her dad was one of the few people in the world she trusted. "I'm leaving home for a while."

"Where to?"

"I don't know yet. Cross state, probably. Maybe farther."

Hank clicked his pen, stuck it in his shirt pocket. His grey hair caught in a breeze, tossing it like a lion's mane. "Okay."

Kathy shifted her satchel from one hand to the other, waiting for something, she didn't know what.

"Something bothering you?"

She shrugged. "I guess."

"Your mama?"

"Oh, God, no. I love Mama."

"Me?"

"Of course not."

"Here?"

Kathy nodded. "Yeah, here."

Hank sat back in the plastic chair. He let out a heavy sigh and stared down his feet. "Okay, then. Okay." He made move to reach into his back pocket where he kept his wallet.

"No, don't, Dad. I've got some saved up from the Waffle House. Not much but enough for a little while. Wherever I end up, I'll be in touch. And I'll send you some of what I make like I've always done here."

"You don't need to."

"I want to."

"All right."

Kathy looked out at the weedy yard where her banged-up Toyota sat, the only vehicle the family had that actually ran for the time being. Her father's rusting truck, which sat cold and dead next to her car, had a bum transmission. Didn't matter much, though. Her father preferred to walk to church or to Beaver Dam, and her mother always stayed home. Kathy wondered how much gas she had in the Toyota tank, how far it would take her. She'd decided to drive until she ran out and that was where she would stay. It would be fate. Or fumes. Whatever.

She looked back at her father. "Is it a sin to kill yourself if you lose your mind before you do it?"

"You gonna kill yourself?"

"No, I was just wondering, is all."

"You losing your mind?"

"No. Not yet." She added a chuckle to let him know she wasn't losing it, exactly. But sometimes she was so ready to climb out of her skin she thought she might just explode.

Hank cocked his head. "Well, you're asking a damn good question, Kathy. I guess you'd need to talk to God about that."

"I guess." God, Hank was always about God. She tolerated it, because she loved him. But God, she couldn't figure out the appeal.

Kathy looked again at her car. She'd bought the thing when she was a junior at Tazewell High, had even painted a green and white Tazewell bulldog on the driver's side door. Six years later, the car coughed and growled and smoked but managed to get her where she needed to go. "I'll call you when I get where I'm going."

"You best call. Your mama will be frantic if you don't."

"I know."

Hank nodded, looked back down at his Bible. Kathy hesitated then stepped over to give her father a quick hug. She hated displays of affection. They made her feel vulnerable, and there was little worse than being vulnerable.

She drew back. "See ya, then."

"Love you, Kath. I'll miss you."

"Me, too."

Hank went back to his scribbling. Kathy went down to her car, checked the gas—¾ of a tank, good—then left in a spray of gravel.

She made it all the way across the state on the gas, secured a smelly one-room, furnished apartment in a 50's-era apartment building on Artic Avenue with an $100 deposit—almost half of what she had on her—then landed the job at the restaurant two days later. She settled in as best she could for a girl who'd never seen the ocean, reading a couple of battered science-fiction novels from a used bookstore, salvaging and fixing a bicycle some rich idiot had tossed out with his back-alley trash, cleaning the apartment, working, sitting on the beach in the chair bought at a souvenir shop on Atlantic.

Six months into her new life now she has no friends but that's okay.

She has a little money in her pocket and that's good. She calls her parents once a week and lies about being happy.

Another herring gull lands near her, and she flicks her foot, sending it aloft. Her mind drifts to the novel she's currently reading, monsters in a basement in New York City, waiting until the woman who owns the brownstone is alone so they can suck her soul, make her pregnant with their spawn, all that typical horror crap. Stupid woman.

Stupid story. But she paid 50 cents for the book and is going to finish it, regardless.

"Kathy?"

She opens her eyes and shades them against the cold glare of the early afternoon. It's her co-worker, Jill, standing over her, dressed in a big wrap-around sweater.

Kathy sits up, stares at Jill. This is weird; Jill and Kathy aren't friends.

And Kathy isn't late for work; her watch reads 1:34.

"What?"

Jill pushes a strand of short blonde hair behind one big ear and grimaces.

Shit, am I fired or something?

"What's going on?"

"There was a phone call for you, up at Ocean Billy's."

Kathy looks over at the pier and the restaurant that sits atop it. Dark shingled walls, neon sign blinking in the window—OPEN— bright blue umbrellas over the outer patio where some patrons like to sit even though it's cold. The restaurant will remain open until the first of December, but then will close until March. Kathy isn't too worried; she already has applications in at al the 7-Elevens, Burger Kings, and Pizza Huts. If that doesn't work out, she'll get a job with housekeeping at one of the year-round motels.

"Don't you even have a cell?" Jill seems a bit put out, yet a bit guarded.

"No," says Kathy. "Who called?"

"It was your dad."

"Oh." *Oh, shit.*

Hank called. He never called; he always let her do the calling. And for him to try to reach her at work was troubling. Kathy's mouth is suddenly dry. "He say what he wanted?"

Jill turns on her toes and trudges toward the splintery steps to the pier, not looking back, her heels flinging out little sand sprays, her hair flapping like yellow wings. "Not really," she calls over her shoulder. "Something about your mom. He wants you to call him back as soon as you can."

"What about Mom?" Kathy shouts, scooping the unfolded chair under one arm and the tote under the other. The chair is ungainly, so she drops it and hurries on without it. If someone steals it, screw 'em, she hopes the cheap seat rips as soon as they sit on it. "Jill, what about my mom?"

"I don't know." Jill reaches the pier, clomps up the steps, and disappears into the restaurant. Kathy grits her teeth, shoulders the tote, and picks up her pace.

Ocean Billy's is dimly lit, with a low ceiling, narrow passages, and loops of fishing net clinging to the wall and filled with assorted plastic sea life. Kathy works her way past the first few tables and booths to the central waitress station, where Jill is scooping up a handful of menus, eyeing the family of five that just went out to the porch. The restaurant manager, Brian Dorren, is leaning forward on his hands, staring at the computer screen. It reflects blue on his face.

"There was a call for me?"

Brian looks up at Kathy. He's not happy. The computer must be screwed up again. "What? Yeah. About fifteen minutes ago. Your father."

"Can I use your phone?"

"Don't you have one?"

"At my apartment."

"A landline? You kidding me? That's all?"

"I'll make it quick. I'll pay you back." She hates being obliged. It's almost as uncomfortable as signs of affection. She raises her brows into the best pleading expression she can muster. It feels creepy.

Brian scoots over so Kathy can reach the phone, which is perched beside the computer monitor. Brian continues to glare at the screen as Kathy punches in her number back on Black Rock Ridge. It rings four times, five, six, then Hank picks up. His hello is weak, like he's down in a well. Not good. Kathy clenches her toes in her shoes.

"Dad, me. Heard you called. I was out on the beach. I'm at work now but don't start for a bit. What's going on?"

"You need to come home."

Her throat clicks. Shit, oh shit. "Why?"

"So... so much happened this morning."

Jill comes back in from the deck, the door slamming behind her. "I wish we would just close the deck after October," she mumbles. "Too damn cold and people complain that their food doesn't stay hot long. Duh."

Kathy backs away from the counter toward the wall, but it doesn't seem to be far enough. She cups her hand around the receiver, whispers, "Dad... what? What happened?"

"You mother's dead."

Kathy drops the receiver. It hits her foot and bounces once. She stares at it on the floor as her vision closes in and the world spins. Then it opens again, slowly, fuzzy around the edges. Brian's fingers poise over the keyboard. "You okay?"

Kathy can't shake her head. She doesn't want to pick up the receiver, but her body bends and her fingers take it against her will. She hugs it to her chest as if that will quiet what her father has to say. Yet she hears him on the line, faintly, "Kathy? You there, sweetie?"

"Yeah."

There are several glasses of water on a tray on the counter, ready to go out to the customers. Kathy reaches up and grapples one, spilling some of it onto the floor. She gulps the water down. She hates the way the water tastes with that slice of lemon on the side of the glass. Who the hell thought water was better that way?

"How did she die?" she manages. It's a whisper.

"Dog bit her. Attacked her."

"What? A dog? A fucking... dog?"

"Yes. There was something seriously wrong with it." He is on the verge of crying now, his voice broken, shuddering. "I don't know, Kathy. Annie was outside hanging the laundry. I told her not to, but you know she wants to do as much as she can when she feels up to it. So she was out there. The dog came out of the woods. She screamed for me; I was on the deck, writing my sermon. I raced through the house and out the back. The animal... dear God, Kathy, it was the most horrific looking animal I ever saw, mangy, red eyes, pieces of it falling off like it'd been in a grinder. There were metal bolts sticking up out of its skull, freakish thing."

"Didn't you stop it? Didn't you kill it?"

"If I'd a gun I'd have shot the moment I saw it, dear God, of course I would have. But there was the hoe, the one by the garden, and I grabbed it and ran and smashed on its back, over and over and over. Chunks of it flew away but it didn't matter. It didn't stop. You mother lost her balance. She fell. The dog bit her on the leg. She screamed. I screamed. I smashed the hoe down on the dog's head and it finally fell over, dead. Annie was still screaming and struggling..."

Kathy could see her mother in the dead grass of the backyard, on the ground, screaming, screaming. There was a scream in Kathy's own throat, burning, but it was locked down like a stone, wedged in place. "Dad..." she managed.

"...so I picked her up, carried her into the house, put her on the sofa. I washed out her leg, wrapped it up. My hands were shaking so hard I know it hurt her, I didn't want to hurt her, but I couldn't help it. I gave her some Tylenol. Then I called 911. I told them to get up here as fast as they could. I begged them. They promised they would. They said just stay calm."

Stay calm? Mom!

"When I hung up, Annie was relaxing some, she wasn't crying anymore, said she the pain was better, and she was tired. She fell asleep, and I thought, 'Oh, that's good. Thank God! She can rest 'til they get here.' I put her favorite blanket over her, and I sat beside her and prayed. 'God, save her, please God, let her be all right.' I don't know how long I sat there, I was numb, sitting, waiting, praying. It was like my heart had stopped moving. Like the world had stopped turning." Hank's words twist. He sobs suddenly. A red-hot spear cuts through Kathy's gut and she folds into it, pressing down into the pain. "I prayed for Annie, that the dog wasn't rabid, that she was just wounded. Then I looked up at her, and she was dead."

"Dad!"

"She was dead. No breath, no pulse. I pushed her heart over and over, to get it to start again but it didn't. It couldn't. She was dead."

"No." *Please no!*

Brian is looking at her now, his brow furrowed. He mouths, "You okay?" Kathy turns away from him.

Hank continues. "I went out to the deck. I fell on my knees and prayed again, more earnestly, prayed that this was a nightmare, not real, not her, not now. This wasn't right! She couldn't be dead. I couldn't wait for the ambulance to come; I couldn't just stay there and hope they'd find us when they'd never been here before. You know how confusing these mountain roads can be. I left the deck and ran down the road, hoping they knew where to find us, hoping they were on their way. I heard them in the distance then, beyond a curve, and I shouted for them as if they could hear me and follow my voice. They made it up to me, nearly ran me over, and then let me in to ride with them back up to our house. It was strange. I felt all would be well at that moment. They were all in white, like angels down from heaven. I climbed out of the ambulance, laughing out loud, certain they could change what happened, could bring her back around to me. I took them in to where Annie was laid out on the couch… and…"

There is a long pause. "And?" whispers Kathy.

"She was gone."

"I know, Dad, you said she was…"

"Not dead, Kathy. Gone. Gone from the living room, from the house. Blanket balled up. Pillow on the floor."

Kathy blinks, swallows dry air. "No, no, no, just hold on here."

"Gone like vanished in the Rapture."

"Wait, not…"

"Maybe our Father has called His own home. Maybe I didn't make it. Maybe I wasn't good enough... good enough to go with Annie..." His voice cracks, spirals upward.

Kathy's hand clenches around the receiver, hard, as if she is grasping her father's arm to make him shut up, shut up and think. "It wasn't the Rapture! I'm here, if you didn't notice, unless you think I'm not worthy of God's love, either! Now listen to me. Maybe she wasn't really dead. Maybe she was just really bad off, and you left her there and while you were on the porch, she got better and got up and..."

"And what?"

"I don't know? Went out back? Walked out into the woods? Maybe she wasn't thinking clearly and just wandered off. Did you even go look?"

Now Hank is screaming. The sudden rush of anger causes Kathy to gasp. "Of course, we looked! We looked all over the woods around the house! For, damn, almost an hour! She wasn't there! I showed the paramedics the dead dog; they bagged it and are taking it to the animal control office down the valley so they can check it out. They thought the metal spikes were peculiar, some kind of gothy or Satanic animal abuse. One of them said his daughter's boyfriend had pierced his nipples and cheeks and put spikes in his own head so he'd look like an alien. They said the dog didn't look rabid, but it was hard to tell for sure, as mangled as he was.

They told me to call and file a missing person's report and form a search party if she didn't come back home soon. Then they left."

Oh, God, what the hell is this? What is going on?

Kathy takes a deep breath. Her heart pounds. "Dad, listen, do what they said. Call the cops. File the report. Get a search party. I'll come home and we'll find her."

"Kathy, your mother is dead! I know *dead*! I've buried dead! I've said services for the dead! I've closed the eyes of the dead and offered prayers for the dead! I've touched the dead! I've held the dead! She was dead!"

Kathy closes her eyes. *This is not happening, this is insane. This is crazy.*

This is Suze Mustard crazy.

"Kathy?" It's Brian again. His face comes into her field of vision, but it's shimmering through the tears she didn't realize she was shedding.

"You look sick. I think you should go home. Want one of the waitresses to drive you?"

Kathy opens her eyes and looks at her boss, standing there with his vest and his nametag and his expression of concern. Suddenly the smell of cooked shrimp and oysters makes her nauseous, and she has to swallow hard to keep down her gorge.

"Yeah, I need to go home," she says. "But they can't drive me. It's fucking seven hours away."

5
Jenkie Mustard

Jenkie sits outside the trailer on a rusted, lopsided glider, one hand holding a cigarette and the other crammed in the pocket of her sweatpants, playing with loose threads around the hole there. The jacket she's wearing has gotten too hot—seems there is some sort of Indian summer going on here in Desper Hollow and she's sweating like a mule—but she won't take it off because it's too much effort once she's sat down. Jenkie's a big girl, five foot eight, tipping the scales at 283. Her seventeenth birthday was yesterday, but she didn't have anyone to really celebrate with 'cause Bink is Bink and the hollows are hollows. She'd thought about walking down to her mama's house but then her mama would want to know where she'd been at and what she'd been up to, and that wouldn't be good, no sir. Jenkie's hair is normally brown, but she recently dyed it dark red. She has brown eyes and a pointed nose like her younger sister Suze had. There are four pierced holes in each ear, but she usually just keeps studs in the lower holes. The others have started to close up.

Today, Jenkie's in one of what Bink calls her "I Hate Granny" moods.

And if there was ever a woman to hate, it's Granny Mustard, even though she's been dead for months. Damn old witch. It's Granny's fault that Jenkie is stuck up in the wilderness that is Desper Hollow in a piece of shit, mouse-infested, leaky trailer with four living dead people and one dead dog locked in the bedrooms who make the place stink like a sun-warmed slaughterhouse. It's Granny's fault, all right. If she'd just decided it was okay to die when she was supposed to die and didn't start looking for a way to stay alive. If she hadn't made Jenkie and Suze work with her over the summer, teaching them some of her magic, her moonshine potions, then Jenkie would still be living at home, going to school off and on and looking for a new boyfriend.

Jenkie draws on the smoke, flicks an ash, and kicks her heel into the dirt. The little bit of sunlight that is able to find its way through the dense trees up and around Desper Hollow sparkles on the fallen blanket of oak and maple leaves.

Now, sure, there were times when Jenkie enjoyed what she was doing. Sometimes she savors being in the mountain wilderness three miles southwest from the rest of the Mustard clan, with no one to tell her what to do except herself, bossing around Bink Bickerstaff (a 30-year-old idiot, once her boyfriend but only for six days, which is when she realized he had some sort of problem with his brain that made him smart about some things but stupid as a gnat about other things), experimenting off and on with Granny's moonshine, eating whatever the hell she wants (Bink makes a run down to a Tazewell once every two weeks for groceries, beer, and gasoline for the generator he's rigged up to the trailer), sending Bink out to trap living prey to feed the hollows, which gives her time alone to masturbate, nap, or watch old video tapes on the machine the hunter left here before he abandoned the place.

Other times, however, a dark heaviness falls on her mind, and she hates it all and wants to burn it to the ground like her sister Suze burned the town of Beaver Dam. Burn the dog (there is only one now; Doug got out and away three days ago when she wasn't paying attention and she's not seen him since and doesn't have the energy to go looking), the hollows, Bink, herself, the dented, mouse-pissy trailer, all of it. Douse it with kerosene, light a cigarette, drop it in the middle of the kitchen floor and let it go up in a blaze of glory.

Behind her in the trailer she can hear the hollows slamming around and growling. They have broken the glass on both bedroom windows, but luckily the windows are just tiny ones, too small for any of them to crawl out through. Now they take turns at the windows, their noses or chins hooked over the rim, drooling, jibbering, snarling at every warm-blooded living thing that happens by—crows, hawks, sometimes even a squirrel. Sometimes one will figure out how to get an arm through the hole and by some miracle of reflex will actually capture a curious sparrow. The bird will be yanked through the window hole and in a matter of seconds, nothing but a couple feathers would drift back out.

Bink is gone for the afternoon, which is fine by Jenkie. She pretty much hates him. And he looks like what you'd think a Bink would look like—short and grimy. He has a beard like a hay bale that exploded from the inside. He has a forehead the size of a toaster and a tic in his eye. He constantly pulls at his nose like there were bugs in there. He's a native of Beaver Dam, son of a miner and a seamstress, but his parents moved to Ohio when he was fifteen, dropping him off at his friend Benny's house where he remained. A demented genius, he tinkers with electronics and made a minor name for himself with his little workshop in the Benny's garage. Bink's the one who rigged up the charger, and he's the one who planted the electrodes in the brains of the dead dogs so Jenkie, remotely, could keep them from coming after her and make them stop or attack.

Of course, he'd also been the one who forgot to shut and lock the metal plate over the roof hole last week, letting one of the hollows—the one who can talk—escape last week. Idiot! Bink said he'd forgotten to turn off the VCR and didn't want to use any more electricity than they needed to, so he'd had hurried down the ladder without securing the panel. Jenkie had shoved him and said fuck the electricity, keeping the hollows locked up was a hell of a lot more important.

So alone now, except for the hollows slobbering at the windows, Jenkie has time to think and get to feeling like shit all over again.

And yeah, it's all Granny Mustard's fault. Back in June, Granny sent an invitation to Jenkie and her sister Suze, two of Granny's great-granddaughters, to come up and visit her in her cabin at the top of Moon Peak at the top of Black Rock Ridge. Okay, sure, "invited" might be too mild a term. Demanded was more like it. Neither liked Granny, both were scared of her, and had only been to the old woman's cabin on Granny's birthdays, when the rest of the Mustard clan took food and presents up to the Mustard matriarch in an attempt to appease her.

Those visits weren't too bad because the adults did all the talking and the kids pretty much hung back and kept their mouths shut. However, Jenkie couldn't take her eyes off the bones Granny hung on strings across her windows like curtains, or the little animal skulls that lined the edges of the porch. Mojo, bad mojo, should anyone cross her.

But up the sisters went on that day, more terrified of not going and what would happen if they refused, bitching at each other in their nervousness, looking over their shoulders to make sure there were no bears or rabid raccoons around, trudging the brambled trail that wound back, forth, and up past the other Mustard homes and barns and corn patches to Moon Peak. They paused at the foot of Granny's sloping yard, took collective breaths and walked up to the ancient cabin.

One thing Granny Mustard was well known for on all the ridges and coves and hollow around and down to Beaver Dam was her moonshine.

She made the best, strongest shine around. One sip would blow your shoes off. Two would light a fire in your mind. Three would send you out of your skull for an hour or two, and that was what her customers wanted.

Granny's stills were located along several small creeks that crossed the lower portion of her property, and she worked them from July until October, distilling hundreds of gallons with the help of several of her sons and grandsons, then hauling it out to sell in the dark of night to men and women who loitered at the outskirts of Beaver Dam or along one of the unnumbered, unpaved roads that traveled into the mountains and died.

These same sons and grandsons also went on yearly raids, smashing other men's stills and beating the shiners into temporary compliance. Sure, the rivals tried to do the same to Granny, though were rarely successful. Granny had too much muscle-heavy family living in cabins encircling her land for her rivals to get through. The few who did, well, they either limped home missing one body part or other, or they disappeared altogether. No one ever called the law on Granny Mustard. They were all in the illegal businesses and nobody needed the light of the law snooping around. And knowing Granny had a touch of ancient magic made leaving her alone all the better choice.

The day Jenkie and Suze went up to Granny's cabin was a hot and strangely quiet one. Summer insects were silent. Crows, though dozens of them hopped about on top of the old woman's clothesline, didn't caw.

Even the wind, which usually whistled or wailed this high up, was still.

The girls found Granny Mustard on her porch, bowing back and forth on the oak sapling rocker, fanning herself with a folded-up magazine, a paring knife and bowl of damsons in her lap. She was a startlingly shriveled figure, arms like sticks wrapped in tissue paper, face like that of an apple head doll with eyes so far back in the skull you could hardly see them except when she blinked.

Jenkie and Suze reached the bottom of the porch steps, stopped, glanced at the little skulls rimming the porch floor. Then they looked up at Granny. You never spoke first around Granny Mustard because if you did you chanced getting a slap across the mouth. She stuck her magazine fan under her arm, peeled a damson in her hand, dropped it into the bowl then lifted her gaze. Her lips parted and a second later came her crackling voice. "I need you girls to help me a bit."

"Okay," said Jenkie.

"Okay," said Suze.

There were three rooms in Granny Mustard's cabin. In the front room were Granny's chair, a chifforobe with a drawer missing, a small table and lantern, a cot, and a tin bedpan. An ancient, hand-stitched sampler hung on the wall next to a nail from which dangled a large beaver pelt. The two windows were obscured by curtains of dusty, yellowed animal bones.

Through the door was the kitchen, and off the kitchen the pantry.

Granny led Jenkie and Suze to the kitchen and pointed at the big metal bowl on the black walnut table she used for washing dishes and cleaning catfish.

"See that in there?"

They looked

In the bowl was a chicken. Well, it had been a chicken. Now it was freshly chopped chicken parts. A head. Feet. Wings. Torso. Not plucked for cooking but just chopped up pieces with feathers poking out. When Jenkie made a mistake of shrugging, Granny whacked her bony hand.

Granny sniffed, pinched her nose, and said, "Dyin' ain't on my agenda. You hear me?"

In unison, both girls said, "Yes 'um."

"Got too much to do."

"Yes 'um."

"So I aim not to do it."

"No 'um."

Jenkie and Suze stood without speaking or moving as Granny Mustard went into the pantry and came out with a jar. "Ain't what you think," she said, shaking the jar lightly and letting the brown liquid slosh around inside the glass. "Ain't shine. Not normal shine, anyway. It's special shine. Special 'gredients. Special power I done put in it."

Jenkie nodded then glanced nervously at her younger sister.

"I need you to help me catch pieces," said Granny.

Jenkie almost said, "Pieces of what?" but didn't want another whack.

"Get ready now," she said, her deep-set, milky blue eyes glinting.

"Okay."

"Lean in."

They leaned in.

Granny Mustard unscrewed the lid of the jar and poured the contents over the chicken parts, like she was adding a marinade. Then she put the jar down and looked into the bowl, one hand on her angular hip, her brows drawn.

The chicken head twitched.

Jenkie and Suze flinched.

The head twitched again, and the beak started opening and

closing, slowly at first, then picking up speed until it looked like a pair of castanets Jenkie saw a Spanish lady use once on TV, back when her family had a TV and it worked.

"Lord a-mercy!" whispered Suze.

Then the legs began to tremble, the claws clutching and unclutching.

"Get ready," said Granny Mustard.

Jenkie's lips curled in between her teeth. She held her breath.

The dismembered wings started flapping futilely. The torso started turning on its axis. Then the parts, in one explosive shudder of feather and flesh, scrambled, flopped, and skittered around the base of the bowl and then up and over the sides. The sluggish torso tried to roll up and out but couldn't quite make it. Granny grabbed for one leg, but Suze instinctively jumped back until Granny barked at her. Suze grappled for the other leg, but it slipped past and plopped onto the floor.

Jenkie snatched up a wing as it scooted to the edge of the table. It twitched and thumped against her palm. Suze dove for the escaped leg, which was now hopping around drunkenly on the worn linoleum. With her free hand, Jenkie snatched up one of Granny's empty moonshine jars from the nearest shelf, dropped to her knees and brought it down over the leg, trapping it against floor. Suze sat up and back, her fists balled, her eyes bugged.

"Head!" said Granny. Jenkie glanced up to see the old woman leaning over, holding one leg and the second wing, with her elbow pinning the roly-poly torso to the tabletop. It had made it up out of the bowl, after all.

"Get the damn head, you!"

Jenkie looked around, keeping the jar pressed to the floor so the leg wouldn't be able to scratch its way underneath. Suze was beyond herself, crying now. "I don't see it! Where is it?"

Granny Mustard jerked her head in the direction of the back door, which was cracked open a couple inches. The chicken head was dragging itself toward the door, trailing a bit of spine, the beak opening and closing, opening and closing, snap, snap, snap. Its tiny eyes glowed a strange, dark red.

"Jenkie, you get it!" Suze said, but Jenkie was still holding the wing and keeping the jar over the leg.

"Don't you dare let that head get out this house!" said Granny. Her little sunken eyes flashed like laser points.

Suze pushed herself up and stumbled toward the door just in time to slam her foot down on the head and hear it crunch beneath the sneaker.

"Damn that, Suze!" said Granny. "Ain't supposed to kill it! S'posed to see how long it lives!"

"I..." Suze began. "I didn't know..."

Granny looked like she'd've slapped Suze if she weren't fighting the other chicken parts on the table. Jenkie's knees were starting to hurt, being down on the floor like that. She wasn't much for squatting or kneeling.

Then the wing in Jenkie's hand stopped flapping. The leg in the jar went still. The torso under Granny's elbow stopped trying to buck itself away.

Granny's cheeks puffed for a moment then she said, "That's it. Not even five minutes. Hell's bells. Well, I'll just have to try again. You girls go toss all this garbage out back in the slop pile, you hear me?"

They heard and they did, stomping through the poison ivy and chicory, past the rotting barn to the slop pile, a low, lumpy hillock at the tree line where all Granny's dead pigs and chickens had been buried and where she tossed kitchen scraps. They were too scared to look straight at each other.

"Maybe we can go on home," Suze whispered as they wiped their hands on their shorts, the chicken parts flung onto the pile with a couple handfuls of dirt tossed on top for good measure.

Jenkie shook her head. "You crazy? She didn't tell us we could go."

"Well, we could say we heard Mama callin'." Suze's eyes were tiny and bright like the eyes of a hog that knew an axe was hovering over its head.

"From a half-mile away? Screw you, Suze! Granny's got better hearin' than you and me put together. She'd hear Mama callin', or not callin'. She'd know we was lyin'."

"I don't want to go in there no more, Jenkie."

"Me, neither. But we ain't got no choice."

Suze grabbed her elbow. "What's Granny doin' in there? What's with that shine all about? What she mean to do? She said she didn't wanna die but what…?"

Jenkie yanked her arm away. "I don't fuckin' know! Now shut up, she's probably watchin' us from the kitchen door."

They clenched their fists and jaws and headed back across the yard to Granny Mustard's cabin. Inside, they found her plucking another chicken—a whole one this time—her arms covered in feathers and tiny spots of blood. Without looking up she said, "Now nothin' you seen today is anyone's business but mine and yours. And it really ain't yours, cept'n I need the extra hands ya'll got. You hear me?"

"Yes'um."

"Yes'um."

They waited.

Granny Mustard turned her head toward her great-granddaughters. It was like watching a hawk turning toward a chipmunk. Jenkie's arms flushed cold. "Ya'll go on now. Come back tomorrow 'round noon. Don't make me send one o' my boys to come lookin' for you."

"No'um."

"No'um."

They walked out of the cabin, down across the weedy yard, onto the footpath, and then ran all the way home.

The rest of the summer, Suze and Jenkie had to go up to Granny's cabin to help her with her experiments. They gathered new ingredients, helped her catch bits of animal that ran all over the kitchen, into the front from, and sometimes out to the porch. They washed jars and dumped animal parts into the compost pile when they were done with them.

But they were always sent outside when Granny got out the book.

The large, leather-bound volume was kept hidden beneath the pantry floorboards. They knew this because after a few days of being sent out to the backyard, Jenkie summoned up enough courage to kneel down in the grass beneath the kitchen window then raise herself up enough to peer in.

The book was thick and old, cracking along the spine and

with pages so yellow it looked like a cat had peed on it. Granny would take it out when she had a batch of shine she wanted to make special. She would line the jars up on the table, take off their lids, and put the book down before them. When she opened the cover, everything around it—the jars, Granny's hands, the tabletop—frosted up, as if the book itself breathed ice.

Granny would read something from a page there, some sort of long and rambling chant in an unrecognizable language of hums, whispers, and moans. Granny's eyes would roll up and go pure white, one of the most horrifying things Jenkie had ever seen. Granny's own breath grew cold and misty on the air. Then she'd shut the book, put the lids on the jars, hide the book away, and call the girls in for whatever chores were next.

Over the course of the weeks the special shine became stronger. The dead animals and pieces of animals came back to life for ten minutes.

Then fifteen. Soon, nearly an hour. They wandered or skittered about, snapping, growling, scratching. If there were eyes, the eyes morphed from black to an eerie red. Granny laughed chillingly once and said, "I'm like them Wright brothers. If they'd stopped trying after their third flight, folks'd still be travelin' round on the ground."

Suze frowned She didn't know who the Wright brothers were. Jenkie did but had no idea how Granny knew. The old lady never went to school, and as far as Jenkie could tell, she never read anything except for seed catalogs, farming magazines, and now that mysterious, leather-bound book.

Then, one evening in late July, Suze went up to Granny's cabin without Jenkie and that's when all hell broke loose. Less than two hours later, Suze was back at the house, searching frantically for a butcher knife and a can of gasoline. Mama wanted to know why but Suze was all giddy and white-eyed, screaming shit like "I got away from her! I did! Woo hoo! And I'm gonna stop her! I'm gonna stop it all! Just watch me! I'll set it right!"

Then she was out of the house again, waving that butcher knife, the gas can slapping her thigh. Mama tried to chase after her but gave up after a couple yards because she had a heel spur. Jenkie said no way was she going to get between Suze and whatever that knife was for. Though she knew it had something to do with Granny.

Of course, it did.

Then Beaver Dam was burning like Atlanta in Gone With the Wind.

Deputy Buddy Floyd found Suze curled up a tree with a bloody stump and the butcher knife and the amputated hand on the ground. The deputy wrapped Suze's stump and got her into the patrol car, then stomped on the pedal to get her down to the hospital in Tazewell. In her haze of pain, Suze managed to tell him that Granny had left her cabin and made it down to town, slobbering and moaning, trying to catch Suze, trying to kill her. Suze escaped to her house, got the gasoline and the knife, then came back to find Granny had already eaten the manager of the Beaver Dam Motel and his wife, and was chomping on Perky, the parrot they kept in the motel office. As Suze faded into unconsciousness she mumbled, "She bit me... my hand. I had to chop off... knew what her spit might do... poison like snake venom..."

Deputy Floyd yelled at her to shut up and be still, but Suze went on, fading out, bleeding out. "We shoulda told somebody. Shoulda told 'em 'bout them chicken heads... them dead foxes and that shine, that bad shine..." Then she went still quiet and still at last.

None of that made sense to the deputy or the personnel at the hospital when they checked Suze's body. None of that made sense to Suze's mama, who cried and drank, drank and cried, locked in her bedroom. None of it made sense to anyone else in the Mustard family, not Granny's sons or grandsons or daughters or granddaughters, who wandered down out of the mountains to the ruins of Beaver Dam in little nuclear family clumps to marvel at the amazing destruction one of their own, and a teenager at that, had wrought. They attended Suze's wake, bringing big platters of cooked chicken that Jenkie couldn't look at, much less eat. They wept as if they really cared, though most of them didn't really, they were just happy it wasn't them doing something that stupid and ending up dead like that.

Granny didn't make it to the wake. This had some of the family wondering if she was sick or just being stubborn. The one and only thing that would get Granny out of her cabin and off Moon Peak was the death of one of her own. She'd tap down the mountainside to the wake, armed with an oak walking stick and wrapped in her smelly old shawl, then stand over the coffin and stare at the dead family member with her sunken little eyes.

Granny's two eldest grandsons, Burley and Calhoun, hiked to her cabin; they found it empty and left in quite a mess. The family searched the forests but came up empty. Two days later Granny's body was discovered in the wreckage behind the Beaver Dam Motel. Her head was bashed in good and solid, brain half out—most likely from a chunk of falling timber.

No one was sure how she was missed; the bodies of everyone else who'd died in town had been discovered right away, but there she was, all white-haired and papery skin and cracked skull, lying in the rubble. Burley and Calhoun rolled her up in burlap, hauled her body up Black Rock Ridge in the back of their pickup, and buried her in the Mustard family plot along with Suze and all the other assorted Mustards going back 168 years.

And that was that.

All done.

All over with.

Or not.

What Granny had started was by no means over. Jenkie felt a secret rush of power, now that Granny and Suze were gone. Burley or Calhoun would take over Granny's moonshine business, probably move up to Moon Peak and live there, the newest rulers of the clan. But nobody else in the family knew about Granny's immortality experiments.

Jenkie was certain she could continue Granny's work. She envisioned herself immortal, like Granny had, and even though Granny had come up short, Jenkie wouldn't. She imagined herself perfecting the shine then revealing her secret, and with the new respect she'd earned from the family she would take over where Granny had left off. Making everybody do what she told them. Punishing them if they didn't. And wouldn't that just rock the mountaintop? Wouldn't that just make life good for once?

She remembered a lot from her time in Granny's cabin. And so she collected her dogs Dan and Doug, a burlap sack, a few sweatshirts she liked, and then sneaked up to Granny's cabin when Burley and Calhoun weren't around. Some of the jars of special moonshine were gone, knocked over and spilled, which was disappointing. But there were six full jars, sealed up with tightened lids, which Jenkie wrapped in the sweatshirts and put into the sack. Then she added a couple pots and pans, several socks filled with the most recent dried ingredients Granny'd used, and that creepy, battered, leather-bound book from under the pantry floor. Holding it gave her the willies; it was as cold as she expected it would be.

Then, with the sack over her shoulder like some weird and sneaky Santa, she headed down the road to where Bink was living with his friend Benny and told him of her plans. She swore him to secrecy, adding, "I'll kill you, you tell anybody." He was cool with that, liking the idea of a secret project, and suggested the abandoned trailer over in Desper Hollow as the best place to do what she wanted to do.

Desper Hollow was a location few people knew about, and those who knew, avoided. There was no reason to go there. It was hard to get into and out of, nestled in the gap between Black Rock Ridge to the east and Ragged Ridge to the west, past the Burris Mount talus slope then down a narrow, steep incline. There was no clear passage at all, what with the lay of granite outcroppings and deep ravines. An overgrown footpath led to it, just wide enough for a carefully driven vehicle to squeeze through. It was a miracle that a trailer had made it there, but no surprise that no one ever tried to take it back out again. The hollow itself was just less than four acres square, a plot where sunlight filtered through the tree branches just once a day and for less than an hour, leaving the rest of the day drenched in shadows. Because of the steep slopes around the hollow, rain didn't just trickle down but poured in like oil into a tractor engine. All in all, one of the last places someone would want to spend much time. But Bink was right. It had the privacy Jenkie was looking for. It had the trailer.

Bink rigged a generator and had a Jeep that was able to tackle the terrain.

Things went pretty well those first few weeks. Jenkie caught and killed mice in a cheese-filled shoebox. Then she brought their little lifeless bodies back to life for several hours, then a day, and then two days by adding new combinations and varying amounts of Granny's ingredients into the shine. The liquid had already been chanted over, so there was no real need for the leather-bound book. But it fascinated Jenkie as much as scared her.

When she dared to touch it, to open it, cold air drifted up from the pages, hitting her in the face and lining her eyebrows with frost. The words inside were gibberish, and not made of real letters at all but weird slashes and curls and dots. The markings seemed to crawl on the pages. She never kept the book open for long, quickly hiding it back inside a kitchen cabinet.

Jenkie went from killing trailer mice to scavenging dead squirrels from the forest around the trailer. The shine brought them back, too, though squirrels tended to be all snappy and chittery and too hard to catch once they got spinning around on the trailer floor. So she ended up squashing them with a brick. Dead birds were next, and voles, and rabbits. A little bath of special shine stirred them from dead death to living death. Bink marveled at it all, said someday this would make them famous.

But it didn't take long for the fun to run out. First of all, she'd hit a wall. She couldn't get dead critters to live past three days. Second of all, even though she'd wanted things to be a secret, a secret was no fun when nobody knew it. And nobody but she and Bink knew what she was doing and so nobody cared. In fact, she'd heard from Bink that her mama thought she'd run away since Suze died. Jenkie summoned her courage again and opened Granny's old book, hoping that maybe she could make the shine stronger by chanting over it like Granny had, a double-dose, if you will. She steeled herself against the cold, and tried, through chattering lips, to make sense out of the gibberish, but her lips couldn't figure out how to form the sounds, and when done, the shine was no more powerful than it had been before she started. She thought about throwing the book away, moving back home. The days plodded along, and life was way, way boring.

Then in mid-August Bobby Boo Anderson wandered into Desper Hollow. And it got good again in a most dark and troubling way.

Dan and Doug heard Bobby Boo first and started growling at the door. Jenkie was on the couch, eating peanuts and dangling a recently dead, red-eyed baby possum from a string like a puppet, making it walk back and forth across her foot. Bink was on the floor on his back, having fallen asleep after a meal of canned chili and applesauce. He snored, and with ever fifth or sixth snore, he farted. The room was rank with the smell. Scattered around him on the floor were wires and bits of snipped metal and screws and pliers and nails; all day he'd been working on a little electrical charger thing. "All police have 'em," he'd said proudly. "They're called tasers. You can stop a man in his tracks. And this one is powerful enough to stop ten men in their tracks. Just in case one your relatives or somebody else gets to wandering too far from home and finds us. We don't want them in here, snoopin'."

"Huh," said Jenkie. "Won't that much electricity kill 'em?"

"Maybe," said Bink with a grin.

"How you gonna know if that charger thing works?"

Bink said, "It works. I know what I'm doing. A bear comes 'round, he's down for the count. A Mustard comes 'round, he's down for the count. Better than a gun."

"Whatever." Jenkie got up to cook the chili. Retarded genius, she thought as she opened the can and dumped the shit into a pan, put it on the hot plate.

So Jenkie was playing with a dead possum puppet and Bink was snoring and farting on the living room floor when the sound of distant footsteps shuffling through leaves drove the dogs to their feet and to the trailer door, where they whined and pranced nervously, their toenails clicking on the linoleum. Bink struggled awake, squinted, rolled to his side and pushed himself to his feet. There was drool in his beard.

"What's that?"

Jenkie shrugged. "I dunno. But it's something comin' this way."

Bink and Jenkie squinted out window. There was Bobby Boo Anderson, or something that looked kind of like him, forcing his feet forward, swinging his arms like some kind of drunk gorilla, and heading toward the trailer.

"What the hell?" said Bink, digging crusty sleep from his eyes.

"That Bobby Boo? What's he doin' way out there? I thought he'd gone to Hollywood."

"That's what his Aunt Dottie said."

"Damn." Bink sucked air through pursed lips. "What's wrong with him?"

"Like I fucking know."

Bobby Boo got closer, his head tipping back and forth like his neck was broken. His eyes appeared reddened, rheumy. Closer now, and Jenkie could see smears of dried blood all over his face and the tattered remnants of his shirt and jeans. There was a big, festering wound on his arm. Animal fur was stuck against his face. He was barefoot, and his feet seem to have been shredded by a hay baler.

"He been eating raw animals?" asked Bink.

"I don't fucking know! Jeez!"

The dogs were way crazy now, spinning and leaping on the floor, howling. And before Jenkie could stop him, Bink opened the front door and the dogs charged out, dove off the steps, and barreled across the rocky stretch of weeds toward Bobby Boo.

"Fuck you, Bink!" Jenkie screamed.

"They'll bite him and chase him away, okay?"

"Bink! You asshole!"

The dogs got within several yards of Bobby Boo and skidded to a halt. Their backs bristled, their lips curled back, baring their teeth.

"Dan! Doug!" Jenkie shrieked. "Get back here!"

But no doing. The dogs were all about Bobby Boo invading their territory, and after a moment's hesitation and with a howl of indignation, they charged him. Bobby Boo swung open his arms like a mother collecting her children. The dogs jumped up, burying their teeth into his shoulders. Bobby Boo sunk his teeth into the dogs' necks, one at a time, tearing out their windpipes. Then he let go of Dan and took a bite out of Doug's spine. Dan struck the ground. His body spasmed in the leaves.

Then Bink, stupid, brilliant, idiot Bink, dashed out of the trailer with his newly invented charger and aimed it at Bobby Boo. He got almost within arms' reach and shouted, "Hey Bobby Boo! This is for you! Woob woob woob!" and pulled the trigger.

ZING!

The barbs struck Bobby Boo in the upper right arm. He dropped Doug but didn't fall to his knees, though Bink had assured Jenkie that was how a charger worked. Instead, he trained his dreadful red eyes on Bink and stretched out his mottled arms.

"Ah, crap!" Bink squealed. He let go of the charger, spun on his heels, and raced back to the trailer. He jumped up the two front steps and into the door but refused to let Jenkie close it.

"No, don't!" he said, shoving her backward. His voice was high-pitched, manic. "This is something weird! We gotta catch this guy! We gotta figure him out."

"He's gonna kill us! Bink, my dogs!"

"Shut up!

"He killed my fucking dogs now shut the fucking door!"

"No!" He pushed her again, harder, and she sprawled on the floor.

Stars blew up behind her eyes.

"Crawl behind the sofa and stay put!"

"I hate you, Bink!"

Through the open door and the sparking stars and the tears she didn't realize she was crying until then. Jenkie saw Bobby Boo reach the front steps, dragging the wires and the charger. He struggled to climb the steps as the flies hummed around him, his tongue dangling out the side of his mouth, grunting like an old man with constipation. Slap, slap, went the tops of his lazy feet as they worked their way upward. This close and Jenkie noticed that both of his ears were gone, and half his nose. His fingers were bones with flesh and muscles clinging on in spots.

They scrabbled at the air, reaching for the open doorway. The smell coming off him was putrid and powerful. Jenkie gasped, sucking in the foul air. Peanuts rocketed from her stomach into her mouth. She hacked them out.

And that was the moment, and only moment, Jenkie did exactly what Bink told her. She scooted her butt around and behind the sofa, where she clung to the ratty fabric, tucked her head, and uttered the one sincere prayer she'd ever said in her life. "God, help me!"

She heard Bink's giddy, insane laughter as he trotted into the narrow hallway, taunting Bobby Boo. "Come on, big man, you want some of me? Huh? Come on, come on! Nyuck, nyuck, nyuck!" She felt Bobby Boo's heavy, sloppy footsteps as he entered the trailer, rocking it on its worn foundation, following Bink. Jenkie crammed her fist into her mouth and screamed. The sound was a squeak, but loud enough.

There was gritty snarling, a shuffling in her direction. Jenkie's eyes flew open. A pair of rotten flesh-covered hands grabbed the top of the sofa. A second later, Bobby Boo's face zoomed over the sofa, stopping inches from her own. The red eyes radiated a cold deeper than a January freeze.

Jenkie's voice fell back into her throat. Her eyes bugged. For the barest moment, she was unable to move, but then as one mangled hand shot out toward her hair, she shoved herself backward so fast the loose nails in the floor caught and ripped her ass through her sweatpants. She slammed against the counter that divided the living room from the kitchen, just beyond Bobby Boo's scrabbling reach. She tucked her head and closed her eyes. *I'm gonna die! I'm gonna get eaten up by Bobby Boo Anderson!* And it was gonna hurt like hell.

Then Bink shouted, "Here, hey, Bobby Boo!" Jenkie's eyes flew open to see Bobby Boo's head creak around to face Bink, who was back in the living room, waving his arms and hopping up and down. "Come here, you stinking fuck!"

Bobby Boo growled and spun about faster than Jenkie could have imagined, spittle and clotted blood flying from his lips. The charger whipped out and around at the end of the wires. Bobby Boo stood and lumbered toward Bink, who dashed back down the hallway and out of sight. Then Bobby Boo stumbled out of sight, too.

Another scream erupted in Jenkie's throat; she slapped her hand over her mouth to shove it down. *Shut up shut up, let him have Bink and then I can get out of here!* She pulled herself up and stared at the open door. *Go, go, get out now!*

Her ass stinging from the nails and her heart pounding like a teenaged boy on a hooker, Jenkie heaved herself up and stumbled around the couch. She glanced down the hall as she fled to the door. Bobby Boo was lumbering through the open bedroom doorway at the end of the hall, unsteadily, shoulders pounding off either side of the doorframe.

Bink's trapped! Oh, shit, Bink's gonna die!

She laughed out loud with relief and horror and the thought of the electrical genius getting killed by a fucking, red-eyed, arm-chargered Bobby Boo Anderson in a piss-shit trailer in the middle of fucking mountainous nowhere. Wouldn't Benny scratch his head over that? Wouldn't his customers marvel at the insanity of it all? "That's a damn crazy thing," they'd say, rubbing their chins and pulling at their beards. "That's almost Suze Mustard crazy, you ask me."

Then she saw a leg shoot out from behind the door and catch Bobby Boo on the shin. He lost his footing and fell flat on his face with a moist thunk. Bink darted from behind the bedroom door and into the hallway. He yanked the bedroom door closed, trapping Bobby Boo.

Jenkie stood still at the open living room door, staring down the hall.

"Got him! Got him!" said Bink, panting hard, his voice twisted into his little girl squeak. "Tripped him and now we got him! Now hurry, Jenkie! Go get me that old roll of deer fencing out back by the tree!"

"What? You kidding me?"

"Get it, Jenkie! Hurry the fuck up!"

The bedroom door began to rattle on its hinges then was slammed hard from the inside, over and over.

"He's tryin' to get out! Hurry! Get the roll! Then get my tool kit off the kitchen counter!"

Run away or help Bink? Get out, go home, let Bink die?
"Jenkie!!"
Or help him and see what happens. See what happens next. Holy shit-olie, what might happen next?!

Jenkie found the roll of chain link and dragged it into the trailer. It was tall and heavy as a mother, and the sharp, twisted wire edges dug deep divots in the trailer floor. Panting, sweating, she wrangled it down the hall to Bink, where the door was starting to crack around the edges.

"He can't remember how to use a door knob! Ha! What a stupid idiot! I wonder what Larry, Moe, and Curly would do at a time like this!" Bink laughed hysterically, both hands gripping the knob, leaning back with all his might in case Bobby Boo suddenly did recall. "Now, tool kit!"

Jenkie retrieved the rusty kit then took Bink's place pulling with all her weight against the doorknob with her heels dug into the floor. Bink hammered one end of the metal mesh wire roll, which was nearly as tall as the door, in place, then secured it with long nails, heavy-duty fencing staples, and screws, all up and down both sides, leaving the remainder still in a roll that leaned against the hall wall. Bobby Boo continued to growl, grumble, snarl, and pound and scratch the door.

"I don't think he can bust down the door, and I don't think he'll figure out the doorknob," said Bink. He spoke rapidly, clearly thrilled and terrified, patting the wire fencing as if it were a friend, or animal. "But even if he does, I don't think he'll get through this. Even a bear couldn't get through this. And I mean a big bear. A big damn bear!"

"You sure?" Jenkie's throat and mouth were dry as sand. It hurt to speak.

Bink rolled his eyes. "I fix stuff, you know that. And this is fixed."

Jenkie touched the wire fencing then flinched as Bobby Boo thumped hard against the door behind it. She thought of Bobby Boo's halting but determined steps. She thought about his tattered flesh and his hideous red eyes and the expression of mindless hunger twisting the features of his face—what was left of them, anyway.

Then she thought of the red eyes that all of the special moonshine experiments had ended up with. Those red, haunting, searing eyes.

Bobby Boo had those same eyes. He moved like a reanimated piece of chicken.

"Shit!" she hissed.

"Shit, yeah!" said Bink. "We caught us one hell of a stinkin' crazy man!"

"No, no, Bink. Don't you know what we got here?"

"Yeah, it's Bobby Boo Anderson, and…"

"Hell yeah, it's Bobby Boo. Or it was. But he's one of the experiments! One of Granny's experiments!"

Bink blinked. "What? Oh, no…"

"Oh, yeah!" She licked her lips. Suddenly her mouth wasn't so dry anymore. "Listen, idiot, you seen what I done here, following Granny's steps. inYou know what I'm up to, you know what's been happening!"

"Well…"

"Well, are you that fucking blind? Are you that fucking deaf? Are you that fucking… what's it when you can't smell worth shit? Whatever. Are you that, too? His eyes is all red, like the animals I been bringing back to life."

Bink left the hall for the living room. Jenkie followed. Back in the bedroom, Bobby Boo continued to grunt and pound.

Jenkie slumped down on the sofa, thinking hard, and it made her head hurt. "Here's what I think. I think Granny had a batch of special shine that she'd fixed up when Suze and I weren't at her house. I think maybe for some reason she killed Bobby Boo…"

"I always thought killing Bobby Boo would be a good idea. What an asshole."

"… and after she killed him she poured the shine on him like I pour it on the dead animals. But I think this special shine was the strongest stuff yet, something I didn't get when I went to her cabin, 'cause there were shattered jars all around, spilled jars."

"So you think little ole Granny killed Bobby Boo?"

"Maybe she did."

"Then poured the shine on him?"

"I dunno. Maybe. Something like that. Maybe he tried to steal some of her shine, or bust up a still, or steal the money she got hidin' in her pantry.

"C'mon now, it ain't like Granny never had nobody killed before."

They sat in silence, thinking. Then Jenkie said, "Too bad the shine didn't work on Granny. If she came back to life she could tell me what that damn book is all about, how to read it, how to use it."

Bink laughed. "Really? You want her alive again? Like Bobby Boo is now? If she was like Bobby Boo I don't think she'd be able to tell you anything at all. That's one fucked up dude."

Jenkie rubbed her ass carefully, testing the gouges from the nail heads.

"Okay, no, not really. But it would'a been kinda cool to see her locked up in a trailer bedroom, trying to get out but so brain-gone that she couldn't even figure out a doorknob."

"Yeah."

That had been three damn months ago. Since then, they had collected a few other dead-alive, red-eyed hollows. Two of them were Dan and Doug, who had come back to life, snarling and stumbling and snared with a rope and tarp then put into the back room with Bobby Boo. Then came along five other hollows, humans this time, captured and stowed away with the help of Bink's charger, now used on the heads and nowhere else.

Jenkie had let one starve, Bink had let one escape (leaving Jenkie to hunt the hollow down), and that has been about the extent of the adventure in Desper Hollow.

Big fucking deal.

The fun has worn paper-thin once more.

Jenkie cusses, kicks at the leaves scattered about her feet, then sets the glider to rocking as fast as she can make it go—squeak, squeak, squeak—hoping the squeaks will drown out her thoughts and the sounds of the hollows grumbling inside the trailer. If she and Suze had refused to get involved with Granny's awful moonshine experiments, then she wouldn't be stuck up here with no boys to flirt with, no phone or computer, and only an old television with a VHS tape player that you have to shake to make work. Oh, and a bag of VHS tapes that Bink stole from the Salvation Army drop off in Tazewell—The Best of the Three Stooges, some Grizzly Adams (which are okay, Jenkie thinks the Griz is hot), five science fiction films from the 1960s, some stupid yoga tapes (yeah, right, Bink), a Gone with the Wind boxed set with damaged box, a bunch of episodes of Jim Bowie, and the complete Alfred Hitchcock Presents.

Squeak, squeak, squeak.

She rocks faster, harder as a wind picks up and the hollows grunt through the broken windows. She plugs her ears but that doesn't help.

"Shut up, Bobby Boo! Shut up, Stead! Shut up all you freaks!" she screams but this only makes it worse. They sound like pigs. Hungry, dangerous, man-eating pigs.

The last time she got into her "I Hate Granny" mood a few weeks back, it had been a freezing, rainy October day. She'd been stirring ingredients into a jar of moonshine, swirling it round and round and feeling dizzy with the movements. "This sucks," she'd said, stopping in mid-stir. "All this work and for what? What's the point?"

And Bink, being Bink, had given her grief.

"Quit your belly-achin'," he'd said, down on his knees in the trailer's living room in front of the TV, untangling a Stooge tape that had gotten caught in the VHS. He loved the Stooges, and fancied himself to be Curly at times, which made him all the more irritating. "This was all your idea, ya know. You was thinkin', 'Oh, oh, it would be so cool to keep doin' what Granny Mustard was doin'. I think that would be fun!' So you did just that. And you got exactly what you asked for."

"No, no, not exactly," snorted Jenkie. She unplugged the hotplate, gave the recipe one last stir then plopped down on the sticky, sagging couch. She kicked off her shoes, found the clippers on the end table, and started clipping her toenails. She hated clipping her toenails. A hassle and awkward and they always grew back. The only pleasure she got out of it was watching the little bits fly through the air. This time, one landed in Bink's beard and he didn't notice. Now that was fun. Briefly.

"Yeah, exactly."

"Cram it, Bink."

A mouse skittered across the living room floor and disappeared in a hole in the floor. "Moe, Larry, cheese!" said Bink in his best Curly voice, and then he giggled and slapped his forehead.

"Shut up, Bink." Clip clip clip. Another piece flew and landed on his shoulder. Good.

"You got what you wanted. So quit poutin'. It makes my stomach sour."

He turned the tape once more, straightening out the last of the mess, and put the tape into the machine. He jabbed the start button. Stooge tape kicked in; the tune "Three Blind Mice" sputtered through the TV speaker. Black and white Stooge heads appeared in a circle on the screen.

Bink pushed the pause button and looked back at Jenkie. The toenail glistened in the beard hair and on his shirt. She caught sight of a couple Cheerios, too, clinging to the cuff of his sleeve. "You ain't got the patience God give a goose. You know how long it took Madame Curie to figure out radiation?"

"I don't give a shit and I don't know who Madame Curie is or was so shut up."

Bink stood up and crossed his arms. One Cheerio fell free. "Why you so mean to me, Jenkie?" he asked.

"'Cause I hate you."

"I know, but why you so mean to me?" Bink's lips drew together, and his eyes squished up. He'd been drinking beer and it made him even more stupid. "I come up here to stay with you, help you out. You begged me. 'Oh Bink. I know you's good with electricity and wires and shit like that. I got a project and I need your help.' Remember that? Beggin' me to help you?"

Jenkie tossed the clippers aside and fumbled for her pack of cigarettes on the lamp stand so she didn't have to look at Bink. "You remember wrong. I stopped by Benny's house and said I had a interesting idea for a project."

"No, you begged me for help. And I said okay."

The match flared, the cigarette was lit. Jenkie blew out the match and flung it at Bink, but it missed. Bink pinched then wiped at his nose, dragging a silvered streak of mucus up and across his left cheek.

"You told me what you was up to, I didn't freak out, now did I? Did I?"

Jenkie clenched her jaws around the cigarette, bending it downward a bit. "No."

"I seen you messin' with dead things, bringin' 'em back around. Nobody but God or Satan supposed to do shit like that, but there you was, doin' it, anyway. I seen critter parts crawlin' and floppin' on the floor, all red-eyed and gurglin'. Some tryin' to bite me in the foot! Did I get scared and run away?"

"No."

"And now you got dead people living here in the trailer with us. And a dead dog. And you got equipment to control 'em all, thanks to me."

"You want a fuckin' prize, Bink?"

He stuck out his tongue and made his best Curly face. "Sointenly! I like prizes, Moe! Give me a prize! Woob woob woob woob!"

"Shit."

Bink's shoulders dropped and he looked sad again. "Just quit being mean to me. Quit your 'I Hate Granny' moods. Just shut up, write those letters I told you to write, and see what happens. Nobody's gonna just stumble into Desper Hollow and say 'Hey, here's somebody what should be famous! Let me give her a million dollars!' Ya hear me?"

Jenkie scowled.

"I said did you hear me?"

Jenkie nodded vaguely, then lay down on the couch and considered what Bink had said. Those damn letters. The thought was daunting. Writing more than a couple sentences made her hand hurt. "Why can't you just send out e-mails for me from down at Benny's house? You write better'n me."

"'Cause it's your project." Bink sighed heavily and sat on the floor again. He whirled around to face the television and reached for the VHS start button. "Write the damn letters, and I'll mail 'em. Okay? Things work out like we hope, we'll get money, big money, lots of money for what we got back there in the bedrooms."

And so Jenkie wrote the letters. Four of them, with addresses Bink found on the internet using Benny's computer. One letter went to the SyFy Channel. One to E! One to FX. One to a new network called Check It Out! Jenkie had seen shows on the first three when she lived at home with Mama and Suze. She'd never watched the fourth network, but Bink told her it showed lots of weird stuff so that made it a good possibility. It took Jenkie a whole week to finish the letters because she had to start over and over when she realized her handwriting was so bad, even she couldn't figure out what she'd put down.

While Jenkie remained at the trailer to mind the hollows, Bink took the letters and mailed them in Tazewell. Now, several weeks later, there had been no response from anyone in Hollywood. Not a "thanks but no thanks" or even a "this sucks, get lost."

"I should just let 'em all out and to hell with it," she mutters to herself. The glider stops rocking and she scratches her belly. She is sweaty under her dyed bangs, and it itches. "Let 'em go, let 'em do whatever they're gonna do. I can't take it much more. It was dumb to do this in the first place. I hate it. I hate them! I hate Granny!"

Wriggling up and out of the glider, Jenkie goes into the trailer and slams the door. The noise and vibration sets the hollows to growling more loudly. They sense it's time they will be fed, and it's actually past that. Jenkie screams, "Shut up!" They don't shut up. She stalks down the hall, past the little room in which she usually sleeps, the non-functional bathroom, and stops just outside the two doors behind which the hollows are kept captive. In front of each door is a tall, sturdy chain link gate that Bink bolted in place with the biggest brackets available at the Tazewell Hardware Store, replacing the roll of fencing Bink had put there when Bobby Boo came along.

There are two hollows in one room—Bobby Boo and the weird talking one—and two others and the dog Dan in the other. There were five hollows a couple weeks ago but the one died because Bink didn't get enough food for all of them. Funny, that a dead thing can starve, but yep, they can. The hollows spend their time scrabbling at the walls, the door, the broken windows, each other. Bits fall off them over time—an ear, a nose, a finger or two, a ribbon of skin. They just walk over the pieces, flatten them against the molded carpet. Bink cut a square hole in the roof over each of those bedrooms. The holes are covered over with a strong square metal plate. When it's time to feed the hollows, Bink or Jenkie climb up a ladder outside, unlock the plate, and throw the living food down inside. They do it real fast, though so far the hollows haven't learned to climb up on each other to reach them through the ceiling.

Jenkie grabs a beer from the refrigerator, twists off the cap, leans against the counter, and drinks it with her eyes closed. It helps, some.

Then she finds her mirror shades and goes out back to where the ladder leans against a crooked oak tree. It's an old, splintery wooden one, so she has to be careful. She drags it to the end of the trailer where the hollows' rooms are. Once it's in place, the legs planted firmly, she heads for the homemade chicken wire pen where Bink put the critters. There are numerous rabbits, a grey fox, squirrels, groundhogs, possums, rats, mice. The animals can't move around much; Bink has tied each of their front legs together so they can't dig or leap away. They stare at Jenkie as she stares at them. Some seem angry; others resigned. A burlap bag hangs on the top of the chicken wire. She takes it off, opens it wide, and dons the thick gloves that were inside. The critters in the pen start to scatter and roll away as best they can, trying to burrow under the oak tree's fallen leaves. Their dark eyes flash in terror.

"Just hold still, this won't be any worse than what a hawk would do to you. As Bink would say, quit yer belly-achin'."

She steps over the chicken wire and snatches up the fox, three groundhogs, and a couple squirrels, mice, and rats. Into the sack they go, struggling and snapping.

It's not easy to carry a sack of twisting critters up a ladder, but Jenkie does it, slowly, pausing after each step upward, coughing, spitting out into the grass. She hates heights and just a couple rungs up she's already feeling woozy. Finally, she's at the top. She leans forward to brace her elbows against the tattered shingles of the roof. The bag bumps and thumps against the guttering. She hoists it up and onto the roof where it continues to wriggle.

She dials the combination for the padlock on the metal plate. The hollows have heard her and are down in the bedroom, trying to get up to the hole in the ceiling. Deep breath, now. She pats her jacket pocket; yes, the charger is there and ready in case. She pats her face to make sure her mirror shades are in place. She always wears them when facing the hollows. Their red eyes spook her, and she has a feeling if they stared at her, right into her eyes, they might weaken her, over-power her, charger or not.

Jenkie shoves her hand into the bag and grabs the fox by the tail. He comes out, yipping and twirling. Taking a breath she flips back the metal sheet, exposing the hole into the bedroom.

The two hollows are directly beneath. Their heads are craned up, red eyes glowing. One is Bobby Boo, all bits and pieces, yet still hanging together. He reaches for the hole, fingers clutching. The other one is Stead.

Stead is staring up, too, but he isn't clawing. He never does. He is the scariest one of them all, because he talks. Because it seems he can think. How he got up through the hole that Bink left unlocked is a mystery. Jenkie thinks he must have somehow crawled up Bobby Boo's shoulders. But no way in hell was she going to ask Stead how he escaped. No way did she want any more interaction with him than she already had.

Stupid, stinking mess, all of it.

She wishes the fox was a fire bomb. *Boom! Bam! Sky high and baked like a pie!*

"Here you go, you ugly beggars!" She hurls the fox into the bedroom below and the hollows fall on it. She tosses in the groundhogs and squirrels then slams the metal plate back in place and locks it.

Back down the ladder, she refills the bag and begins to climb up to the hole in the roof over the second bedroom.

Halfway up she hears Bink's Jeep grinding and puttering up to the front of the trailer. The engine cuts off. The car door opens, slams. Bink shouts, "You got a letter! Jenkie! Holy shit, guess what? The guys from the Check This Out! Network wrote back!"

Jenkie drops the bag of critters on the ground (screw 'em, they aren't going anywhere) jumps from the ladder causing her fat feet to sting, and limps around the trailer to find Bink grinning, and waving an envelope in the air.

6
Jack Carroll

This one's going to be good. This is going to make a name for me, going to get the ratings and the numbers Nate has been hoping for. This is going to bring in the big bucks. A stepping stone to better things for me.

Jack stares out the window of the plane at the yellow, orange, and scarlet folds of the Appalachian Mountains below, his arms crossed lightly, his tongue still tasting of the beef fried rice he'd eaten at the Charlotte airport during the 2-hour layover. He'd sworn to his boss, Nate Rothman, head of the newly-launched television network, Check This Out!, that this trip was worth the airfare and the time, I mean, come on, a hillbilly who keeps a bunch of people locked in bedrooms and believes they are zombies and wants a reality show based on it all? Golden. Priceless. And of course, there are no zombies, there never were zombies beyond the imaginations of Romero, Matheson, Savini, and a couple other twisted minds.

And certainly, the young woman who claims to have some is bat-shit nut-soid. But! he emphasized, pumping his fist to show his confidence, just to get cameras into that backwoods region, to film her in her delusions, in her weird day-to-day encounters with whoever else lives with or near her, now that would be a reality show people would tune in to week after week since that the fascination with rich housewives and bickering bubble-haired beach babes had waned. He already has a title in mind for the show, "Madness in the Mountains."

Nate, a middle-aged guy who chewed down his anxiety with countless packs of spearmint gum, stood in his small corner office with his hands in the pockets of his expensive, Hollywood-casual, I'm-unaffected-by-much-and-unimpressed-with-you jeans. He'd read the woman's letter to Jack and then laughed hard and long, swearing, "What the fuck do people think? We'll film any piece of trash idea they send our way?"

Of course, Jack bit back his reply that the Check This Out! Network was all about trash people threw their way. The goal was to offer American—and hopefully, someday, global—audiences the strange crap they couldn't find anywhere else on the tube. Nasty crap. Strange crap. Make you cringe crap. Stuff you'd never seen anywhere else crap. The shows in development include a poorly-written but fairly-well acted dark comedy serial about a woman who works as a hooker in her home and keeps various snakes on hand to entertain her customers and a reality show in which the crew documents the life of a bearded lady and her alligator-skin husband as they travel the country in a circus on the verge of bankruptcy. There is also a talk show called "Oh, My God!" where guests discuss their various religious beliefs (the more obscure, obscene, and unsavory the better) a couple stupid game shows that involve whipped cream, thumb tacks, and motor oil, and finally "You Think That Tastes Weird?", a cooking show where people come on and whip up their favorite bizarre concoctions and then offer them for free to people on the street. "Mad in the Mountains" is just as good if not better than some of the ones already purchased, even if Nate is doubtful.

"You know what you're going to find out there?" Nate had told Jack on the phone right before Jack boarded the plane out of LAX with Sam Pearson, the eternally patient cameraman. "Some crazy chick with a couple chickens on the roof and rat nests in her brain. You look at her wrong and her pa's either gonna put a bullet through your head, corral you into a shotgun wedding, or go all Deliverance on your ass. Literally. Some people think the big city's a scary place? That's nothing to compare to the backwoods."

"I hear ya," said Jack. He rolled his eyes at Sam, who only shrugged and reshouldered his carry-on. "But I have a good sense about this. If it turns up empty or I get screwed by this gal's papa, I'll pay you back for the airfare."

"And if you get killed?"

"You don't have to pay for the funeral."

"Huh," said Nate.

Now, as the plane begins to descend into the Roanoke airport, Jack tosses a handful of Tums into his mouth and chews them up. Sam snorts, coughs, and grumbles awake in the aisle seat, then turns to Jack. His face is nearly as red as his hair, and scrunched up from sleeping with the side of his face mashed into his arm.

"We there?"

"We there."

"Feel like I'm going home to Tennessee," says Sam, his voice cottony from sleep. "Makes me think of my mom's walnut pie and apple fritters. Man, you haven't tasted good 'til you've tasted those."

"Yeah, well, you'll just have to enjoy them in your imagination, and I'm going to need you to help me out with more than camerawork. You know the language of these mountain people. Might require a bit of translation."

"They aren't aliens, Jack. They speak English."

"What kind of English, though? I have a hard time with Southern accents. And there might be things like hillbilly gang signs I want to make sure I don't accidentally use."

"You worried all of a sudden? You getting nervous?"

"No, I just want my bases covered. I want this to work more than anything I've wanted to work in a long time."

"Sure. I got you covered." Sam shakes his head, slightly bemused, and then digs under the seat for his carry-on even though the plane hasn't stopped yet.

The Roanoke airport is easy to navigate. With their baggage claimed and rental car signed for, within the hour they are heading southwest in an all-wheel drive Mazda Tribute, steering southwest along Interstate 81 and then exiting at Marion to head due north into the mountains. Jack's booked a room at the Blue Creek Motor Inn in Tazewell for tonight. Plan is to get a solid night's sleep, meet up with this Jenkie woman at her trailer in Desper Hollow tomorrow, take two-days' worth of film footage for a pilot episode, then head back to Los Angeles to let Nate see the findings.

He'd gotten a tetanus shot prior to leaving the city, though Sam had laughed and asked what the hell he thought he would be getting into, a septic tank?

"Can't be too careful. I don't have a natural immunity like you do."

The road to Tazewell winds, undulates, meandering up and up through forested stretches and past farms with fields stripped clean from their harvest. Fall is creeping toward winter; trees are shedding their leaves, with an equal amount on the ground and on the branches. Steep peaks rise on either side now, some softened with evergreens, others topped with craggy, jutting granite. Sam plays with the radio, bringing in a local station out of somewhere near there. The songs are a peculiar selection of bluegrass, rockabilly, and gospel. Jack can barely stand it, but Sam taps his foot and drums his fingers cheerfully on the window glass. When he begins singing along to one, that's when Jack has had enough. He flips the switch and turns it off.

"No can do, man."

They reach Tazewell late afternoon. It's a small, pleasant town, reminding Jack of something out of a 1960s television show. They find the Blue Creek Motor Inn on the main drag. It looks like its online photo—a simple, two-story place with little charm but a great price, and it's moderately clean and moderately comfortable. Sam claims the bed nearest the bathroom. "I have a weak bladder," he confesses, and Jack answers, "Dude, TMI."

They call in a delivery from Pizza Plus and then over Cokes and a large, everything-topped pizza, lay the plans for the following day. There is no way to call this Jenkie Mustard character and let her know they are coming, but some guy named Bink Bickerstaff had sent an e-mail reply to the network letter, describing how to get to Desper Hollow, being you couldn't find it on Google maps.

"We take this easy and carefully once we get to Desper Hollow," says Jack.

"No threatening moves or facial expressions. Let them know we're friendly."

"We aren't facing grizzly bears, Jack," says Sam. "Just chill out or…"

"Or they'll smell the fear on me, right?" Jack chuckles, then coughs up a bit of pizza crust that got snagged in his throat.

"Don't go in all hyped up and expecting the worst. There are some good people there, just like good people in Los Angeles."

"There are good people in Los Angeles? When we get back, why don't you introduce me to a few."

"Ha. Seriously. Haven't you ever heard the old saying, 'You find what you're looking for'?"

"Yeah, and I'm looking for some great, over-the-top maniac shit that will make a good television show. If I didn't think I was walking into something bizarre, if I thought Jenkie Mustard was sweet and innocent like Elly May Clampett, I'd have stayed back in California."

"You'll find all kinds, Jack."

Jack takes a swig from his Coke can, kicks off his shoes, swings his legs up on the bed, and lays back. There's a crack in the ceiling in the shape of a limp penis, complete with balls. "I forgot to tell you that, before we go up there, I want to buy a gun."

"Fuck, really?" Sam gets up from his bed and tosses a pizza rind into the trash. He licks his fingers and wipes them on his shirttail. Then he touches the camera case on top of the dresser, as if he needs to make sure it's safe and not still out in the car.

"Well, I couldn't exactly bring one on the plane."

"You really want a gun? Seriously, Jack?"

"You have something against protection?"

"I have something against going into a place like an invading army. It's bad…"

"What? Mojo?"

"Kinda."

"Really, I want a gun. There must be a gun shop in Tazewell, or somewhere between here and Desper Hollow. You think?"

"I don't want to think about it. I can just see it now, you shooting someone accidentally, and being thrown into jail by some backwoods lawman. Now that would play right into your stereotypes, wouldn't it?"

"I'm not unskilled with a firearm."

"Not unskilled. What a weird way to put it."

"I can shoot, okay? I used to shoot skeet."

"Where?"

"When I was growing up, my parents belonged to a country club."

Sam laughs. "Last time you shot was then, what, fifteen years ago?"

"No. Twelve."

"Shit."

"I know about the safety, I know to keep the damn thing pointed down."

"That eases my mind."

"I'm getting a gun, Sam."

"Okay, fine, I'm not going to argue with you. I'm too tired. But it might not be as easy as you think. I think you have to register or something. Maybe give a blood donation, a kidney."

"I'd look it up online if this place had Wi-Fi. Can you imagine, a hotel this day and age?"

Sam grunts.

"So first thing I get the gun. Then we gas up and follow the directions this Bink person gave us to get to Desper Hollow. Looks to be way out of the way. I hope the rental has good shocks. Be ready to film as much as you can of the trip from here to there. Set the location, let Nate see what a wilderness were going into, so he can feel the intrigue, the mystery, the potential danger and weirdness. Maybe we'll spot some outhouses and long johns hanging on wires."

Sam plops down, pulls off his jeans, and then climbs in under his covers. "Whatever, Jack," he mutters.

Jack turns on the television, flips through the channels, cusses when he can't find his network among the choices. Within two minutes, Sam is snoring. Jack balls up a napkin and throws it toward the trashcan. It bounces off the end of his bed and falls to the floor. He turns on a re-run of Jersey Shore, cusses, and settles in to watch.

7
Armistead

He stands at the wall beside the broken window, his arms crossed, watching the others suck the bones of the animals that have been dropped through the ceiling to the floor. He got a few of the mice, one of the squirrels, but that was it. The other snatched up the rest as quickly as his sluggish arms could move. Now the other is wandering back and forth over the filthy, well-worn carpeting, chewing the final bits and snarling at him.

There are flies in the room, though they are groggy with the cold. They land on his face, his hands, buzzing curiously, walk about a little, probe his skin and the exposed muscle, and then fly away. It's as if something in him and in the other turns the flies away once they have a taste. Some flies cling to the walls, some investigate the bone and foul liquids that litter the floor.

There is no sense of time in this room, only a sense of space. The Hunger is brutal in his gut and brain, burning and sawing, a constant agony that drives his teeth down against each other. He has sensed his jawbone crack several times but hasn't felt it. He has sensed two of his toes come off but hasn't felt them.

Who am I? he wonders. He stares at the wall, past the gobbling, shuffling other, hoping to find something on the water-stains that reminds him of something. Anything from before. But they are only stains, dark brown stains that run down to the floor.

Why am I?

The other veers off his usual course, bumps into Armistead, growls. Armistead shoves him away and he returns to his pacing. Back and forth and back and forth. Then he wanders over to the window and sticks his hand out.

Who am I?

It's nighttime, Armistead knows that much. He can hear nocturnal animals outside, calling, hooting, screeching to one another. He knows that sound, the sound of longing, the sound of desperate searching. Mingled with the sounds of the night-creatures and the growling of the other in the room with him, he hears still more like them in the room next door. Snarling, stumbling. Groaning, thumping. Driven back and forth, around and around, going nowhere but always going. He feels a momentary sense of sadness for them, for the other here with him. For their longing. Their searching.

There is the sound of loud music, too, down at the other end of the trailer. He doesn't know the music, but it is irritating, with a rhythmic thud that he can feel through the floor. He hears a man's laughter and a woman's heavy cough. The cough belongs to the One With No Eyes. The one with the charger. The one who brings pain that rivals the Hunger.

There is no rest in this dreadful, foul room. Nothing but stink and growling and longing and Hunger. Armistead moves to the center of the room. He stares at the wall, then at the other, then up at the hole in the ceiling. He remembers that he escaped… yesterday? Last week? How long ago? And why is he back now? Why did he let that happen? This, he cannot remember. Did he go through the hole up there? Maybe. He can't be sure. And his uncertainty makes him furious and overwhelmed.

Why am I?

There is a commotion at the window, and the other grunts and snaps his hand back inside. In his grasp is a fluttering bat. It flutters only a moment, for it is bitten in half in a matter of seconds. Small rivulets of blood bubble at the corner of the other's mouth.

Armistead looks at the door. Unlike the other, he knows how to use the knob, but he also remembers there is a heavy steel gate on the other side. Yes, he escaped. But how did he do that? He knows it was not through the door. If he can remember what he did, he will try again. He looks up again at the hole in the ceiling, and the metal that blocks it. Did he go up and out?

He must escape again. He must stay gone and not be captured. And if he cannot succeed, he must find a way to die. Unlike the other stumbling about in this room, Armistead knows he is cursed. The other is cursed, too, but he is empty, unaware, reduced to an eating machine with no thoughts, no purpose other than to kill and eat and kill and eat. He is clearly driven by the same Hunger that Armistead is but has no need to make sense out of it.

Night, day, night, day. How long has he been here? How long must he stay? If he could starve himself to death, he would. But the Hunger is a terrible and powerful master, one he cannot ignore.

Who am I?

Why am I?

When the other finally stumbles away from the window, Armistead goes to it and looks out and up. It is hard to see the sky. There are trees everywhere, bending down over the trailer like dark sentinels that shiver in the wind. There are slices of navy blue beyond them, however, and a sliver of white moon. The shape of the moon is something he thinks he knows but isn't sure. Something sharp. Something shiny and cold.

The other comes back to the window, slaps at Armistead but Armistead snarls and the other moves back and away, red eyes cold, staring. It begins to pace once more. Back and forth and back and forth.

Black creatures flutter in and out among the trees. Armistead can sense the warmth in their bodies, the blood coursing there, and the Hunger turns in his brain and belly, and he groans in distress, bears down into the pain, bites into his lower lip and takes a piece off it. He spits it out onto the floor.

He considers the moon again, the sharp shape hanging above the trees. Sharp. Wait, yes. Sharp. Sharp cuts. Sharp cuts down, destroys, kills.

He has a vague memory of swinging something sharp, back and forth, clearing a small plot of land. A curved blade swinging, slicing, cutting down. When was that? Why was that? If he could find something sharp like that now, could he destroy himself? Could he kill the brain that torments him so?

Yes...

But there is nothing sharp in the room. Just pieces of flesh and bone and the worn carpet and the stink and the rusted air vents and the cracked window. And the other.

"I must die," he says aloud to the sky and the other glances at him suddenly as if he is a food source, but then turns away. "I must die again."

He closes his eyes. A fabric of memory floats past, fragile, translucent, pale blue, trailing warmth. What is that? Why can't he recall? There is a flash of light behind the blue, and it breaks apart to reveal... nothing now, only the darkness behind his eyelids.

He opens his eyes again to the nightmare in the room.

No more! I cannot live this non-life! I must find a way to end this!

But then he hears a voice beneath his own, bolder, greater than his own.

NO.

The power of the voice startles him. It resonates through his whole body, causing his fingertips to dig into the windowsill and his spine to stiffen. He recognizes the voice on an untouchable level. But he cannot name it. It is not the man at the other end of the trailer. It is not the One With No Eyes.

"What?" he says. "Who are you?"

And then again, deep in his brain, a voice that for just that moment stays the Hunger and gives him a strange sense of dizzying lightness.

You will not destroy yourself.

Armistead tilts his head back in an attempt to see the moon, but it is gone now. Was it the moon? Does the moon speak?

"Please! Who said that?" But there is no reply. There is nothing but the fluttering, leathery creatures and the wind and the maze of black tree branches.

At the other end of the trailer, the One With No Eyes begins to yell at the man, curse him, and stomp around.

And there is that. There is always that.

8
Kathy Shaw

The double-wide looks exactly as it did when she left home in May, same mildew clinging to the side where the sun never shines, same dead plants in pots on the deck that her mother had quit caring for when she got really sick and neither Kathy nor her father bothered with because there were plenty of other things to bother with. Her father's chair is still on the deck, a yellow legal pad on the railing with a small rock on top of it so it won't blow off. Hank's Chevy truck parked at an angle in the gravel.

A bumper sticker on his truck, which has been there for years, is worn mightily on the edges but you can still read the sentiment. "God is My Pilot, Not My Co-Pilot." Parked in the grass off the edge of the driveway are a dented pickup truck and three cars. They belong to church members; she can't remember who.

The family cat, Puffster, trots up to Kathy's car as she turns off the engine, waiting, watching, until Kathy climbs out. It's mid-afternoon, and the air is cold enough to chill her cheeks and hands and send a shiver across her shoulders. Puffster purrs loudly and winds herself around Kathy's leg, thrilled to have her mistress home. Kathy puts the cat on her shoulder, scratches the cat's head, and carries her up onto the deck. She pushes open the sliding door and steps into the house.

"Dad? Are you here?"

Kathy stares at the sofa where her mother died... or didn't die... and she begins to breathe heavily. She puts Puffster down and stands with her hand to her heart. She lets her gaze travel about the living room, Annie's favorite room, decorated with bits and pieces that meant the most to her.

A mahogany rocking chair with an embroidered cushion Annie had made the year she and Hank were married. Framed photos of Annie's parents and Hank's parents. A hand-painted Shaw family coat of arms Hank's ancestors had brought over from Scotland a long time ago to settle in the wilderness of western Virginia. The crest features a knight's helmet, three small hawks with wings extended as if flying heavenward, and a hand holding a sword. The family motto is written in Latin beneath the artwork: Fide et Fortitudine. Her father explained to her when she was younger that it meant "By Faith and Courage." "We are poor but we are faithful," he said. "We are common but we are courageous. This is your heritage, Kathy. Not a thing of pride but a thing of inspiration." Kathy didn't like being poor or common, but she liked the image of the rising birds, flying up and away.

Kathy touches the arm of the sofa. There is an imprint of her mother's head still on the little blue throw pillow.

Mom... Mom what happened? Where are you?

Hank comes out of the bathroom, drying his hands on an old, blue towel. It's strange, he doesn't look older, as Kathy thought he might, but younger, as if grief and fear and uncertainty had dredged up something in him, a vulnerability that had been buried under years of determination. His blue eyes are bright and hard. There is several days' growth on his face, which is dark rather than grey.

"Kathy." He drops the towel on the dining table and lifts one arm, perhaps hoping for a hug, but Kathy just takes his hand, squeezes it briefly, lets it go. If she hugs him, he might cry. If he cries, she will cry. And she won't be able to bear any of it.

"Sweetie," he says. "I'm so glad you came home. The search party's out, a new crew of ten of the congregation. We've been searching around the clock, all night, this morning. They sent me back home for a while."

He kicks off one shoe, peels off the sock; the blisters on his feet are swollen and oozing. Kathy grimaces.

"I'm not staying here, though," he says. "I'm just going to change my socks."

"You should bandage your feet, too."

"New socks'll do it." He goes into the small laundry area off the kitchen, tugs socks from the dryer, comes back. "These are better, thicker. No time for bandages." He puts on the socks then his boots. He sucks air slightly at the pressure.

"Dad..."

"It's all right. I can still hike."

"Damn, you're hard headed."

Hank almost smiles. "Not unlike your mom." The near smile quickly fades. He goes to the sliding door and opens it for Puffster. Hank's hiking stick, fashioned years ago so he could walk the forested slopes and talk to God without taking a major tumble, is propped up beside the door. It's a nice piece of work, done himself with a pocketknife, oak carved with wavy patterns that look like sunrays and mountain ridges. The tip is tamped metal, sharp, to best grip the earth.

Puffster exits, and then turns around as if she has changed her mind as Hank closes the door. Hank comes back to Kathy and shoves his hands into the pockets of his thick denim jacket. "She's been gone more than twenty-four hours now. I have a call into the State Police. And the church folks have been wonderful, searching all yesterday afternoon with me, and throughout last night. It's slow going. The land is tough; it's hard. God meant business when he created these mountains."

"But He didn't create them to keep you from finding Mom," says Kathy.

"I didn't say that. God is good, Kathy."

Kathy bites back a retort. She's used to her father's religion, she's grown up with it, though she's heard he wasn't a God-loving man before he was married. His beliefs are the source of his strength and his primary comfort in life. It makes him a kind and patient man. But usually, Kathy doesn't want to hear about what God's done or what He hasn't done. Because none of it makes much difference. People do or don't do their own thing, and nobody she knows of ever got struck by lightning or saw angels.

"Let me get some water and my hiking boots. We can hurry and join up with the searchers."

Hank nods, steps aside. But then he catches her arm, and she flinches and turns back. His brows are drawn, his jaw tight. "She was dead, Kathy. I know it. As God is my witness."

Kathy opens her mouth, not sure what she is going to say even as the words come tumbling out. "Okay, Dad. I believe you. She was dead. But now she's gone. And we'll find her. Okay?"

Hank stares at her an uncomfortably long moment then lets go of her arm. He returns to the sliding door, where Puffster has returned and is staring inside longingly.

Twenty minutes into the hike and Kathy is sweating, drawing in air through her mouth, her lungs working hard against her ribs. Her throat stings. Hank, four paces ahead with his hiking stick, calls over his shoulder.

"You all right?"

"I guess I lost some stamina living at the beach."

"Can you keep up? If not, go on back. I don't want anything to happen to you."

"I can keep up." She pulls a rubber band from her coat pocket and quickly braids her hair into a slightly lopsided ponytail that she tucks down the back of her collar. A loose strand catches in her mouth and she spits it out. Sometimes she thinks she should just go on and cut her hair off short.

The forested earth slips out from beneath her feet, pine needles, silt, slimy humus of compacted leaves and bark. She pulls herself upward by grabbing branches and small saplings. One is uprooted in her hand, and she tosses it aside. She pushes on, leaning forward against the rise of the land. A tiny black snake slithers away from her boot and disappears into a lump of wet leaves.

Hank locates the search party with his walkie-talkie, then directs Kathy to follow him over a steep knoll and then down toward Barter Creek. "They're just a half mile southwest. We create a fan, and move outward together, spreading out slightly from point one but always being within shouting distance of one another."

"Okay." Kathy follows, over matted strands of honeysuckle, wide grapevines, and vicious patches of thorny greenbriar. She trips, scraping a long but shallow gash in her left hand, then rights herself and continues on as sweat cuts down her chest to the waistband of her jeans. The walkie-talkie protrudes from Hank's jacket pocket, bouncing against his hip with each step, sputtering and hissing.

And though she has fought hard over the last day not to, to keep her thoughts under control and on other things, anything, stupid, worthless things, petty things, she begins to imagine what might have truly happened to her mother.

Her mother, attacked by a dog in the backyard. She dies. But, no, she isn't really dead. Hank in his panic and grief, thinks she is. When he isn't watching she wanders away in a crazed state, up into the forest of Black Rock Ridge. Hobbling, struggling, without her cane to help her. She finds a cave, perhaps, or a pile of fallen trees, and lies down, exhausted, confused, unable to continue. Then night comes, and the temperatures plummet below freezing. She curls up against the rocks, or the logs, breathing heavily, casting clouds out around her bare head. She cries, confused, now dying certainly. She calls for help in a faith whisper, for her husband, or her daughter, or God to rescue her. But no one comes. They can't find her. They're looking but can't find her.

Mom.

She curls up more tightly, head into her chest, trembling with fear and a cold certainty that she will die. She was not dead but now she will die.

No, Mom. I'm sorry. I shouldn't have left. Oh, God damn it!

Hank slides down a steep incline, rights himself. She hears him gasp quietly. His feet have to be incredibly painful.

If I'd been home, this wouldn't have happened. I would have watched you while Dad went outside. I would have seen you awaken, kept you from leaving.

"Mom…" says Kathy, her voice breaking.

Hank looks back, stops, his hand on the trunk of an elm tree. His eyes are tight, his cheeks drawn. His grey hair lifts and falls in a breeze. He didn't wear a hat. He should have worn a hat. "Kathy. I know. I'm sorry. You can't know how sorry."

"We'll find her."

"Yes."

"I mean it. We'll find her."

He nods. "I know."

They reach the creek. Hank is limping, Kathy is out of breath but forces herself to keep up. Her left hand burns from the gash and she squats for a moment to let cold water flow over it. They follow the winding creek bed, stumbling over rocks along the bank.

"How close are we to the search party?" she calls.

"Maybe three tenths of a mile."

Still so far to go.

Then Kathy stops. She glances up at the cedar and vine-choked rise to her right. Turns her head. Listens.

Hank keeps on, crunching against the riverside rocks, leaning forward into his hiking stick, free fist at his side, clenched in determination.

There is a shimmering sound, that of branches being shaken. A deer?

Possibly. But a deer would be keeping still in the presence of humans. Several pebbles roll down from the dark shadows of the tightly-pressed trees.

Several more. Then stillness.

A squirrel. A big squirrel, or several, chasing each other. That was what it was.

Kathy swats a late season fly from her ear, turns, takes a step forward.

There is a sudden, loud rustling in the trees on the knoll. And what sounds like raspy breathing, heavy, wet.

That's not squirrels.

The cedar branches begin to spasm, back and forth, smacking into each other. Dead needles fly. And now a growling, low, rumbling...

Kathy catches her chest. "Dad?" She stares at the trees, afraid to move. Afraid not to move.

... growing louder, threatening, almost human.

Kathy shouts, "Dad!"

Hank turns, stares at Kathy and then at the tree branches as they slam against each other as if trying to give birth to some hidden terror. He throws down his walkie-talkie and races toward Kathy.

The growling becomes a screech.

And then Annie Shaw bursts from the cedars, eyes blood-red and popping, her mouth open impossibly and hideously wide. She howls like a banshee, her legs wobbly, her arms flung outward as she skids down the knoll. Her hair is wild, crusted with leaves and sticks and dried mucus that glints in the sunlight.

Kathy screams, scrambles backward, trips over a large stone, and falls into the creek. She lands hard, falls, striking her head on a submerged log.

She bites the inside of her cheek, tearing out a chunk of flesh in a bright flash of pain. Stars shatter her vision, and it draws in on itself, dark as midnight. She gasps, comes up choking on the gritty water she's sucked in, spitting blood. Her vision opens again to reveal her mother, Annie, clambering into the creek, head wobbling, tongue lolling, hands opening and closing like claws.

"Mom!" Kathy scoots back in the water, her hands up, waving her mother away. "Oh, my God! Dad!"

"Annie!" shouts Hank. He does not see his wife's face. There is unabashed joy in his own.

Annie's flesh is covered in filth and wood ticks. There are green splotches on her face. One eyelid is gone. Her lower lip is ragged, as if she's been chewing on it. Her flesh is pale and tattered at the ends of her fingers.

"Oh, shit, help!" Kathy scoots backward again, runs into the creek bank. She rolls over, tries to get up, slips on the slimy moss of the creek bed and goes down.

And then Hank is there, splashing into the creek, tossing the hiking stick aside, and grabbing for Annie's shoulder. He spins her around, cries out, "Annie!", but his expression, which was open and full of hope and delight, twists instantly into one of horror. Annie gurgles then plunges her face toward Hank's arm. He jerks it away before she can bury her snapping teeth into the flesh. With a cry of disgust and grief, Hank plants his foot against his wife's chest and shoves hard, sending the woman sprawling into the creek. Kathy crawls up onto the bank, sobbing, staring at her father in the middle of the water and her mother, now a hellish specter of her former self, clumsily trying to regain her footing.

"Dad, what's wrong with her?" Kathy cries. "What's wrong with Mom?"

Hank stands, the creek water flowing around him, his legs slightly apart, arms out for balance. In his hand is a large rock. He is weeping.

"Dad!"

"Be quiet, Kathy!" he roars. Kathy catches her breath; she's never heard him speak like that before.

Annie makes it to her feet. Her dress is soaked and wrapped around her thin legs. A large strip of flesh has ripped off her shin in the fall. It hangs down, but no blood flows from the wound. Annie snarls, licks at the air, and then hurls herself forward. Hank cries toward the heavens, then stares at his wife and throws the rock at her head. It strikes her skull, bounces off. But the blow is enough to cause her to go down again, this time to her knees. She wails, kicks and scratches at the water, the rocks. She snarls and blinks her horrid red eyes, licks her cracked white lips.

Hank snatches the hiking stick from the bank and points the metal the tip at Annie. "Annie, I'm sorry. I'm so, so sorry!"

"Dad!"

"Don't watch, Kathy!"

But she watches.

With a cry of anguish, he jams the stick into Annie's left eye, then pushes until it's driven a good six inches into her head. Annie squeals, flails her arms, chomps her teeth, and kicks at the water.

Kathy stares, her hands over her mouth.

Annie snarls again, this one sputtering, weakening. Then her remaining red eye rolls up in its sockets and she drops like a dead fish on a harpoon. Hank jabs the stick in another inch, then lets go. He pants heavily.

They both stare at the dead woman in the creek. Kathy, soaked, shivering, watches as her mother's hair is caught up in the current and pulled back and away from her tattered scalp. A single red oak leaf floats by and snags on her outstretched fingers.

At last, barely a whisper, "Dad?"

Hank shudders.

"Dad, what happened? What happened to Mom?"

He shakes his head.

"You killed her!"

He says nothing.

"You just killed her. Didn't you?"

Hank draws the hiking stick out of Annie's eye. It comes out with a soft, sucking sound that makes Kathy gag. He wipes the tip of the stick off in the weeds. "No. I didn't kill her. I told you. She was dead. She died back at the house."

"No!" She feels as if she's going to faint. The world shakes beneath her feet. "No! She was alive! She heard us, followed us..."

"She attacked you."

"Yes, but she was alive! Some kind of alive!"

Hank scratches his face, the scrubby growth of beard. He frowns, but not at Kathy. He is deep in thought. Then he says, "We must bury her, quickly."

"What? Dad, no. You aren't thinking clearly. We... you... killed Mom! Somebody's going to find out you killed her. Oh, my God, will you go to prison?"

"Don't use God's name in vain."

Kathy glances at her mother in the creek and puts her hand to her mouth. "What was wrong with her? Why did you kill her?"

Hank puts his hand on his daughter's shoulder. That is enough to make her legs give out from under her and she collapses. She covers her face with her hands. Hank's hand remains on her shoulder, and he kneels beside her. "Kathy. Listen. I told you. I didn't kill her. She was dead. She was trying to kill you."

"It... it looked like that, but it couldn't be, Dad. That's impossible. Mom wouldn't do that... wouldn't be like that..." The words fade out and away.

"I finished what nature tried to do but wasn't able."

"No, no! Stop it! You make no fucking sense!" She twists out of Hank grasp, holds her head, and rocks back and forth. This is not right, this is not real, this is not happening. No, no, no, no. Hank wipes his mouth, closes his eyes for a moment, and then wades back into the creek to retrieve Annie's body. He hauls her onto dry land.

"I've got to bury her, quickly, up the slope a ways," he says. "I'll do it alone if you would rather wait here."

Kathy nods. "I'll wait here."

She looks at the creek, watching the water swirl and flow, unable to block out the sound of her father huffing as he drags her mother's corpse up into the dense forest. She waits and watches the water, thinking how this creek flows into a river, and that river to the ocean. If only she were back at the beach now. If only she'd not come home to this. Or if she'd stayed home in the first place and had never left, none of this nightmare would have taken place.

Bad things flowing into bad things, making a greater bad thing. Is that what's happening now? Her father had mentioned an evil in his letter, but she had chalked it up to Dad being Dad, and all his talk about what was godly and what was not.

It is a long time before Hank returns. His sodden pants legs are now also covered in mud, bits of leaves, and grit. He doesn't say where he buried Annie. He only says, "Kathy, would you pray with me?"

She shakes her head.

And so he kneels by the creek on the wet grasses, his head bowed, his hands folded and shaking. She can't hear his prayer, and she doesn't want to. But it is clearly filled with anguish and repentance and a begging so deep it cuts her soul.

When done, Hank stands, calls the other searchers and tells them they could stop looking. When asked why, he says, "Let's meet at my house. Then we'll talk."

"What are you going to tell them?" Kathy asks as they take the steep slopes home.

"I'll tell them we found her, and she was already dead. That we don't care for them to see her because animals have scarred her face, but that I have put her in my bedroom and covered her body."

"But that's a lie, and you've always said…"

His eyes, usually so soft, are stern and wounded. "That must be the truth for them, Kathy. The real truth would be beyond cruel right now."

"Dad…"

"Please now, no more questions."

But there are more questions. So many that they knot in her mind so tightly that it is all she can do to follow her father home and not get lost in the dense forest, herself.

9

Jack Carroll

Jack finally snags himself a gun, a used .38 Smith and Wesson, and a box of cartridges for $200, more than he'd planned but a decent deal according to Sam. He snagged it from a strange little man who'd been standing in the parking lot outside the Skinner's Gun Shop in a Tazewell strip mall because the background check would take too much damn time.

The man, a grizzly old fellow not quite five feet tall, one eye white as milk and the other near black, dressed in dirty, oversized coat and cowboy hat, was waiting there in the cold, staring at Jack and Sam as they went in the shop and then as they came out again.

"Hey, boy!" he called.

Jack said to Sam, "Don't acknowledge him."

Jack unlocked the Tribute and climbed in the driver's side. Sam shook his head, bemused by Jack's discomfort in a small town, and gave the old man a nod before getting into the passenger's seat.

This was all the old man needed. He strolled over to the car.

"Shit, look what you've done," mumbled Jack. "Don't you know better than to make eye contact with people you don't know?"

"Ah, he probably just wants a couple bucks."

"Not from me."

"Stingy."

"Mental."

"Hey, boys," said the old man as Sam rolled his window

down several inches. "Find what you need in there?"

"Yeah, we're fine, thanks," said Jack, and he turned on the engine.

"You have a good day, now."

The old man didn't step back. "Ain't got no bag or box," he said.

"Seems you didn't get nothing in there."

"No, well, thanks for your concern." Jack gave Sam a look that he hoped would break the other's friendly spell and make him roll up the window.

"You lookin' for a gun?"

Sam pointed at Jack. "He is."

"Sam, fuck," said Jack.

"Drive over other side of the road and I got something you can use." The old man pulled a handgun out of the pocket of his coat. "$300. Got the ammo, too."

"Shit," said Jack.

"We'll take a look," said Sam. He gave Jack a look, and Jack said, "Ah, screw it," and drove off the lot across the street and parked in front of an abandoned auto mechanic shop. He sat back and crossed his arms. He'd give Sam one minute. That was less time that it would have taken to fill out that damn permission slip over at the gun shop.

The old man crossed the road, grinned, pulled the gun back out of his pocket and shoved it though Sam's open window. "$300. Works good. Box of cartridges, full up. You want a gun, you got it."

"You sit outside the gun store and just wait for people to come out?" asked Jack.

The old man chuckled.

"Isn't this illegal?"

"Free enterprise, my friend. We're Americans, ain't we? Go on, hold it. It's a good one."

Jack let out a noisy breath and reached for the gun. It was solid, polished, looked to be in good shape. But what the hell did he know about firearms?

"Let me," said Sam. He took the gun, opened it, looked inside, shut it, held it, balanced it. Said, "Let me see the cartridges." The old man gave him a small box. He looked at that two, carefully. Then he said, "$100."

The old man scoffed. "No."

"Fine, then." Sam held the gun and cartridge box out the window.

"$250?" said the old man.

"$200."

The old man spit on the ground. He rubbed his forehead under his cap. "Okay, you got me, brother. And don't ever say nobody in Tazewell treated you good, you hear me?"

"No problem there," said Sam.

So now they have a gun. And a box of ammunition. And an hour or so travel ahead of them. They fill up at the Marathon gas station then drive out of town, heading northwest, past an appliance store, a post office, and a county courthouse complete with a statue that looked at a quick glance, like a local Civil War hero. Some tidy homes and steepled churches, and onto state roads that continued up and up, back and forth, around, down, then up again, farther still, over narrow bridges and through more stretches of dense forest, past barns returning to the earth from whence they came and small fields with curious cows standing with their noses pressed through pipe gates. A turn due west at a tiny spot of a settlement called Tiptop, and then onto an even smaller road. Higher, higher into the mountains, yet the tallest peaks ahead of them seemed to maintain their distance. Sam has the camera trained out the window, catching footage of weed-choked house trailers, occasional brick homes on far hillsides, healthy crops of rusted cars behind wire fences bearing weather-worn warnings to "Keep Out!" They cross the same creek several times, and a river, and now a railroad track that seems to be going in the same direction they are. Sharp switchback turns take them higher into the mountains, around rocky bends cut into the steep land by road builders, slowing when then road narrows to a single car width, watching the drop off to the side, down, down into the tree-filled maw of Mother Nature.

They squeeze pass several cars and motorcycles going in the other direction, and some larger trucks bearing the name

"Beaver Dam Mines," that seemed to own the road and caused them to steer the rental up against the dented guardrails.

The farther they go, the more claustrophobic Jack feels. The tall trees, towering ridges, the sharp turns and steep embankments, with no sense of distance but the clicking of the odometer on the dash. He finds himself catching his breath, letting it out, wondering if something might come crashing through the brush onto the road like that creature in the old Bogie Creek movie. His hands grow damp around the steering wheel, but he doesn't wipe his hands off because he doesn't want Sam wise to his discomfort.

At last, a paved road leads off to the left, marked with a small rectangle sign, "State Route 687." And beneath that, "To Beaver Dam and Beaver Dam Mines."

"Okay, slow down. That Bink dude said turn here," says Sam. "Can ya feel it, Jack? We're getting close to zombieland! It's almost showtime!"

"I don't feel anything but the need to take a dump. This Beaver Dam best have a restroom."

"We don't go as far as Beaver Dam. We take a right two miles down this road before we get to the town."

"I don't give a shit. We're going into town. This I will give a shit."

"A country boy would just pull off and go behind a tree."

Jack stares at Sam. Sam shrugs.

Jack's sense of discomfort is growing and his patience waning. He's tired of driving, tired of feeling out of his element, particularly tired of Sam's smug expression of comfort and stupid mountain quips. The farther he gets from LA, the more his body tenses. The more he has a sinking feeling that things will go wrong even though he was the one spouting courage and certainty when selling the idea to Nate.

"I'm not going behind a tree," Jack mutters. "There is 'when in Rome' and there is 'when in the middle of mountainous nowhere.' I'm not shitting on a bunch of leaves and have a mountain lion come up and bite me in the ass."

"Suit yourself. You're the boss, boss."

"I'm not the boss."

"Whatever you say, boss."

They drive on.

The railroad track parallels the road to the left, appearing briefly now and then behind trees. Shadows strobe the road; a deer dashes across, followed by a fawn. A large truck rumbles toward then past them, bearing the Beaver Dam Mines sign on its door. A small gravel stretch bears off to the right and just past it, a large green sign,

"Beaver Dam, Unincorporated."

Jack slows the vehicle. "Unincorporated? What's that mean?"

Sam puts the camera down. "Means it's not separate from the county. Means no police force, fire department. They don't collect taxes as a town."

"In other words, bum fucking nowhere."

"I grew up in an unincorporated town. Good place. Nice people. Damn, but you're ignorant. And arrogant." Sam smiles but Jack can see the challenge in the cameraman's face.

"Okay, whatever. I'm sure they're lovely folks. Bake cakes. Shake hands. I really don't care if they collect taxes as long as they have a working toilet."

But the town isn't much of a town. There is an Exxon gas station and convenience store, obviously newly built, and a couple new trailers set up along Main Street with signs on their windows reading, "Beaver Dam Grocery" and "Beaver Dam Pharmacy." The rest of the town is flattened, razed, leaving charred lots to either side of the street.

Sam films through the window. "That Bink dude said something about the nearest town to Desper Hollow having a fire last summer. Didn't realize it took most of the town down."

Jack pulls up in front of the Exxon station, stretches his shoulders, turns off the engine. He can see a man inside the plate glass window, staring out at him. "Probably gets very few out-of-towners," he says. Inside he's thinking, This is like *The Hills Have Eyes*. I've got a gun in my pocket, but we haven't even loaded it yet. That'll be effective if I get attacked.

While Sam moves out into the middle of the street to film the town of Beaver Dam, Jack stalks into the convenience store, bowels rumbling.

The place smells new—new paint, new wood, new packaging and ceiling tiles. He inclines his head and pulls on a smile for the man, who has turned from the window and now watches him from behind the counter.

He's an older man, sixty or so, cigarette pack in his shirt pocket. His nametag reads "Simon."

"Hello, there," says Jack. He's got to move soon, or he'll embarrass himself worse than he's ever embarrassed himself before. It's all he can do to keep from tap-dancing on the floor. "Restroom?"

"Getting gas?"

"Ah, no. Do I need to?"

"Restrooms for customers only."

"Really? How many customers do you actually get?" Ah, shit, wrong thing to say. The man's gaze narrows.

"Where you from, fella? Richmond?"

"No, no, father than that." He tries not to tap dance on the floor. Got to keep cool. Look cool. "Hey, if I get some candy bars would that work?"

The man shrugs, nods, pulls a key from a nail and passes it over. Jack hurries to the men's room as, outside, a coal train rumbles by.

Relieved in more ways than one, Jack returns the key to Simon then selects a couple Hershey bars, two bags of Cheetos, and a six-pack of cold Coronas. As the man swipes his debit card, Jack says, "What happened to the town? Wildfire or something?"

"More like Suze Mustard."

Jack signs the slip, slides it back. "What's a Suze Mustard?"

"Suze Mustard's a who." The man leans on his elbows, doesn't move to bag the snacks. "Great-granddaughter of Granny Mustard. Burned it down in July. Mine folks starting to build it back up. Got this station, couple stores. But looks like that's about all they're gonna do. Think they changed their minds when they saw how much it would cost."

"Was this Suze woman…"

"Girl. Only fourteen."

"Okay, was this Suze girl any relation to a Jenkie Mustard?"

The man spits air. "Oh, you bet. Suze was Jenkie's little sister. They're a bunch of Mustards around here. Dangerous, mad bunch." His face angles. "How you know Jenkie?"

"Well..." Jack hesitates. He doesn't want to tip his hand as to what they're doing in the area. Still, the idea that Jenkie—the supposed zombie owner—is related to the girl who torched a whole town. "I don't really. Just heard her name mentioned, down in Tazewell."

"Oh, yeah? Who was talkin' about Jenkie? Nobody seen her 'round here for months. Her mama Penny said she probably ran off like Bobby Boo Anderson ran off, out to Hollywood or something to get into movies. Like either one of 'em has what it takes. Bobby ugly and dumb and crazy. Jenkie dumb and crazy and dumb."

"I don't recall who was talking about her. I think it was at the... ah, the motel? Maybe she did run off, came through Tazewell on her way out." *Shit, Jenkie Mustard is crazy. Her whole family is crazy. Now if we can get some of the other relatives to join in the show, this will be a winner, no doubt about it.*

Jack's sense of unease and claustrophobia begins to fade, replaced by renewed excitement for the project.

"So what you boys doin' up in Beaver Dam? You geocachers?"

"We what?"

"Geocachers. Used to have some of them people coming into Beaver Dam lookin' for caches. Some outsider had hid one in little plastic box under the front stoop of the Beaver Dam motel. If you're lookin' for that, 'fraid it got burned up with the motel and the folks inside it."

"No," says Jack. He looks out the big window to see Sam walking back to the Tribute. "We aren't looking for a geocache. We're... making a nature documentary. Filming trees, plants, animals in the fall, all that shit, you know."

"Why's your buddy filming Beaver Dam? Fire was long ago. Suze did it. Not nature."

"I think maybe he's just testing the camera out to make sure it's working okay. We came a long way on a plane. Camera might have gotten jostled in transit. You know how those baggage handlers can be."

"Not really."

"Well."

The man taps one finger on the counter. "You just be careful. Don't go wanderin' Black Rock Ridge too far up. Mustards all over the place up there. They don't take to people comin' around uninvited."

"We're just going to keep to the main roads."

"Ain't no main roads. Just roads."

"Okay, well, we'll keep to the roads, whatever kind they are. Film out the window, that kind of thing." *Film out the window? Oh, yeah, that sounds professional.*

A woman comes into the convenience store. She's young, pretty in a stoic, introverted kind of way, early twenties, long brown hair in a braid that hangs down across her shoulder. She's dressed in jeans, hiking boots, a blue wool coat that is a couple sizes too big for her. A colorful but dirty hand knit scarf is wrapped around her neck. Her hands are drawn up in the sleeves. She glances at Jack then out the window at the vehicle and Sam, who is now sitting in the passenger's seat with the door open. Then she looks at Simon.

"Hey, Kathy," he says. "How you doing?"

Kathy lets out a silent sigh, shakes her head. "Good as can be expected."

"So sorry about your mom. We'll miss her. Penny'll be at the wake this afternoon."

"Yeah, thanks." Kathy looks at Jack again. She looks angry, defeated, scared.

"We're praying for you all. A loss. She was a sweet woman."

"Yeah," says Kathy. "She was. I need to get a few things."

"Sure. Take your time."

Kathy turns away, goes down one narrow aisle and selects some cans from the shelves. Jack wants to watch her, opens his mouth to say, "Sorry about your mother," but he knows that will likely spook her, coming from a stranger. He asks for a bag, which the man gives him, stuffs the snacks inside, and goes out to the car. He hands Sam the bag and the beer and gets behind the wheel.

The girl's car is a real piece of crap. No front bumper. Dented rear door. Paint gouged in numerous places. It makes Jack feel embarrassed a bit, with his new shiny rental. He wondered what she thought of him. If she even did. If it even mattered.

Places to go, zombies to meet.

Another mine truck drives by, then a car, and then nobody.

"Let's get out of here," he says to Sam, and they do.

10
Kathy Shaw

She forces herself to drive slowly on the way home, though her body is shot full of adrenalin and everything inside her screams, "Hurry!"

But she does not want to hurry. She knows what she must face at home.

In the bag on the passenger seat beside her are several cans of diced tomatoes, a box of quick-cook rice, a carton of milk, a couple bananas, a pack of bar soap, and some coffee singles. She didn't really need to get this stuff today, it could have waited, but she wanted to get out of the house. Needed some air. Needed to be away from Hank for a while.

She prefers to shop in Simon's gas station convenience store rather than the makeshift trailer grocery, which is dimly lit and cold and the woman behind the counter there most of the time, May Lee, is an angry old bitch who used to work as one of the Beaver Dam Mine secretaries until she developed throat cancer and couldn't man the phone anymore. The mine insurance got her cured, but now she whispers, and her whispers are always pissed off, like the person who comes in to shop gave her the cancer.

A car passes her, heading toward town. But only this one car. Little traffic takes this road now. A newer road has been carved out from the other side of the Beaver Dam Mines now, making more of a straight shot down toward Tazewell. It's like the mining company owners, who swore it would rebuild Beaver Dam, have hedged their bets a bit. They aren't really keen on putting much more money into it as they originally suggested they would. And so they aren't really keen about people driving through the remains of the town. Doesn't make for good PR, doesn't bring about the best image for the area or the business. Best to encourage folks to drive in from another direction so they don't have to pass what is still a shitty-looking place.

For out of the July ashes, a distorted, stunted version of the town has arisen. Smaller, uglier, colder, with little sense of what it had once been, like a dead thing forced back to some form of life. It will probably never be as it was before it died. A shell, a hollow place, full of ghosts and memories and echoes. Kathy wouldn't be surprised if a brand new, tidy, clean, and modern town was at this very minute being erected on the other side of the mines. Maybe name it Beaver Dam 2, like it's a movie sequel.

Up an incline, around a curve, and there is her father's church, the New Light Church of the Creator. It's a small building, recently painted with a new coat of white by Hank and the hiker, Armistead, who'd come through in August. The double, arched doors on the front are bright red, though it's not a Methodist Church. Hank explains to those who ask that the red represents the Middle Ages tradition of sanctuary. When he bought the land and built the church sixteen years earlier, Hank said, "No one will be turned away. Everyone will find safety and peace inside these doors." And he'd been true to his word. Wanderers, locals, tourists, believers, doubters, people angry with God and people who had no thought of God at all. Hank truly loved them all, never preaching to convert but being kind to each as if they were his closest friends. When the Shaws' crops came in, Hank portioned some of it to offer congregation members whose own corn or beans didn't fare as well. The same with hams, or eggs, or chickens. It was all from God, Hank said, and he was only giving to others what God wanted him to give. While Wednesday night and Sunday morning offerings brought in just enough to pay the church's electrical bill and taxes, with a few dollars left over at times that went to the electric bill for his own double-wide, Hank never complained about money. "God provides," he said. The disability check Annie received for her multiple sclerosis and the money Kathy brought in from work kept the family poor, but no poorer, Hank pointed out, than most anyone else in the mountains.

Kathy once challenged Hank, "But why does God provide so much for the mine owners? They have millions. And even Granny Mustard is hardly destitute. We both know she rakes in the cash with her shine business. But look at us. We can barely make it."

Hank's answer, "We're making it. We're eating. We're staying warm. We're surviving. Do we really need more than we have?"

Kathy had lots of answers for that on the tip of her tongue. "I'd like money to go to college."

"I'd like to build a real house with more than one bath, one that has a big, walk-in tub for Mom."

"I'd like to be able to get a car I can trust, and not wonder every few miles if the whole thing is going to rot out from beneath me."

"I'd like you to be able to get new carpeting to replace that crap on the floor, to get a new sofa to replace the sagging one, to put in a new washing machine to replace the one that died seven years ago, to put in new weather stripping around the doors and windows."

But she didn't say them. She knew what he would say. It was always the same answer. Always "God is with us. We are all right." Kathy could see Hank's heart on his sleeve, and it was a good heart. She didn't have the heart to hurt that heart. She stops the car in front of the church. The big sign reading,

"Worship With Us. 10:30 Sunday Mornings. 7:00 Wednesday Evenings. All Welcome. Minister Hank Shaw" now has a pot of burgundy mums propped up at its base. Likely a local lady dug up some from her yard and put them here in memory of Annie.

"Mom," whispers Kathy.

The wake will be today, up at their house at noon. Congregation members will bring squash casseroles and apple pies, chocolate cakes, and fried chicken. The women will hug Kathy and pat her on the head as if she is a child. The men will hold their hats and nod respectfully as Hank stoically talks about love and eternal life. The children will play outside mostly, for even though they are familiar with death and its rituals, they don't care to stare at a homemade pine coffin on a table in a living room and wonder what the body looks like.

And in this case, they will have no idea in spite of how much they might imagine. Because Annie is buried up in the forest in a four-foot-deep grave covered with soil and moss and cedar branches. Annie, with her ruptured, damaged body, has been left where a coyote can dig her up should he smell her, and then buzzards can enjoy her remains. For in the coffin in the Shaw living room, a coffin Hank sealed tightly under the white lie of "She asked that when her time come, there be no viewing," were one hundred and ten pounds of shortened two-by-fours and old bricks, duct-taped together and wrapped in thick oil cloth so no strange movement would be detected when the pallbearers take her down to the church graveyard this afternoon. Mike, the local gravedigger, will have the hole ready, a six-foot deep rectangular pit at the far corner of the church property where Annie used to sit on a little wrought iron bench when the heat of summer services got to be too much for her. Everyone will pray, there will be more hugging and more condolences, then folks will head home, no one the wiser. No one having an idea of what Annie Shaw's final minutes were like or that her husband had killed her. Okay, that her husband stopped her even though she was already dead and was trying, in turn, to kill her own daughter.

We're all Suze Mustard crazy now, Kathy thinks. *It's contagious, this insanity.*

She considers the sign again, how lovingly the letters had been painted onto the white plastic. Maybe Hank could have an in-home church down in Virginia Beach. Right there in her apartment. She can keep working, he can keep preaching. They would be far away from Beaver Dam and Block Rock Ridge and the Mustards and whatever horrific evil had taken hold of her mother. They would never speak of what happened to Annie again.

"Let him say yes to a move," Kathy says, not quite a prayer but an appeal, nonetheless. She bows her head and cries for her mother, for her father, for herself. Then she digs the tears away from her face, presses the gas, and drives home.

11
Jack Carroll

"This what it was like where you used to live?" Jack leans forward, teeth gritted, fingers clutching the steering wheel. The Tribute bounces on the rutted gravel road like some kind of old-fashioned Grapes of Wrath jalopy. Several times they've hit potholes hard enough to send Jack to the ceiling.

Sam grins. "Oh, sure. And worse, some spots."

"We'd get insurance on this car?"

"Yep."

"'Cause it's not going back to the airport in the same shape we took it away in."

"Slow down some, that'll help."

The road, little more than powdered gravel and hard-packed dirt, is even steeper now. Every so often, Jack has a flash of the Tribute flipping over backward and then tumbling down, down, like the bad guy's car following the chase at the end of an old detective movie. But the vehicle clings like a mountain goat, and up they go.

Sam has the directions out, printed from the Bink dude's e-mail.

"We've gone ¾ mile on this stretch, now watch for a turn off on the left. Hold it, okay, there it is, beside that old sycamore, see?"

Jack says, "I don't know sycamores from a tree."

"A sycamore's a tree."

"Shut up." He slows the car, steers left. Presses the gas gently. On and upward they continue. There are several house trailers and cabins this high up, some nearer the road, some up on weedy clearings. Dogs on heavy chains challenge them, barking, growling, and leaping to the length of the chain's reach. Clotheslines stretch from porches to tree branches, weighted down with yellowed sheets, socks, and faded towels. Chickens peck weeds, run away at the sound of the engine. Every so often they see a person—a man tinkering on the engine of a truck, a woman beating a rug over a porch railing, a child running and waving as if the Tribute is some kind of one-float parade.

"Right here," says Sam.

Jack steers right, and up they continue. He glances in the rearview and goes dizzy for a moment, seeing the trees and ridges and distant valley below them. He looks back at the road. His fingers grip the wheel even more tightly.

"How much farther to Desper Hollow?"

"Looks like about two more miles."

"Looks like about? I thought the directions were pretty specific."

"Yeah, well, this Bink dude said it was point eight miles from the last turn to this one, so he's clearly not as careful as I'd have hoped."

"How do you know this was the correct turn, then?"

"Because, Jack, it's the only one that had an old broken sink lying beside it."

"Somebody could have moved the sink."

"And it was off by less than a tenth of a mile. We'll just have to trust the sink hasn't been tampered with."

The Tribute skids a bit on the rocky road; Jack sucks air. "Damn, I hate this place."

"You'll come to love it. Beautiful, breath-taking scenery. Fresh air. Oh, and there's money to make and a boss to please, just keep reminding yourself."

A minute later they bear to the left, driving over a downed piece of barbed wire. The trees here seem all the denser, all the darker, all the more oppressive. They lean in like ominous and curious monsters, some branches reaching down as far as the vehicle's roof and dragging their branchy fingers along the top.

Then Sam says, "Okay, now we need to be even more careful."

Jack stops the car. "Wait... More careful than what?"

"Don't stop, Jack."

Jack starts driving.

Sam waves the print out. "Didn't you read all of this Bink dude's e-mail?"

"Sure. Didn't I?"

"It was near the bottom, under the directions."

"I think I did."

"Among other things, he tells us what the weather might be like and how we should make sure we have plenty of gas in the tank, and what restaurant is best in Tazewell. Then he says 'Oh, yeah, when you get to your last left turn, keep your eyes out. This is deep Black Rock Ridge territory. Lots of Mustards here."

Jack stopped the car again, and frowned at Sam. "The guy at the Exxon mentioned the Mustard family. I told him we were going to stay on the road, not go anywhere uninvited. So we should be okay, right?"

"The Bink dude seemed to be suggesting that this whole area is an area that they'd consider strangers to be uninvited."

"No, listen to me. We should be all right, right?"

"I hope so. But we can't just sit here, we have to keep..." The end of the sentence drops off. Sam points up ahead. There, in the shadows in the center of the road are two large men. One has a shotgun over his arm. The other, a shiny something that looks like a machete.

"Holy shit!" cries Jack. He slams the Tribute into reverse. The engine roars. "We gotta back out of here!"

"We can't!"

A glance in the rearview reveals another large man in the middle of the road, tapping the butt of a large revolver against one palm, mouth in a sneer. All the men wear wide-brimmed hats. None of their eyes are visible.

"I'll run him down!"

"And the other will shoot us through the windshield or we'll be charged with murder. Play it cool, play it easy. We can do this," says Sam. "I think we've just met some Mustards."

The men walk silently toward the car.

12
Jenkie Mustard

She made brownies in the toaster oven last night, but the men from Hollywood haven't come and now she thinks they were lying, and she's majorly pissed and so has eaten more than half the pan. Bink is out back, tying up the legs of the newest catch. A couple possums, two squirrels, rats, mice, four groundhogs. A good number for the day. But he told Jenkie this morning that as winter sets in, it'll be harder and harder to find food for the hollows. They tried snakes and salamanders a while back, but cold-blooded critters didn't work. The hollows just walked over them, crushing them into the bedroom floors with all the rest of the crap. She doesn't know what they will do when it's winter and the warm-blooded animals are hiding out or hibernating. Maybe they could go on a pet roundup, steal some dogs from the folks over on Black Rock Ridge. Her mama has chickens and a shit load of barn cats. Burley Mustard raises goats. The Shaws, and most everyone else, have pigs. Jenkie might not be fast, but she can be sneaky.

Jenkie takes another bite of brownie. They aren't so good after the first eight, but they're filling and at least that's something. She tosses the pan down on the counter and storms out to the front steps. It's cold today. No more Indian summer. She can see her breath. A breeze catches her red hair and throws it against her face, into her eyes. It doesn't smell too good. It's oily and crusty. She thinks she should wash it, because maybe the TV guys will come anyway, even as she guesses they won't. She thinks maybe she should take a shower, too, but that would mean going down to her mama's house and trying to avoid the inevitable questions as to where the hell she's been, or all the way up to Granny's cabin, which, as the crow flies, is the closest house to Desper Hollow. Granny's place has a big washtub and a pump. Bink can only bring so much water to the trailer in jugs, and they drink most of that, or boil dumplings or potatoes in it.

But if the Hollywood guys come and she stinks, that wouldn't be good.

Though the hollows stink as bad as anything can stink.

And she's certain the TV guys aren't coming.

The hollows scrabble and groan down the other end of the trailer, sticking noses out of the broken windows, then hands, clutching, missing a finger or two, blotched and blue and purple. Always reaching for something, and even when they catch something, never satisfied. Every so often, she can hear Dan's throaty, dog-like growl beneath the others' chattering, slobby wails.

"Shut up, Bobby Boo!" she calls. "Shut up, Stead! Shut up Dan! Shut up all of you! You got another hour before I feed you, so cool your jets!"

They don't cool their jets. Jenkie drops down in the glider and rocks back and forth.

Squeak, squeak, squeak.

She doesn't have her sweatshirt on, and she shivers.

Squeak, squeak, squeak.

Once more, she thinks of how good it would feel to burn the shit down or blow it up. Then she thinks how Bink is warm blooded, and he might satisfy the hollows for a whole day, should she shove him down the hole in the ceiling.

Bink comes around the trailer, rolling up the twine he uses on the animals' legs. "I'm going down to Benny's." He tosses the ball of twine to Jenkie, and she misses. It hits the ground and rolls a few feet. Bink pulls at his nose. His beard is full of crumbs from the morning toast.

"Why?"

"Why not?"

"I hate you."

Bink says, "That's not nice! Woob woob woob!" He slaps himself in the face like Curly does in the videos, does a little run in place. Jenkie hates Curly almost as much as she hates Bink. She doesn't get the appeal of the Stooges. It's like watching three Binks be stupid for laughs, and it's never funny.

"Ya want to be like Curly you gotta shave your head and your stinkin' beard," she says.

Bink scoffs. "You don't know nothin' 'bout the Stooges. Curly had lots of hair, and if he'd let it grow out, he'd-a looked just like me. He'd-a been a handsome man, just like me."

Jenkie crosses her arms and looks out at the trees.

Bink pulls his Jeep keys out of his pocket. "What you gonna do while I'm gone?"

"Why do you care?"

"'Cause you got that damn 'I Hate Granny' look on your face again. I get the feeling next time you get like this, you gonna do something really dumb."

"Go to Benny's. Make some fuckin' electrical thing. Fix some fuckin' TV or some kid's remote control car. Just get out of here."

Bink shrugs, takes a step, turns back. She can see he really is concerned she'll do something stupid.

"Why don't you do another shine experiment?" he says. "You ain't done one in a while. Try another combination of ingredients."

"Can't get nothing to live past a couple days, you know that."

"You don't win by quitting. That's how I got so good with electronics, you know. Hey, somehow Granny got things to live a lot longer than a couple days. She got 'em to live, what, forever maybe? We got the proof in the trailer."

"Granny was smarter than me. I'm stupid as hell. All I got to show is stuff she already done. Ain't got nothin' to show of my own. I'm glad them TV men didn't come here. They'd've laughed their asses off at me. They'd probably sue me for makin' them come all the way out here for nothin'."

"Jenkie..."

"Just go!"

"Really?" Bink's face changes and it's different now, different from any way she's seen it before. "Okay, Jenkie, have it your way. I'm going. I'm gone. Don't expect me back. You're on your own now."

But she pushes. She can't help it. "Fine! Just fucking go!"

He fucking goes, driving off in the Jeep with a spray of dust and disintegrating leaves.

Jenkie storms back into the trailer, jams in an exercise tape, turns up the music so she doesn't have to hear the hollows, then gets out Granny's pots, recipes, and the bags of ingredients. One of the bags has a ragged hole in the side. She peeks in to find little beads of mouse poo. She throws the bag toward the plastic trashcan; some poo falls out and spatters on the floor.

She pulls the leather-bound book from the cabinet and places it on the counter. It's so cold. She stares at it, hating it, fearing it, wanting to know its power, wanting to understand it like Granny did. She traces the faint gold design pressed into the leather cover—a knight's helmet and the fading outlines of three winged birds rising up.

"Where'd this come from, Granny?" she whispers. "Where the hell'd the power come from? I want to use it. I want to be like you. I don't want to be like me anymore."

Slowly, she turns back the cover and feels the frosted air rising from the brittle pages and stinging her lips. There is no title page, like the books she used to have in school. There is no author or copyright date. No pictures. Only the pages with the chants, chants in the unrecognizable language.

There are only two jars of Granny's shine left, and one is just quarter-full. Jenkie opens this one, and frowns. Once the shine is gone, it's gone.

She doesn't know how to distill anything. Even if she did, Desper Hollow is nowhere near a creek, and she doesn't have a still. And there will be no more corn or barley until next summer.

And, of course, she doesn't know how to read the damn chants.

Holding up the jar, she gazes at the clear liquid. The living room light swirls with it, distorted, as if broken apart by the power in the jar. Jenkie never did like the taste of shine too much; it bit her tongue and chewed her gut. But what would happen if she tried this shine? What if she added her most successful combination of bloodroot leaves, pine bark, bracket fungi, and crushed black widows and, rather than pouring it onto dead creatures, drank it? What would the shine do to something that wasn't dead yet? Would it kill it? Would it make it live longer? Granny never drank the special shine. In spite of everything else in her life, Granny was one careful, calculating old woman.

But Granny's months-dead now. It's pretty damn clear she never did get the right combination of shine-blend and chant, or she'd be up on Moon Peak, still. Now Jenkie is in charge of it all.

What would happen if she mixed it up and drank it down? Would she turn into a hollow? Or would she become immortal, like Granny had hoped all along? Why didn't Granny write all this down? Screw Granny and her secretive, selfish ways.

Jenkie holds the jar with both hands. She stares at it, at her distorted face reflecting in the glass, at the light spinning and breaking and reforming itself. She lifts the jar to her lips, tips it ever so slightly. The liquid rolls toward her tongue.

Then she puts the jar down and heads out back to the pen to select a mouse or vole to kill. Maybe a bit more dried bloodroot would up the revival rate to four days instead of three. Maybe some of that mouse poo sprinkled in for good measure. Can't know until she tries. She might as well keep trying.

Ain't nothing else to do in Desper Hollow. Ain't nothing else to do with my life but play with the lives of other things.

13
Jack Carroll

"I've been on this earth twenty-six years and five months, and of all those days, this is the worse of my entire life."

"Just shut up, Jack" says Sam. "We're lucky to be alive."

"Alive? Yeah, alive. And that's about all we are."

"Better'n dead."

Jack stops on the trail, leans over to catch his knees and his breath. He spits sour saliva into the leaves. "So we're not dead, but we're in the middle of fucking nowhere with no car, no money, and no real idea where we are. No food, no water! Yeah, we're gonna die, Sam, and don't try to tell me we aren't. This is just a long-drawn out way to do it."

His heart and head are pounding, as much from exertion as the fear that snaps at his heels. His throat is scraped dry from breathing through his mouth. His lips are cracked.

"We aren't that far from Desper Hollow. Maybe a tenth of a mile, maybe two."

"Fuck Desper Hollow! We need to turn around and go back down. I can't go up anymore."

"Back that way?" Sam inclines his head. "Back where those guys were? Seriously? You want to do that? You heard them, what they'll do should they see us again."

Jack doesn't reply. He doesn't want to go back that way anymore than he wants to go forward. He just wants to stand still and let whatever God there might be descend on a cloud and lift him the hell out. Why was deus ex machina reserved for Greek tragedies? Why the hell couldn't real life be like an ancient play where the rescue of the good guys was assured?

It had scared the bejeezus out of him, the encounter. He'd never been as terrified in his life and was actually quite surprised he hadn't pissed himself. Even back in Los Angeles, when confronted by gang members on a dark street corner, thugs who had threatened him, knocked him down and broken his tooth, and then stolen his wallet, he wasn't as afraid as he had been when meeting the Mustard brothers.

They'd surrounded the car, as well as three huge mountain men could, brandishing various weapons and grinning like they had just discovered some fat, delicious wild pigs snared in a trap.

"Cut the engine!" the one with the shotgun called. Jack had hesitated, certain this was just some kind of stress-induced vision, certain this kind of stereotypical hillbilly couldn't have been for real. But he was. So were the others. The shotgun was aimed at Jack's face. Jack cut the engine.

The two men in front of the Tribute grinned in unison. Jack glanced in the rearview to see the other man grinning, too. *Holy shit, we just drove onto the set of Deliverance!* Jack thought. His butt cheeks clenched defensively.

Out of the corner of his eye, Jack saw Sam slide his hand up along the door to press the lock button.

"What good will that do?" Jack whispered.

"Probably nothing," said Sam.

Oh God, oh God, oh God. This is it. We're done for. They'll find our corpses, our skeletons, years from now when someone buys this mountain land to build a ski resort!

"Sam," whispered Jack. "These are your people. Our lives are in your hands. Don't let us die."

Sam swallowed loud enough for Jack to hear. The sound wasn't encouraging. Sam said, "I'll do what I can."

The first big man, the one with the shotgun, came around and stopped at the driver's side door. Jack could see his eyes now, tiny things, enfolded in weather-worn flesh. The man jerked his thumb at the door.

"Unlock that damn thing and get out."

Oh my God! What is worse? To die in the car or die after I've been raped?

"I said open the door and get your asses out here."

For some reason he couldn't understand, his hand decided to take the chance with getting out. Maybe he could run away? The video he'd seen about defensive actions said that if you ran in a zigzag pattern, chances of a bullet striking a killing blow was reduced.

But did that also apply to a shotgun shell? Would a shell to the leg kill you just as sure, make you bleed out slowly?

Jack got out. Sam got out. They looked at each other over the roof of the Tribute.

"Name's Burley Mustard," said the man with the shotgun. He jerked his head in the direction of the man with the machete. "That's my brother Calhoun. And back there's my cousin, Pete."

"Pleased to meet you," said Sam. This almost made Jack laugh out loud. Almost.

There was a long pause. Then Burley said, "And you?"

"I'm Sam Pearson, this is Jack Carroll."

Burley nodded. "Okay, then. What you boys up to up here? We don't 'member nothin' 'bout two outsiders comin' up our neck o' the woods.

You 'member hearin' anything 'bout that, Calhoun? Pete?"

The other men shook their heads, pursed their lips.

"Oh, well we're making a film," said Sam.

"Film?" Burley punched Jack lightly in the chest with the muzzle of the shotgun. Cold raced Jack's veins. "What kind o' film?"

"Nature film," said Sam. "Birds, trees, insects. That kind of nature."

"Yeah?" This was Calhoun. He walked around behind Sam and touched his back with the tip of the machete. Jack gasped, silently. *Oh, God, no no, please.* He could see Sam's eyes twitching at the corners.

"Yeah," said Jack, surprised at how steady his voice sounded coming from a throat that was tight as a tick. "We're making a documentary on the beauty of the Appalachians. You live in a magnificent part of the country, Mr. Mustard."

"Oh, we do, we do," said Pete. He came up beside Calhoun, waving his revolver. "And we like it... unspoiled... as some folks might say."

"Oh, you bet," said Sam. "It reminds me of where I was born and raised. Nothing prettier than the mountains. I miss my home so much. Just being here makes me think I should go back home. Visit my Mama, my granddaddy."

This piqued Calhoun's interest. "Where you from, exactly? Not here. Never seen your face before."

"Kentucky, other side of the mountains, Harlan County."

"You don't sound like a mountain boy."

Sam pulled on a grin. Then he pulled on his accent, deep, rounded, full-fledged Southern mountains. "Well, that's because if I talk the way I'm used to, the way I was raised to, my friend here can hardly understand but every third word I say. Pathetic, ain't it?"

"So where's that boy from?"

"California."

Burley huffed. "California? Ain't that nothin' but Nancy boys?"

Jack's heart stopped for an entire five seconds. Then it started again.

"Hell, no," he said, hoping it came out as stern and manly, but hearing his voice crack.

"Shit, no," said Sam. "Jack's a good guy. Got a gorgeous wife, shit, wish you could see her."

"Pictures?" This was Burley.

There was a photo of Jack's recent girlfriend, Miriam, in his wallet.

She'd dumped his ass right before the trip east. He said, "Yeah." He pulled his wallet out, flipped it open with trembling hands, held it out to Burley.

"Fuck yeah, I could eat that," said Burley. He passed the wallet around to the others, who licked their lips, rubbed their crotches, and handed the wallet back to Burley. Burley then searched the wallet, thumbing through the credit cards and receipts while the shotgun lay across his arm. He lit up even more when he saw the bills.

"Cash here," he said, pulling out all the paper money. "How much you got here, Jack?"

"I... I'm not sure. Hundred dollars, maybe?"

"Looks like more 'en that. Here, Calhoun, count it for me."

Calhoun counted it, shook his head, then counted again, mouthing the numbers as he went, his chipped teeth scraping on his lower lip. "Wow, this boy's got close to three hundred dollars here."

"What you need three hundred dollars for up here on Black Rock Ridge?"

"Ah..." said Jack.

"Food," said Sam. "Place to stay. Gas for the car. C'mon, man, you know what folks need money for."

"You out to buy you some shine?" asked Pete. His voice was suddenly darker than before, grittier.

Jack looked at him, shook his head. "Shine? What's that?"

Sam waved his hand as if waving away gnats. His accent got even thicker. He bobbed his head in a way that Jack hoped looked casual and unafraid. "No, sir we ain't after shine. We're after some good film footage of piliated woodpeckers and some American chestnuts, if there are any growin' in these mountains. I'm sure you know, like most folks, that most of 'em die of the blight well before they reach maturity, but there's always hope, ain't there? Always a little glimmer in the night. And we hope to record some bobcats, though as you know they're really elusive. Sly as foxes, silent as fog, my Mama used to say."

Burley's brows drew together as if considering what Sam had said or trying to understand it. Then he pointed into the Tribute. "What you got in there?"

Sam shrugged. "Camera, suitcase. That's about it."

"What's in the suitcase?"

Fucking clothes, moron! Jack wanted to scream.

"Clothes."

"More money?"

"No, I don't think so."

Burley rubbed his chin. The gun wobbled in the crook of his other arm. Then he said, "Tell you what, we's gonna believe you. Let you go on your way. Make your film 'bout them pilly peckers and bobcats."

Sam nodded. "I 'preciate that."

"But we want your car, your suitcase, and I'm gonna keep this money here." He tossed the wallet back to Jack. But just as quickly, he took it back, removed the photo of Miriam, rubbed it on his crotch, then gleefully stuffed it into his pants pocket along with the cash.

Calhoun put the tip of the machete down on the road and wiggled his fingers at Jack. "Keys to your car."

"Well, it's not our car, actually, it's…"

"I don't give a flying pile of pig shit whose car it is," snapped Burley.

He was pissed now. No need to press it. "It's mine. You hear me?"

Jack nodded. He tossed the keys over.

"You boys got phones?"

"Of course."

"Phones, too."

Sam and Jack handed over their phones.

Then Burley stepped so close to Jack, Jack was afraid the man wanted to either kiss him or bite off his nose. "Now," he said. His breath was of cheese and booze. "Now, you are gonna stay on roads, and you ain't gonna go looking for your critters off the road. Right? You gonna make your little movie, then hike back down the mountains. You understand?"

Jack nodded.

"'Cause we run into you two again, we ain't gonna be so nice."

"Okay."

With that, Burley, Pete, and Calhoun climbed into the Tribute, gunned the engine, tossed Sam's camera case out the window, which he dove and caught, and drove off down the direction Sam and Jack had come.

Sam and Jack stood without moving or speaking for several very long minutes. Then Sam said, "Shit, that was close."

"Close?" yelled Jack. "Close? How much closer, short of anal violation or murder could they have come? They took the car, they took our suitcases, they took all my money. You know what this means, don't you?"

"It means we still have the gun you bought. It's in your coat pocket."

"Yeah, I know, but it's not even loaded, Sam. The box of bullets is in the car's glove box."

"Oh."

"So this is what it means—it means we die here. It means we die of thirst, starvation, and they find us shriveled up beneath one of those American chestnut trees you were talking about!"

"Well, actually, the American chestnut tree is no longer…"

"I don't give a flying fuck, Sam! The only thing I have is wallet with no money. My new gun with no ammunition. Oh, that's helpful."

Sam kicked a rock. It rolled and bounced down the road. Then he said, "So you want to just stand here, or do you want to keep on heading for Desper Hollow?"

"What choice do I have?"

"Those two. That's pretty much the extent of it."

And so they are hiking, panting, sweating, hurting. Jack's mind bounces back and forth between a certainty that the men are coming back up to get them, that the vague, fragile hope that Jenkie Mustard really isn't a crazy old mountain woman but a mildly delusional gal who has a nice truck to carry them back to Tazewell where they can rent another car, and that this is his last day on earth whether he move forward, go back, or stay put.

Fucking shit-hole mountain mutants!

"At least they didn't steal your credit cards," says Sam.

"Yeah, you can eat plastic, so I hear. Lots of nutrients."

Sam punches Jack in the arm, hard. Jack throws a punch back, but it's pathetically weak.

"Just shut up," says Sam, "You were into this trip, so excited about a new discovery, a certain money maker. Well, not everything comes on a silver platter. Some things you genuinely have to work for."

"Who are you, some kind of fucking philosopher?"

"Just repeating what my dad taught me. That which doesn't kill me makes me…"

"Makes me furious and tired and hungry and thirsty and car-less and money-less and stranded and near dead."

"You're nowhere near dead. But if you keep talking like that

I'm going to get pissed and kill you and then you'll not only be near dead you'll be dead-dead."

Jack scowls.

Then the two men freeze. They hear the sound of an engine up the way, and they dart behind thick, thorny brush. A Jeep passes by, heading down the mountain.

"A Mustard?" says Jack softly.

"Like I would know?"

"Was this idea the biggest mistake of my life or what?"

Sam only shakes his head. They go back to the road. Jack takes five steps, stops, hang his head, his chest furious at the treatment it's receiving.

"Let's stop a bit."

"Up this way just a little farther, then west a little bit more. You can do it."

"Fuck off. I'm going to stop for a while. I've got to rest, dude. I swear to God."

Sam is exasperated and he cusses under his breath, but Jack can tell he's wrung out and on the edge, too. They find a patch of soft ground behind a small, mossy knoll, sit with backs against solid trees, and even though Sam had not wanted to, they doze.

Jack awakens with a start, having dreamed of hillbillies cooking him in a pot like the cartoon cannibals from the 1930s. He's covered in sweat even in the chill, his eyes crusted and some kind of insect welts on his neck. He nudges Sam awake, who immediately looks embarrassed that he let himself sleep.

Sam coughs, spits out silt that had found its way into his mouth.

"We've got to move."

"I'm still tired."

"Yeah, well, it's not that you can't do it as much as you have to do it. We're really deep in Black Rock Ridge. I don't doubt there are more Mustards all over. Wouldn't be surprised to find they'd been watching us from overhead, like a bunch of monkeys."

Jack swears, nods.

They find the pathway off the road, a churned, flattened portion of vegetation leading down a steep slope into dense trees and shadows. "This can't be right," says Jack.

"It's right as long as the Bink dude was accurate."

"I feel like we're walking into a trap."

"Maybe."

"Screw you."

"Might as well go for broke."

"We already did that."

They slip and slide down the pathway, balancing themselves with arms outstretched. Sam's camera case bounces on its strap. Jack breathes through his mouth, making his throat all the more dry, all the more sore.

It's getting late; the sun is low.

"Tire tracks," says Sam, pointing. "The Bink dude said he drove a Jeep. Yeah, this has to be right. That was probably the Bink dude in his Jeep, driving past us. I think we're heading right."

"Screw you."

"No time now. Maybe later."

Further down, heels dug in so as not to topple forward, they reach a level bit of land. Then another stretch through a tight, winding passage.

Finally, up ahead, a trailer. A dented, rusted piece of metal with some kind of old rocker-glider out front.

"Guess that's it," says Jack.

"Guess so."

They look at each other. They take simultaneous breaths, and they walk to the trailer.

Jack hears the sounds first, and he stops and gives Sam the hairy eyeball. "Damn, sounds like zombies to me."

Sam takes several more steps then stops. "Sure does."

"And of course, that's impossible."

"Sure is."

Jack's pulse picks up. He grabs Sam's arm. "Are we supposed to shout or something? Didn't I see that in a movie somewhere? When you come upon a hillbilly home you're supposed to let them know you're out there, so they don't get spooked and blast you to kingdom come?"

"Actually, Jack, you're right about that. Though we don't like being called hillbillies."

"Mountain-billies, then."

Sam cups his hand around his mouth. "Hello, there! Hello! Sam Pearson and Jack Carroll here! Hello!"

There is a sound now of a dog barking inside the trailer, though it doesn't sound like any dog Jack has ever encountered before. It's a strangled howl, a garbled bark, like the animal has a rope too tightly around its neck. Immediately following that is a howl that sets the hair on Jack's neck straight up.

They stand there, Sam with his camera case slung over his shoulder, Jack with his hands in his jacket pocket, touching the useless gun, trembling inside his coat, staring at the trailer.

Then the door opens, and someone appears on the steps.

"Holy shit, that's some scary girl," Jack says through clenched jaws.

"Is that Jenkie Mustard?"

Sam glances at Jack, shrugs.

The girl coughs, scratches her ass, and calls, "You fuckin' better be the TV guys."

14

Kathy Shaw

They sit in the silent church, side by side on the front bench, Kathy's brows drawn and her fingers clasping her knees, staring up at the altar and purple velvet cloth that drapes it. Yellow and gold potted mums have been placed on the altar between two wooden candlesticks bearing white candles, one of which sits at a slight tilt. The candle flames have been extinguished; the wicks blackened. A framed photograph of Annie, taken before she was ill, has been removed from the altar, and Hank holds it in his hands. He rubs one thumb along the side of Annie's face. Behind them, one of the arched red doors is open, letting in chilly late afternoon air.

Annie was always pretty, even as she struggled over the years, but this photo is especially beautiful. She was Kathy's age when it was taken, hair of like color but curlier and shorter, face rounded, dimple on one cheek. The photo was made down in Tazewell at Randall's Photography Studio to go into the paper for her engagement announcement. There is hope and expectation in her eyes and the hint of girlish impishness in her grin. She and Hank were married twenty-seven years. One home between the two, and one child. And now, only one remains.

"Everybody's left, Dad," says Kathy. Daylight is nearly gone now, absorbed into the lightlessness beyond the plain glass windows and the trees that surround the churchyard. "We should go home."

Hank sighs without sound. He puts the photograph into his coat and zips it up. "No, I'm going to stay here a while. I need to pray."

Kathy taps her teeth. There's tons of food at home, and, after a day with no appetite, she's finally hungry. The wake ran long—until after three. Then the burial in the churchyard at four. Folks came inside the church for some words, more condolences, and prayers after that. It's nearly 5:30 now. Night falls fast and hard in the mountains in November.

"Pray at home," says Kathy. "Come on, please? Let's eat, then you can get some sleep."

But Hank only shakes his head.

Kathy's toes dance inside her shoes; frustration catches her gut. She studies her father then says, "I've been thinking. I know you have your church here, but there are people all over needing a good preacher like you."

Hank closes his eyes. His hair, which he'd raked back with his fingers, falls down over his forehead.

"And I don't want to sound too practical at a time like this, but we have to think, Dad. There will be no more disability checks. You had no life insurance on Mom. I'm living in Virginia Beach now. You can't make it on your own."

He looks up at her, sharply. She can see the anger just below the surface.

"Please, I don't mean to be disrespectful." She turns toward him, and tries her best to keep her voice even, kind, and not trembling with the confusion and grief that churn her heart. "I have a place, an apartment. I am able to pay for it on my own. You can move in with me. You can preach out of our apartment until, perhaps, we can find another place that would hold more. Think about it, please."

"No."

"Mom is gone now. There is no other family here…"

"My congregation is my family."

"Did anyone offer to let you move in with them? They brought food and they brought drink, but did they offer you a place to stay?"

Hank stands up abruptly and stalks to the altar. He places his hands flat against it and bows his head.

"You can't pay the taxes, the utilities, the repairs on your own. The fifty dollars I send you each month only covers half your groceries."

"I'll eat less, now there's one of me."

"You don't need to eat less. Actually, you should probably eat more. Move down to the beach with me. I get to take leftovers home from the restaurant, and it's good, filling, healthy stuff. Sell the church, Dad. You'll get something for it, I'm sure. We can live on the cheap, you and me. We can make a new start. Don't stop preaching, but please stop suffering."

Hank shifts his weight from one foot to the other. Kathy can feel his rage, his despair, his fear, his faith burning off him in waves. There is no way she is going to get him to do what she asks.

"Dad?"

He turns from the altar. "I'll move in here. I'll live in the church."

"What? You can't. There's no central heat. There's no kitchen, there's nothing but this one room, these benches, windows that leak cold air."

"There is God. God is with me, always, in spite of all the wrongs I've done."

"What wrongs? You're the best man I've ever known."

Hank shakes his head. Kathy looks away. Her own anger and fear bubble up, thick and painful. "Dad," she hears herself saying. The words are bitter and burn her mouth, and she spits them out. "Please, please tell me what really happened to Mom."

Hank slams his fist on the altar and Kathy looks back. His expression is stone hard. "Don't ask me that, don't ever ask me that."

"But you know! You killed her…"

"I did not kill her."

"… you buried her in the woods, and you were terrified. But you never really seemed surprised. It's as if once you saw her face, you knew what was wrong."

"The dog killed her. I only brought her the peace she would not have had otherwise. Peace that I owed her."

"Stop talking like that! Tell me what the hell is going on?"

"I've said too much. This isn't for you to know. No more questions, Kathy."

"I'm no child. I'm an adult. I am your daughter. I was her

daughter! Tell me! What was wrong with Mom?"

"Go home. Leave me alone!"

"No!"

Hank kicks the front bench, sending it over backward and sliding into the one behind it. He roars at the ceiling then turns on Kathy. She's never seen such rage, such fear. His face is flushed red, his eyes terrified.

"It's my fault! God help me, what happened to her is my fault! How she was is because of my weakness!"

"How?" Kathy steps back, not certain he might strike her. "How can it be your fault? You didn't make her act crazy like she was!"

"Oh, but I was the beginning! I started it all. Granny Mustard! If I hadn't given in!"

"What about Granny Mustard? You're not making any sense!"

"I gave in and look what evil has arisen! I prayed for help to come once I realized something awful was going on, once I saw what Suze Mustard had done to Beaver Dam. But no help came. I prayed and there was no answer. Just silence. An empty, dreadful silence. And then your mother was killed, and... and I had to kill her again. It was then I knew the truth."

"Dad! What is the truth?"

"Go home, Kathy! Leave me alone! I've got much to atone for, and I need time alone with God to do it!"

Oh shit, oh, shit. He wants to kill himself!

"I won't go. Dad, sit down. Please, please. I won't ask you any more questions right now. Okay?"

He stares at his hands. Kathy wants to scream. She wants to comfort him somehow. She wants to both knock him senseless and hold him. He terrifies her.

"Please, Dad? Let's just sit and be quiet."

Hank sits, his breathing fast, heavy, his eyes staring ahead at the altar as if it were either his salvation or his curse.

Kathy sits beside him. She steels herself and takes his hand. It is a strange, unfamiliar feeling, holding his hand—his fist. It's knotted, rough, and dry. A working hand. A praying hand. Uncomfortable to touch. But she doesn't let go. "Nothing makes sense right now, not what happened to Mom, not anything about Beaver Dam or Granny Mustard or what you've done or not done. What does make sense is you, and what a good man you are. Come home with me. If you need to pray, you can pray there. I'll… I'll even pray with you if you want me to." She isn't sure she can but it's all she can offer at the moment.

He doesn't look at her but doesn't pull away. "You'll never know." He stares at the altar. "You can never know. Leave it alone. Let me handle it."

They sit that way for many more minutes.

"Will you come with me? Please?"

He takes a long, silent breath. "For now. Only for now. I'll pray and prepare myself."

"Prepare for what?"

He doesn't answer.

No. God, no.

Hank stands and the two of them walk home in the darkness without speaking. There is much Kathy wants to say, but there is no way to speak the words. And no way to even form the complete thoughts from which the words would come.

15

Armistead

He hears voices outside in the fading daylight, calling out toward the trailer. Men's voices. He goes to the window, shoves the other away, and snarls at him to keep him back.

The sun is very low now, with twilight beginning to crawl out onto the yard from the woods. Bats stitch the air with their oily wings, leaves tumble across the weeds, a rabbit, out late, darts beneath a tangled brush.

From the other room, Armistead hears the dead dog trying to bark.

There are two men at the far side of the yard. They look hesitant, standing back, looking at each other then at the trailer. Armistead senses these men are not like Bink or the One With No Eyes. He detects harmlessness there, a vulnerability or innocence.

He also detects their warmth on the air, and the hot blood in their veins and the living currents in their muscles and bones.

The Hunger flares and he wails through the window. It's been too long since he has eaten. His mind cramps in extreme pain.

The men glance at the window, say something to each other that Armistead can't hear.

Then there is a squeak as the front trailer door opens, and, glancing to the left, Armistead can see the One With No Eyes standing on the steps. Her face is completely visible, and it is surprising to see that she does, indeed, have eyes, and they are small and deep set. Her round, full body makes the Hunger rise up again, hotter and more demanding than before. Her brain, her arms and belly, her thighs and buttocks, how they would sate him, how they would save him from the agony!

She calls out, "You fuckin' better be the TV guys."

One of them says, "Yes, that's us. Jack Carroll and Sam Pearson. Are you Jenkie Mustard?"

"Of course, I am. Where the hell you been?"

The men glance at each other again and then walk toward the trailer.

Armistead begins to writhe with the agony of the Hunger. His arms thrust through the open window. But then the other is behind him, pulling him back and knocking him down.

Armistead clambers to his feet and slams into the other, but he won't let Armistead get to the window. They haven't been fed this day. At least he doesn't think they have. And so he is weak, and the other is, too, making it a stand-off as to who can have the window at any particular moment. Armistead shuffles to the locked door, touches the knob, rattles it, and of course it is locked like it is always locked. And the gate is on the other side. He paces, back and forth, every nerve on fire with the Hunger.

He glances up at the covered hole in the ceiling. Where is the food?

"I hunger! I hunger!"

The other grunts, glances back at Armistead, but stays at the window, clawing out at the air. One of his red eyes is no longer in the socket but hangs down his cheek on a cherry-red cord of muscle.

Armistead hears the men enter the trailer. He goes back to the door and begins to pound.

"I hunger! How much longer must I hunger?"

And the voice he'd heard before speaks clearly in his mind, over and beneath the Hunger, over and beneath the desperation, bigger than it all.

Not long now. Not long. It will all be over soon.

Armistead puts his hands to his chest. One set of knuckles burst through into the rib cage. No blood, no pain. He addresses the voice.

"How soon?"

Soon.

"I hunger! I want to die!"

No.

"I want to die!"

No. You have a task to accomplish. You have something to learn.

Armistead puts his forehead against the wall. "Please..."

It will be over soon. I promise.

Soon.

16
Jack Carroll

It is the shittiest place he's ever seen in his life, and he's seen shitty. The front steps wobble, as does the inside of the trailer. Every footstep sets something to rattling or shaking. The walls undulate with the wind. The living room floor has a partial carpet, matted, mouse-chewed, filthy. Linoleum shows where the carpet is not; it was probably white and black at one point, now it's mostly mildew black. There is a sagging sofa, one straight back chair, and a television with a VHS tape player sitting on the floor. The only light comes from one yellow bulb burning in a ceiling socket. There is a dead mouse on the floor.

A little kitchen area is separated from the living room by a counter that is littered with jars, bowls, mugs, a hotplate, and toaster oven. There is a narrow hall off the living room, leading to a couple doors that have big metal gates bolted in front of them.

But more than what Jack is seeing, it is what he hears and smells that causes his stomach to cramp and his mind insist, This is some bad crap right here. *Get the hell out, man. You do not want to be here.*

The sounds are grunts and moans. Thumping, groaning from down the hall behind the locked doors. Sounds of desperation and despair and agony. Animalistic yet not quite. There is a human element there. It's all Jack can do to keep from slapping his hands over his ears.

The smells are urine and feces. Rancid sweat and heavy decay. So strong that Jack's throat burns. Sam, ever the face and voice of calm, is clearly horrified. His eyes blink way too fast and his smile is locked in place so hard that his cheeks twitch.

Jenkie Mustard is heavy and imposing, with dyed red hair that looks like it hasn't been washed in months. There are pimples up and down her face and neck. Her eyes are strange; they flick back and forth as if there is some kind of internal disconnect. Though at this point and place in time, nothing would surprise Jack.

"Set down," she says.

They set. Sit. On the smelly sofa. She takes the straight back chair, coughs without covering her mouth.

"You the guys from Hollywood, right?"

"Los Angeles," says Jack. His mouth is dry. His heart beats hard. "Like I said, I'm Jack Carroll. This is Sam Pearson."

The girl frowns. "Wait, you ain't from Hollywood!"

"Well, kinda. We're from the Check It Out! Network, if that's what you're wondering about."

"Yeah, that's what I'm wonderin'." She grins then, a big, sudden, scary grin that slashes across her big face. "Cool! You guys came! Bink ain't here, though. He went to Benny's. Don't know when he's gonna get back, though. He tinkers with shit down there. He's the one made the charger and the remote control for Dan."

Jack's thoughts tumble over one another. He wants to take a deep breath to bring his nerves back down, but it smells too bad to do that. And so he counts— one, two, three, four, five, six— calm down, keep cool, you're the pro here, she's just a harmless mountain loon—seven, eight, nine, ten...

It helps, some. So does breathing through his mouth rather than his nose.

"So, Jenkie, why don't you tell us what you've got goin' on here," says Sam. He's pulled his Southern mountain accent back on again, but Jack can hear the tension beneath the smooth, easy words. "We read your letter, and it definitely had our attention. Had our boss's attention, big time. Enough to fly us out here and have a look-see."

Jenkie licks her lips. "Well, I done some stuff up here I don't think nobody else ever done in their lives. Stuff that'll make a great television show! But wait. Hold on. Did you boys walk here? You didn't have no car?"

"We have a car… had a car," says Sam. "Unfortunately, we met with a bit of trouble on the way. But thanks to that Bink dude's… I mean Bink's directions, we were able to find our way just fine."

Jenkie tries to cross her legs, maybe to look more ladylike or mature or sophisticated. It doesn't work; they are too big to cross. "What kind of trouble with your car?"

Jack isn't sure how much to tell her. Most likely the men on the road are related, last name and all. But Sam says, "Some kind of misunderstanding between a couple men and us, that's all."

"Ah, shit. One of 'em Burley?"

"Yeah. And a brother and cousin, I think he said."

"Those assholes," Jenkie bounces her heel on the floor. "My cousins, all of 'em. Think they own the roads that go 'round Black Rock Ridge. Mean bunch when they get it in their heads to be mean. Good thing you weren't the law! So they take your car?"

Jack and Sam nod.

"You didn't tell 'em just go to hell?"

"Ah, no," says Jack. "They were armed."

Jenkie laughs. "I'm sure they were! You not from around here, so you don't know Mustards. Nobody messes with Mustards. You's smart not to mouth off to 'em. All they took was your car?"

"And some things in it," says Jack. "And my money…"

"But I have my camera, so we're all right," says Sam, trying to brush it off, trying to sound in control. To sound competent and comfortable in this, the shittiest, creepiest place Jack has ever set foot in. Jack squares his shoulders and attempts to follow suit.

"Now," says Sam. "I'd like to set up my camera and film our initial discussion. You okay with that?"

Jenkie's lip hitches. "Um, do I look okay?"

"You look fine."

She looks like hell, thinks Jack, but then reminds himself that that is a good thing. *That's what we wanted, it's what Nate wanted. Crusty, crude, and clueless. And whatever story she has to tell us will be a great lead in for a pilot. Then she'll show us what kind of dogs and rotted pig meat she has in the backrooms that she claims are living dead people, and we'll be on our way to a hit show. We'll be fine. We aren't really in danger. It's just my big city nerves trying to pull this cash cow out from under me.*

Sam gets out the camera, checks it, holds it on his shoulder, and takes turns pointing it at Jenkie and Jack.

Jack: Why don't you tell me a bit about yourself.

Jenkie: Well, I'm Jenkie Mustard. Nice to meet you fellas. And everybody watching the show, you know. (Smile) Uh. I live up here now, in Desper Hollow. That's in Virginia. Appalachian Mountains. I'm seventeen. I don't live at home no more. My mama doesn't know where I am.

(Laugh.)

Jack hesitates. *She's not even a legal adult. She can't agree to do a show. Ah, fuck it. We'll edit that part out.*

Jack: Okay, so you live way out here in Desper Hollow in this trailer.

What would you say, you're maybe three, four miles away from the nearest house or cabin?

Jenkie: (Shrugs) I dunno. Probably a mile or so from Granny Mustard's cabin, but that's a steep walk up the mountain side. Nothing else for, yeah, maybe three miles. A damn long walk if you ain't got no car, and you ain't got one now 'cause you's dumb enough to have a run in with my cousins and they done stole it from you! (Laugh.)

Fuck. Might have to edit that out, too.

Jack: How long have you been living in Desper Hollow?

Jenkie: Since July. Since Suze burned Beaver Dam down and Granny Mustard died.

Jack: Okay, let's rewind a bit. Tell us about Suze burning down Beaver Dam. Heard some about that at the Exxon station.

Jenkie: It's got a gas station now? Bink didn't tell me that. Huh.

There is a loud wail and crashing from down the hall, and both Sam and Jack jump in their seats. *Oh, God, what the hell is that, really?*

Jenkie waves her hand, brushing it off. "Don't worry 'bout that. It's just 'Stead. He's the weirdest one of all. You'll see. But let's keep on with the interview. I can't wait to be on TV! My mama gonna shit a brick she sees me bein' famous!" She drags her fingers through her sticky red hair, pats it down even though it's so oily it's flat against her scalp already.

Jack: So Suze is your sister?

Jenkie: Was. She's dead now.

Jack: I'm sorry. I didn't know that. So she burned down the town and that made you escape up here to Desper Hollow? Were you afraid she was going to burn you up, too, so you decided to hide? Some kind of sibling rivalry?"

Jenkie: Some kinda what?

Jack: Argument between you two.

Jenkie: Huh-uh. She died same night she burned the town. Cut off her hand. I came up here to keep on doin' what Granny was doing. I got her jars of special shine and her bags of ingredients and her book, that ugly old book over there.

Jenkie points to the kitchen, but the lighting is bad and neither Sam nor Jack can see what it is she's pointing to, but that's pretty much a moot issue. Right now, they're interviewing a kook with things growling and slamming around in the back rooms, and the crazier they can get her to talk, the better it will be.

Jack: Okay, not sure I'm following al that, but continue, please. You said in your letter that you have brought dead things back to life. Is that right?

Jenkie: (Scowls.) I don't lie.

Jack: I didn't mean to insinuate that you did…

Jenkie: I wouldn't have written you that letter if I was lyin', now would I?

Sam: No, I don't think you would have. But the audience is going to want to hear that you're honest, truthful.

Jenkie scowls then scratches at a pimple.

Jack: Tell us how you bring dead things back to life, Jenkie.

Jenkie: Well, you missed one I done a couple hours ago. That mouse there on the floor. Didn't live but ten minutes after I brung him back 'cause I got mad and squished him.

Sam: Why'd you get mad?

Jenkie: I didn't think you boys was comin'. I was really mad about that.

Jack glances at Sam, who is still filming. He can't imagine what this girl is like when she's really mad.

There is another crashing sound in the back rooms. He is dying to know what is back there and yet he dreads it to the depths of his soul. But I'm the professional here, he tells himself. I have to let this girl tell her tale.

And just not sit too close to her should she get really angry.

He backs up about two feet.

Jack: How do you bring dead stuff back to life?

Jenkie: It's like this. I find dead critters, or I kill one. Then I take some of Granny's special shine—over in those two jars on the counter—and I add some of the ingredients I've got from the woods. Bug legs, deer hair, dirt, crushed up bark, oh, I've tried lots of stuff to find the best combination, just like Granny did. I mix it in the shine. So far, the best stuff to mix in is black widow spider guts, bloodroot juice. Stir it up, sprinkle it on the body of the dead thing. It brings 'em back for a couple days.

Sam: That's incredible.

Jenkie: I said I ain't lying!

Sam: No, incredible can mean good. Really good. Now you mentioned an old book. What's that for?

Jenkie: Magic chants.

Jack: No shit?

Jenkie: No shit.

Jack: Can you read some chants to us? That would be great.

Jenkie looks suddenly uncomfortable. She rolls her lips in between her teeth. "No. They're secret. Just for me.

Sam shrugs at Jack. Jack says, "Okay, fine. But can you bring something back to life for us?"

Jenkie: Yeah, 'course. I got some critters out back in a pen. You can pick out what you'd like me to kill.

Sam nods, and as Jenkie hoists herself up off the chair, he gives Jack a look that says, Is this some fucked-up shit or what? And it takes all of Jack's strength not to whisper, "I think we should get the hell out of here."

Jenkie snatches a flashlight from the top of the television and goes to the front door. She turns back. "What you gonna call the show? I got some good ideas if you don't."

Sam says, "Oh, we're still chewin' on that."

Jenkie says, "I like 'Jenkie Mustard and Her Monsters What Come Back to Life.' That good?"

"Ah… not bad," says Sam.

"Or 'Jenkie Mustard and Her Dead Things That She Brung Back to Life.' That good?"

"Maybe," says Sam. He adjusts his camera, continues to film.

Jack follows the two of them outside by the sputtering beam of the flashlight. He didn't think he'd have to watch things die. The wind is starting to blow, and it feels like rain is imminent.

As they pull the door closed behind them, Jack notices a sudden silence in the trailer. He pauses, listening, wondering if whatever was making this noise has tired out, maybe fallen asleep, please God. But then another pathetic, screeching cry pierces the air. And the terrible, dog-like growls join in.

Jack hadn't thought there would truly be things in Desper Hollow that sound like zombies. But there are.

He hadn't thought he'd really be scared.

But he really is.

17
Kathy Shaw

Hank falls asleep as soon as they get back home. Kathy watches him from his bedroom doorway. He is still tense, even in slumber, tossing, tangling the blankets. He is a haunted man. It's no wonder. He believes his wife died. He believes he had to kill her a second time. He believes he did something terrible to bring it about and that God has not heard his cries for help or forgiveness. He believes he has a terrible penance to pay.

And, Kathy thinks as Hank clenches his jaws, turns over again, and groans as if in pain, it all has something to do with Granny Mustard.

But Granny's dead now. Dead and buried. There is no way to find out what is tormenting her father. He won't talk. And Granny can't.

Kathy turns away, mind racing, her heart torn. In her bedroom she climbs out of her church clothes and back into her jeans, sweatshirt, and boots. She turns on the television and watches some show she can't even register, and then turns it off again. She fixes herself a fried egg and can't eat it. She goes back to look at her father, sleeping. The night is wearing on and he continues to sleep restlessly, in torment.

Kathy goes out to the deck, stepping over Puffster, who isn't sure she wants to go out or stay in. Kathy leaves the door open a crack so the cat can make up her mind.

Someone who'd attended the wake had left a sweater on the railing.

Kathy picks it up, turns it over in her hands. Looks like Mrs. Dill's. The elderly lady fashioned the best, softest sweaters, scarves, and shawls in the whole area. It was a shame she didn't have a computer or a grandson with one. She could make some good money with an online store.

It's after six now, a November night that has fallen hard as stone. The wind is up. It's a damp wind, a cold wind. Kathy tucks her hair down the back of her sweatshirt. Dead leaves roll across the deck like hollow, dead things chasing after each other.

Dead like Mom.

Dead like Granny Mustard.

"Granny Mustard," she says to the leaves. "What did Dad ever have to do with that old woman? That terrible old bitch from Moon Peak? He never talked bad about her, and he never had dealings with her."

An owl called in the blackness of the nearby trees.

"But he says he did."

Maybe Hank was sliding into dementia. Though he wasn't quite fifty.

That was too young to lose one's mind to such an old person's disease.

Wasn't it?

Kathy shakes her head. "He's no more got dementia than I've got purple eyes."

Then what? Post-traumatic stress from her mother's disappearance and horrible demise?

Kathy leans on the railing, the sweater dangling from her hand. She lowers her head and feels the hot pressure of tears pushing up behind her eyes. *If I'd stayed home, none of this would have happened. It's not Dad's fault, it's my fault.*

But then she stands straight and digs tears away. Anger stirs, bright and powerful. "No, it's not my fault. It's not Dad's fault. If it has something to do with Granny Mustard, then it's her fault. It's her family's fault. They've been the terror of Black Rock Ridge for way too long. They've been the faults of too many things for too long. We've been scared of them like a bunch of rabbits are scared of a hawk."

She doesn't know exactly what she's going to say, but fuck it, she is going to confront the Mustards. She's going to stand up and demand to know what connection Granny had to her father, the peaceful, kind, gentle minister of the New Light Church of the Creator.

She goes in for her warmer coat. Then she writes a quick note and puts it on her father's nightstand.

"Dad, don't worry. I haven't wandered off. I'll be back soon. Rest, please. Pray if you must but stay put. I mean it. Don't go anywhere. And don't blame yourself for anything. I know where blame lies, and it isn't here. Love, Kathy."

Her father never owned a firearm, but there are knives in the kitchen and a straight razor in the bathroom. She throws them all into a plastic trash bag and hides it under her bed. She considers his hiking stick by the door, and then decides to take it with her. The tip is deadly. She's seen how it can kill.

Before she steps back outside, the wind has picked up and rain is falling, lightly, and within a matter of seconds, hard.

"Shit."

She stands at the sliding door, staring out at the rain. Puffster, who'd gone out, streaks back inside. Kathy's reflection is faint from the light of the corner lamp and distorted where the water slides down the other side of the glass.

Everything seems distorted.

But she is not weak.

She will go speak to the Mustards.

She grabs her poncho from the closet and puts it on over her winter coat.

Even though a rain like this makes the roads muddy and difficult she'll take it slow. She'll take it carefully. But she won't give up until she has an answer.

Before she leaves, she goes back into Hank's room one last time and untangles the blankets even as he sleeps. She lays them atop him gently, hesitates, then kisses his fevered forehead.

"If God exists, then may He give you some peace."

And then she heads out to the car.

18
Jenkie Mustard

It starts to rain as she kicks around inside the animal pen, fanning the flashlight back and forth, deliberating on which would make the most dramatic come-back-to-life for the TV guys. Neither guy seemed to have a preference, so it's up to her. She needs something good for a show. She doesn't want them leaving before she impresses them. She has to make them want to stay and keep filming. Tonight. Tomorrow. However long it takes to make a show. A week? Month? Whatever.

Though they can't leave tonight, at least. They wouldn't get far in the rain in the dark on foot.

She wishes Bink was here. She really hates him right now. He doesn't usually spend the night at Benny's. Must have gotten into some project that ate away the hours before he realized it. Well, screw him. This way, she'll get all the glory. And rightly so.

The TV men stand shivering and stamping the wet ground. The cameraman isn't filming; he's tucked the camera into his coat. The raindrops are big, coin-sized blots that smack her head, streak her face, blur her vision.

"Hold on, I'll get something," she says.

She spots a cornered groundhog. Big, fat, furry. That should do. She grabs him up by his little tail and climbs back over the fencing. He wriggles hard, his bound front legs pawing at the air. His muddy paws fling clots of dirt.

"Back inside!" she instructs, and back inside they go. Jack, the one without the camera looks less than excited about the whole thing. She has to make sure everything goes just right.

Jenkie pushes the front door closed with her foot, directs the men to sit on the sofa once more. They do. She drops the groundhog on the rug; it rights itself and stumbles behind the television.

She finds the butcher knife in the drawer, opens the half-filled jar of shine, considers adding a bit more poo to punch it up a bit but then doesn't. For all she knows, more would be less, and cut the survival rate down. If only this kind of thing had some sort of clear sense to it all. But it doesn't. Not yet. But she's not really dumb like she told Bink. She's smart. She's smart like Granny Mustard. She'll figure it out soon.

Jack watches her carefully. The camera guy, whose name she can't remember, is fiddling with the camera. She hopes the rain didn't ruin it.

Jenkie lowers herself to the floor and sits cross-legged. Immediately, her knees start to hurt. Usually, she experiments on the kitchen counter, but she needs to be where they can both see. "That camera workin'?"

Sam shakes his head. "Yes, just making some adjustments is all."

"Good, 'cause you'll want this part in the first episode. Folks gonna want to know about what I can do." She grapples for the groundhog, drags him out by a hind leg. He kicks, twists around, and tries to bite her.

She thumps his head with her knuckle.

A loud wail issues from down the hall. It's Stead again. Then there is pounding, hard, against the door, over and over and over again. There is a rhythm to the pounding. This is a first. It's like Stead is trying to spell out something. Say something.

Fucking hollow, we don't care what you're trying to say!

Then she hears Stead's voice, "I'm here! Hear me!"

From the look on Jack's face, it's clear he can't really understand Stead's garbled words. That's good. However, it's also clear that he's damn scared. He stares over at the hallway. He's trying not to look scared, but his eyes are big and the muscles in his neck are all corded up.

"I said that's just Stead," says Jenkie, shaking the groundhog by the tail. "Ignore him for now."

"But… what is he? What am I hearing? This is…"

The camera guy lowers the camera from his shoulder. "Yeah, it's getting too loud to get much good from this interview, Jenkie."

Jenkie jabs the tip of the knife into the floor. It wobbles a little. The groundhog struggles. She's getting pissed. "Didn' you read my letter all the way through? I said I got some hollows back there. Okay?"

"Hollows?" asks Sam.

"Yeah. Okay?" *Fucking rain, fucking Bink! Why isn't he back here where he belongs?* "Hollows. I call 'em that 'cause they ain't got nothin' going on inside them 'cept wanting to eat all the time."

"Can't we just take a quick…"

"No! I don't want to show them to you yet. I want to do it slow like they do on TV. Lead up to it, and then, wow! Don't you know how this is supposed to work?"

Jack holds up one hand. "Okay, fine," he says. He's staring at the groundhog and breathing kinda heavy. The other guy has the camera on his shoulder again, and it's pointing at Jenkie.

"All right, then, this is what I do. Watch." She puts her knee over the groundhog's neck. It squirms and makes a shrill, high-pitched chittering sound, which usually makes her laugh, but this is serious business now.

These men got to see she's got what it takes for fame and fortune. Jenkie pulls the knife from the floor and poises it at the back of the creature's neck.

Jack looks up at the ceiling.

"What's matter? Can't watch?"

"I don't care to watch something die. I'll look once it's done."

"You some kinda vegetarian?"

"No."

"Animals gotta die if you gonna eat 'em."

"I realize that. This is different."

"Not so much…"

Stead slams against the bedroom door over and over again. The trailer shudders with the impact, the walls vibrate. Dan, in the other room, howls with one of his own, a shrieking, piercing wail.

Jenkie's had it.

"Damn you all to hell!"

She pushes herself up. The groundhog hobbles behind the TV again.

Jenkie snatches the charger from the kitchen counter and storms down the hallway. She hears the two men following after.

"Don't film this yet!" she screams.

"Doesn't matter what order we get it in," says the cameraman. "We can fix it in editing. This sounds like it's going to be a really good..."

"No!" She turns on them. They are just a step behind her and nearly collide into her. She shoves the guy with the camera back. He stumbles and drops the camera. It strikes the floor with a solid crack.

"What the fuck? You broke my camera!" he shouts, and now Jenkie is both furious at Stead and furious at the cameraman and furious at Stead and every fucking thing in her life.

"Damn you!" she screams. "Fine, just get out of here! I never wanted to be on a fucking reality show anyway, it's all a bunch of shit! TV's a bunch of shit! You're a bunch of shit! Get the hell out of here!"

Jack suddenly loses the expression of ill-ease he's worn since entering the trailer. He shoves her hard with both hands. The charger goes flying.

Jenkie loses her balance, stumbles against the mildewed wall, and then rights herself.

"We aren't leaving!" Jack says. "We came all the way up here because of your letter. We lost our car. I lost my money. We walked until I couldn't walk anymore, all because we wanted to see if you were as insane as we thought you were or if there was a worthwhile story up here. Now I know it's both. You're fucking insane and there's something going on, something awful and so worth filming. You aren't kicking us out until we see it. Until we film it! So open the damned door and give us a look!"

"No!" Jenkie snatches the charger from the floor—it takes several tries—and points it at Jack. She's panting, hard. Sweat rolls down her nose. "And if you don't leave I'll get you with this. It brings a hollow down for the count, and I bet it'll smoke you dead in your shoes!"

But then Jack draws something out of his pocket that makes her lower the charger. It's a gun.

Jenkie starts to shake. Her dream is melting like snow, melting into a puddle on the floor of this mildewed trailer. *Why can't things go right? What the hell is wrong with her life*???

"You're going to do exactly what we ask you to do," says Jack. His words are trembling, but the gun isn't. "I have no qualms about shooting you right here in your little stinking trailer, because we're so far away, who the hell would know? Right?"

Jenkie blinks, balls her fists. Anything she wanted to say slides back down her throat.

The cameraman holds his camera, turning it over and around, probably trying to see if there is any hope of it working. Bink could probably fix it, if Bink were around. But Bink, being Bink, is off doing his own thing. Probably making some new kind of electrical toy. Probably watching Three Stooges with Benny and drinking a six-pack that he'd promised to bring back to her. She can't imagine he was telling the truth when he said he wouldn't come back.

She can't imagine he would really leave her on her own.

Stead wails and pounds, Dan howls, the other hollows growl and thump and snarl. Jenkie stares at Jack, narrowing her eyes as best she can to drive him out and away, but he just stands there, staring back, the gun pointed at her chest.

Then she breaks, turns toward the door, and waves the charger in the air like a white flag. "Okay, fine! Have it your stupid way! You want to see what's going on here, then you'll get an eyeful!"

And if I can find a way to kill them before they leave, I'll do it. This is my secret and until I'm ready to get credit for it, until I know I'm going to get famous for it, it's gonna stay my secret.

19
Jack Carroll

The sounds down the hall finally get the best of the girl and she's mad as hell. She drops the butcher knife, lets go of the animal, and forces herself to her feet with an audible grunt.

"Fuck it!" she screams, fumbling for a little purple metal box amid all the jars and shit on the kitchen counter, and storms down the hallway.

Sam is immediately up with the camera, chasing after. Jack joins them, his mind reeling, his stomach clenching against the even more powerful smell of thick, putrid-sweet decay in the hall.

This is what he's here for, he realizes. To see if worst, unexplainable, supernatural nightmares can be real or are always just figments of bug-chewed brains and overactive, childish imaginations. Even more than the simple idea of the reality show, this is it. Because it's the root of it all. If it's imagination, the show is one thing. If not, it's an entirely different show altogether, and one that will turn a lot of things on their heads.

He doesn't really want to see what is behind the doors but can't not see it. He imagines deformed members of the Mustard family, crammed in there, locked up, believed by Jenkie to be the living dead. Starving, crazed, banging around, screaming to be released.

Or zombies. Hollows. Real ones.

Fucking shit.

He has to see. He has to know.

Then Jenkie spins around and knocks Sam down and the

camera sounds broken. She orders them out of her trailer and threatens them with that thing that looks like a homemade taser. But Jack has the gun. He pulls it from his pocket and trains it on her with all the outward confidence of Clint Eastwood.

She fumbles, sputters, then says, "Okay, fine! Have it your stupid way! You want to see what's going on here, then you'll get an eyeful!"

She digs down into her front jeans pocket—a tight squeeze—and comes out with a key ring bearing three keys. The things behind the doors growl and scream, pound and thump against the walls.

Can I look? wonders Jack. *I have to, but can I? What I see I won't be able to un-see.* His hand is slippery on the gun's grip. She can't find out there are no bullets. She has to believe his ruse. Beside him, Sam looks at once furious, determined, and frightened in this rapidly snowballing, rapidly deteriorating situation. But he's got the camera back up on his shoulder. Guess it wasn't damaged beyond use, after all. Or he's pretending it works.

Jenkie sticks a key in the lock on the door of the room at the end of the hall. Obviously someone switched the knobs around at some point, letting Jenkie lock and unlock at will. Good move, actually.

She looks back over her shoulder. "You'll get an eyeful," she says, sarcastically. "These are Granny's creatures. I didn't make these but give me time, and I will. I don't know exactly how she did it, but she did. She died too quick and never wrote it down, but I'll figure it out. I ain't dumb. I got good genes like her. Smart genes." She puffs up her chest, tosses her head and her sticky hair flops heavily.

"Okay," says Sam.

"Put the gun down. I'm doing what you asked."

Jack shakes his head. "I don't think so. We really don't know each other that well yet, Jenkie."

"I hate you."

I'm not surprised.

The key turns in the knob; it clicks open. "These hollows been livin'

gosh, months now, 'cept for one that didn't get enough to

eat. She died a while back. That was Bink's fault."

She stuffs the key back into her pocket then reaches for a long blue bungee cord that dangles from the knob. Pulling the end up, she clips it to the right side of the gate. She turns the knob and pushes the door open.

"Let me introduce Stead and Bobby Boo." Then Jenkie quickly scoots behind Jack and Sam.

"Oh, fucking shit," says Sam.

He and Jack instinctively move backward. It's all Sam can do to hold on to his camera.

There are two... things... inside the room. Dead things, dead people, strips of flesh hanging off them in grey sheets, flies buzzing around them, landing briefly, then flying away. Their eyes are red as hot coals. One of them, a tall monster dressed only in threadbare jeans, shoves the other out of the way and lunges at the gate, slamming his... its... body against it and thrusting both degraded arms out through the metal bars. The gate shudders and squeaks on its hinges. This one has but the one eye. The other dangles down his cheek and bounces as he moves. There is a hole in his stomach and shimmering, undulating organs are visible.

"Oh, my God," says Jack. "What is this?" But he knows. Jenkie wasn't lying in her letter. She has living dead here in Desper Hollow. She has zombies in these rooms.

The zombie at the gate growls and clutches, scratching at the air, stretching as far as it can to reach Jack or Sam. Its tongue hangs out of the front of the mouth—less a mouth than a gaping hole about three inches across with no lips to speak of. The teeth clack rapidly against each other, and two break and fly out of its head and land of the hall floor. The stench is overwhelming and Jack's stomach clenches. From behind the second closed door there is louder grunting now, and that dog-like, strangled bark.

"Bobby Boo used to live with his Great Aunt Dottie down the bottom of Black Rock Ridge," says Jenkie. Her voice has mellowed now.

Clearly she's pleased they are so terrified. "Somehow, Granny got him like this. Don't really know how, but she did. He was a mean cuss when he was alive. Always yellin' at people like he was king of the hill. Always tellin' 'em to get off the road, to get out of his sight. Now, ha, ha! I get to be queen of the hill and he ain't goin' nowhere!"

"So," Jack takes a breath of the fouled air, swallows down a hint of vomit, and slows his words so he can get them out. "Bobby Boo died and now he's alive."

"Yeah. Duh."

The other one slams his shoulder into Bobby Boo, squeezes to get up against the gate, shoves one hand out, also grasping. This one is shorter and isn't as far gone as the other. His eyes are the same dreadful red, and patches of his face and neck are skinned off. He's missing a ring finger, and his hand is blotched with white and green patches. A small section of his chest is caved in. He has almost a full head of dark hair. His dreadful gaze flicks back and forth between Jack and Sam.

"And that's Stead," narrates Jenkie. "Armistead-something. Can't remember his last name, if he told me. Stead's a funny one. He's not from around here. I met him once when he was alive and down at Hank Shaw's church, helping the pastor clean up some brush and do some repairs. Nice lookin' fellow, you ask me. We talked for a minute. He said he was hiking north and was just passin' through, payin' his way by helpin' folks." Jenkie spits air. "Passin' through? You kiddin' me? Folks don't just pass through here. Ain't a straight shot to nowhere. I think he had something else in mind, though I don't know what that could-a been. He didn't act like no drug runner or shine runner. He showed up the top of Desper Hollow just a couple days after we caught Bobby Boo. Bink lured him in here, too. Bink's good like that. Though he ain't good for much else most the time."

Jack feels himself nod. He glances over to see that Sam is no longer filming. The camera is down and he's just staring, his jaw slack, his eyes unblinking and huge.

Jenkie coughs, sneezes. Maybe the stink is getting to her, too. "The two in the other room are pretty much the same as these. They're Judy and Robert Floyd, or they used to be. Old as night, crippled up, lived not too far from Calhoun's parents' place. Never went nowhere in years. Bink found 'em wandering when he was out catching critters for Bobby Boo and Stead.

They was stumblin' around, bumpin' into each other, all red glowing eyes and smellin' like death. Judy had a half-eaten rabbit in her hands, Robert was tryin' to get at it, but she just growled at him. Bink thought, holy shit! Two more hollows! He led 'em here, and fuck was they slow for bein' so old! Bink could only lure Judy into the trailer. Robert was damned hard headed for a dead man. Bink had to use the charger on him, and then dragged him up the steps and down the hall to lock him in with Judy. Had one more hollow for a short while 'til she starved, some woman Bink found on the road when he was heading out to get groceries. He charged her, chained her to the bumper, hauled her back. One of her arms got ripped off along the way, but that don't seem to bother hollows none. They's always fallin' apart."

"Are there more zombies… more hollows, I mean… out in the mountains?"

"I don't think so. I think we got 'em all."

"How do you know?" Jack asks, never taking his eyes of the slobbering monster beyond the gate just a few feet away. He can't look the thing directly in the eye. He fears it would be like looking at Dracula… sucking him in, draining his will…

"Well, we got all these in August and ain't seen no more since."

Jack is confused. "So, did Granny Mustard pour shine on all five of them? I thought you said she died. Did she die in the fire?"

"Yeah."

"Then how…?"

"I don't know that yet!" Jenkie stamps her foot. "How they get to be hollows now might have something to do with their spit, with their bites. Fuckin' Bobby Boo bit both my dogs, turned 'em to hollows. But I don't know for sure how Bobby Boo got that way at first. All I know is they all got red eyes so it's all part of Granny's doin'."

Then Stead is hurled away and down again by Bobby Boo, whose arms, shoved through the gate bars, seem even longer now, as if they've come unhinged from their sockets. Sam and Jack step back another step.

Bobby Boo drools, waggles his jaw.

"They eat live stuff," says Jenkie proudly.

As if on cue, Bobby Boo turns his blood-red eyes toward Jenkie and lolls his tongue at her.

"They ever eat… people?" manages Sam.

"Ha!" Jenkie laughs hard. "Not that I know of but sure, they'd eat people if they got a chance. Bobby Boo tried to eat me when he first got here. No, they ain't vegetarians!"

"Oh, my God," whispers Sam.

Jenkie notices his camera is lowered.

"Hey, what's the matter? You see all this and don't think it's worth filmin'?"

Sam glances back at her. He blinks. "What?"

"I said ain't this good enough for TV, after all your demanding and threatening me with that gun?"

Sam glances at Jack for help. He seems paralyzed with terrible wonder. Jack waves his free hand. "Of course, it's good enough. Maybe the battery's run down. Sam's doin' his job as best he can, trust me."

"Or maybe he's just scared!" Jenkie laughs. "Yeah, that's it! You big tough Hollywood boys… oh, 'scuse me, Los Angeles boys… come up here and found more than you bargained for. It's too scary to film? Ha! Well, here it is. Right here in front of you. Why don't you just take a closer look?"

With that she kicks Sam in the back of the legs, and he falls toward the gate, slams into it, cries out in terror. Bobby Boo howls and catches Sam's forearm with one set of bony fingers. Sam struggles, shrieking as loudly as any of the hollows as Bobby Boo hauls him up close, pulls the arm in through the gate, and takes a bite out of it. Sam screams. His feet slip out from under him, and he goes down, temporarily out of the zombie's grasp. But Bobby Boo is quick. He squats down and grabs Sam's arm again, bringing it through the bars and back to the lipless, slobbering mouth.

Jack drops the gun and dives for his friend, landing on his knees and catching Sam's free arm as Sam screams, twists, and sobs.

"Let him go, you fucking shit!" yells Jack. He pulls hard,

bracing his heels against the floor.

Bobby Boo buries his teeth in Sam's elbow and tears away a healthy chunk. Dark red blood spurts and runs down Sam's body and legs to the hall floor. Sam's head lolls in exquisite pain, his arms out as if crucified, his body stretched between the zombie and Jack. Jack's shoes slide in the blood as he tries to get traction.

"Help me," Sam whispers, the words bubbling red.

ZING!

The barbs of the taser whiz past Jack's head, but just miss the zombie's right temple. They embed themselves in Sam's neck.

"Shit!" screams Jenkie, and she yanks on the wires, hard, and the barbs pull out, taking hunks of Sam's flesh with them.

"I got you, man, hold on!" Jack pulls harder but the zombie's grip is powerful. He angles his mouth for yet another bite out of Sam's arm.

Then Bobby Boo flies backward with a grunt and thud, and Sam goes limp, free.

Jack scoots back in the blood, dragging Sam with him. He looks up to see Stead at the gate now, staring down at them with his burning red eyes.

His arms reach out through the gate's bars.

But Stead's fingers aren't slashing or clawing. They are turned up. As if in questioning. As if pleading. The eyes don't appear totally void, but there is something behind them, something intelligent. Something...

"Ah, fuck, I broke it!" wailed Jenkie.

...something with a touch of concern? A remnant of humanity? Or something else?

Sam flops over on the floor, writhing, bleeding profusely. The dark red, growing puddle reflects light from the hall's single ceiling bulb.

Jack snatches the gun and crams it into his jacket. He forces himself to his feet, locks eyes for the briefest moment with Stead, then unhooks the bungee cord from the gate. The zombie's mouth moves, and it forms a word that sounds so much like "help..." but that's impossible. The dead can't think, the dead can't speak. Jack yanks on the bungee cord; the door catches the zombie on the back, but instead of fighting, he just gives Jack the oddest look and then steps away, allowing the door to close.

"Give me the key!" He turns to look at Jenkie, who is standing, wide-eyed and furious, staring not at the dying man in the hall but at the shattered taser on the floor.

"I dropped it!" she says. "I stepped on it! I don't know how to fix it!"

"Give me the fucking key, Jenkie!" Jack steps to her, shakes her hard, until she looks up at him. Her lip is snarled, much like the zombies in her backroom. She makes no move, so he shoves his hand down her jeans pocket and digs until his fingers catch the ring. He pulls the keys out and hurries back to the door, where he secures the knob. Then he bends down and as carefully as he can, slides his arms around Sam's chest.

"Would you fucking help me?" he yells, but Jenkie won't be ordered around, she's all about the broken taser and the fact that nothing good has been filmed and the idea of a reality show is bleeding away as surely as Sam's life blood.

Jack drags Sam into the living room, rolls him up and onto the sofa.

Sam is still alive, still breathing, though the steady bleeding and the hitching of his chest are not good signs. Jack grabs the butcher knife from the floor and cuts the bottom off his shirt. He ties it tightly around Sam's arm.

It covers most of the wounds but not all. He shrugs out of his jacket and cuts off a sleeve to finish the rest.

Jenkie stands at the counter and watches, her face pouty, holding the ruined taser. The wires trail; at the end are the barbs with little chunks of Sam clinging to them. "I hate you all," she says.

With his friend bandaged as well as he can be bandaged in that shitty hellhole of a trailer, Jack glanced around for a phone. He saw none.

"Where's your phone?"

"What makes you think I got a phone?"

"You don't have a phone?"

Jenkie shakes her head.

"You got some first aid stuff here? Some way to disinfect this and fix it up?"

"No."

"Damn you and your monsters!" Jack kneels on the floor beside the sofa and takes his friend's hand. "Hey, Sam, hey! Listen. I know it's raining, I know it's dark, but we're getting the hell out of here. I'm going to get you to a doctor."

Oh, God, where the hell is a doctor in these mountains? Are there doctors? Real doctors? Witch doctors?

Sam coughs. Spits up blood. Foamy pink bubbles dribble from his nostrils.

"I know you're hurting bad but just hang on." Jack eased Sam off the sofa and onto his shoulder. He tries to stand up but couldn't.

"Fuck!" He looks at Jenkie. "Do you have a wagon, something?"

"Wheelbarrow out back. It's rusted."

"Is it big enough for Sam?"

Jenkie shrugs.

"Go get it!"

"No! You messed it all up! It was going to be good. It was going to be great! And then your stupid camera guy goes and gets himself bit up and now the taser's broke and why the hell didn't you shoot the hollow? You shoot 'em in the head and you kill 'em. I'd rather have one dead hollow and a TV show than a dead cameraman and no TV show at all!"

"The gun doesn't have bullets, you bitch!" Jack says, then can't believe he said that because that was an ace-in-the-hole, something he could use should he need it again.

"What? Ha!" Jenkie's mouth widens in a grotesque grin. "You boys is dumber than I even thought!"

Jack orders, "Watch him." He gets to his feet.

It's raining even harder now, a cold, sleety rain that stings and burns.

Jack finds the wheelbarrow behind the trailer, next to the animal pen, and it is, indeed, rusted beyond use. One wheel is gone and there is a hole in the bottom. He curses, races back into the trailer, screams at Jenkie, then scoops Sam up off the sofa. This time he gains his footing. Sam's breathing is even shallower now.

"You're a murderer," Jack says as he eases adjusts Sam over his shoulder. "He dies it's on your head." Then he makes his way outside, down the wobbly steps in the rain.

Jenkie calls after him, "Ha, ha! Left your camera! Stupid ass Los Angeles boys!"

20
Kathy Shaw

The car slides in the mud but Kathy's determination and anger is enough to keep it on the road. The engine whines, the windshield wipers slam back and forth, battling the storm. Kathy forces the vehicle through the slop and gravel to Penny Mustard's little tar-shack house. It's the closest Mustard house, and a Mustard is a Mustard. Penny certainly knows something. Her daughter Suze burned down the town then screamed about Granny Mustard as she faded into death in the deputy sheriff's patrol car.

Kathy parks in the weeds, runs through the rain, and pounds on the door. Lights are on inside. The chimney leaks grey smoke that dissipates in the downpour. Someone is home because she can hear laughing.

"Penny Mustard!" Kathy calls. "I need to talk to you!"

The laughing sputters to a halt. There is a pause, and then the door is yanked open. Penny is there, dressed in a well-worn pink acetate robe that has been hastily and sloppily tied. Her makeup is smudged, and her jet-black hair is standing out in all directions. She is grinning. She is quite drunk. Over her shoulder, Kathy can see old Yard Putcher, one of Beaver Dam's miners. He is twice Penny's age, bald except for a mustache, skin leathery and sagging. He appears to be naked, and Kathy is thankful that Penny's full figure fills the doorway.

"What the hell you want out in this weather?" says Penny. Yard says, "Let's have us a threesome!" and Penny says, "Shut your pie hole, Yard."

"We have to talk," says Kathy. "Send Yard back into the bedroom. I need to come in."

"I'm busy, little girl," says Penny.

"And I'm not in the mood to waste my time!" says Kathy. She pushes past Penny into the house and catches a glimpse of Yard and his knobby knees and hairy chest and fading erection. Penny chuckles once, then put her hands on her hips. This hikes her gown up a bit, but not too far. Thank goodness.

"Yard, this has nothing to do with you," says Kathy. "Get out of here. I need to talk to Penny alone."

"Well, shit," Yard mumbles, and he turns and wobbles away, shuts the bedroom door. Penny glares at Kathy. "Since when does the preacher's daughter act like such a little bitch?"

"Sit down, Penny. This won't take long, I promise. But I need some truth from you."

Penny snorts, but she sits. The flower-patterned sofa creaks beneath her. The room is very warm, almost uncomfortably so. A bright, crackling fire burns in the fireplace. An old dog, part hound, part setter of some sort, lies by the hearth, its greasy fur reflecting the glow.

"Now what the hell you want?" demands Penny. "I swear, your daddy know you were acting like this he'd have your hide."

"He doesn't have anyone's hide," says Kathy. She sits down on the rocker across from the sofa. She remains on the edge. She has things to do, places to go, once she knows what she needs to know. "But he does have some kind of ghost nipping at his heels. A Mustard ghost."

"Ghost?" Penny laughs. "Your daddy believe in ghosts? Not countin' the Holy Ghost, that is."

"Granny Mustard," says Kathy. "My father had something to do with her before she died. I don't know what it was, but it's tearing him apart. I have to know. I have to help him before it's too late. And I figured you'd have some idea of what I'm talking about."

"Why should I?"

"Being as Suze burned down Beaver Dam and swore Granny was behind it."

Penny reaches for a bottle of beer on the end table. It tips over and spills. "Shit." Kathy jumps up and catches it before most of its gone. She hands the bottle to Penny.

"Thank you."

Kathy sits back down, grips her knees impatiently. "Well?"

Penny takes a swig, another. She frowns at the floor.

"I was so sorry to hear about Suze," Kathy adds. "I'm sure that was so hard on you."

"Yeah." Penny is growing more pensive now that Kathy helped her with the beer and mentioned the loss of Suze. She sits without speaking for a long, frustrating minute. In the bedroom, Yard can be heard burping and flopping over on a creaking bed. Then she says, "There's nothing I know 'bout your dad and Granny, Kathy. Suze and Jenkie spent time up at Granny's during the summer. Something spooked Suze, spooked her bad. Could be Granny was testing moonshine on them girls. When they came home they smelled like it. But what girl ain't tried out shine? Specially 'shine their own family makes?"

"I wouldn't know."

"They spent every day up there. Went regular, though didn't seem to like it much. Came home, never told me 'bout what they were doin'. I figured at least they was staying out of trouble, not gettin' laid or gettin' pregnant."

"Back up, Penny. Back up before the summer, even before Suze and Jenkie started visiting Granny. Did you ever hear Granny say anything, anything at all about my dad? Maybe about his church? Did she have a grudge against him for some reason? Did she think his preaching was talking against her moonshining business?"

Penny upends the beer bottle, draining it dry. She puts it on the end table and wipes her mouth. "Can't say I heard nothin' like that. Not all Mustards is close to Granny. Was close to Granny. Just her grandsons in these last years. Them boys kept the moonshine competition at bay. They protected Granny's business. If anybody knows about who Granny liked and who Granny hated, it'd be Burley or Calhoun. Maybe Pete."

Kathy's jaw tightens. Burley. Calhoun. The worst of the Mustards.

"Okay," she says. "I'll go find them. I know where their house is."

She stands up, rubs rain from the back of her neck.

Penny shakes her head. "They ain't home. They moved up to Granny's cabin for the time bein'. They plan on takin' up the business, and they gotta do it from on top of Moon Peak. And they's not to be sneaked up on, Kathy. Can't say that enough. They ain't to be sneaked up on or riled."

Oh, shit. Granny Mustard's cabin? Penny's right. I can't go up there! Nobody who's not a Mustard dares go up to Moon Peak!

"I hear you," says Kathy. "Hey, will you come with me? I can pay you some money. Fifty dollars?"

Penny shakes her head.

No, nobody but a Mustard would go up to Moon Peak.

But Burley and Calhoun would be the ones to know about Granny's relationship with Hank Shaw. And Hank is distraught. Hank is suicidal.

Kathy can't help him unless she knows the truth. He is her father. She loves him.

And as Hank always said, "The truth shall set you free."

Though he never said the truth couldn't be dangerous as hell.

21
Armistead

The other has blood on his face and neck, and he runs his fingers along it to bring it to his mouth so he can lick it all off. It is fresh blood. Human blood.

Armistead stares, watching.

Some bits of the flesh the other had ripped from the arm of the man in the hallway has gone down his throat into his stomach but then fell out a hole there onto the floor. He scrapes it back up and stuffs it down his mouth again.

Armistead wanted some of the arm, no, he wanted the whole man, he wanted to pull him into the room and savor the warm and the blood and the bowels and the muscles and the brain matter and the energy that would come with it, energy that would sate the cursed Hunger. He is so hungry now he can barely move. It wasn't hard for the other man to push him back from the door.

But there was something in that other man's face for a moment, a flickering hesitation and wonder… a recognition that neither the One With No Eyes nor Bink had ever seen.

And it was clear the man had seen something in Armistead that was different from what he saw in the other hollow.

For that reason, and of course for his weakness, Armistead had not fought when he was pushed back, and the door was locked.

Why am I?

What am I?

He waits, listening. All he can hear is screaming and arguing in the hallway on the other side of the door and the hollow in the room with him, eating chunks of flesh that had fallen out of his abdomen.

Then the voice that drowns all the sounds out.

Very soon now.

The voice surrounds him with a warmth that he wants to grab and hold on to. A sense of blue, of light, of buoyancy fills his mind, if only for a moment. It is familiar but he cannot recall why.

You will know what to do, Armistead.

Armistead moves to the window, looks out. There is no moon, only rain, only blackened branches scraping the grey night sky.

"Who are you? Tell me!"

Very soon now.

You will know. You will remember.

22
Jenkie Mustard

Screw them all! Now I'm gonna do what I've wanted to do for a long time! Won't Bink crap his pants when he comes up here and gets a good look! Whoo! It's gonna rock his mind!

The TV guys were out of the trailer, and they weren't going to get far.

Jack was carrying the cameraman over his shoulder but was stumbling every few feet. What a laugh! They'd screwed everything up, and now one of them was going to die and so ha ha!

"I'm no murderer!" she screams out the front door. "You were just careless, that's all! So get the hell out of here! Assholes!"

Blow it all up! Burn it all down!

If she can't have a TV show, then she'll make one big show all herself.

There is gasoline for the generator in plastic containers out back. She has matches in the kitchen.

Blaze of glory, just like Suze!

She wonders if hollows will scream when they burned up? It will kill their brains, that's for sure. A charcoaled brain is no brain at all. If she can figure out the camera, she will film it. And yeah, then people will watch it and say, "Wow, Jenkie!" and they'll remember her just like they remember Suze. Only Jenkie won't have to cut off her hand and kill herself for the fame.

Jenkie goes outside, hunching over against the downpour. Jack looks back at her, but she can't see his face for the night shadows and the rain.

Hurrying to the rear of the trailer, she grabs two full,

five-gallon gas cans then hauls them back inside. The hollows are making more ruckus than ever; guess they can smell the blood in the hall. That, in addition to the fact that Jenkie hasn't fed them today.

She unscrews the caps, splashes the living room and part of the hallway with gasoline. Some gets on her feet but hell, she'll be careful. She's not going to burn herself up. She's not that dumb.

The bedroom doors groan and creak as hollows slam themselves against them with all their might. The trailer walls rattle in response. "Shut up!" Jenkie laughs.

She snatches her matches and cigarettes out from between the sofa cushions, throws on her heaviest sweatshirt, pulls up the hood, and tucks the camera beneath her arm. She glances around, ecstatic with what she is about to do. Then she darts into the kitchen, snatches Granny's leather-bound book from the cabinet, stuffs it inside the sweatshirt and tucks the hem down into her jeans.

Stead is no longer howling, but the other hollows continue at the top of their dead lungs. Dan barks, sloppily and loudly. "Cool your jets!" Jenkie shouts. "Ah, fuck it, yell as loud as you want. Won't matter in a couple minutes, anyway. Yell, you hollows! Scream! Let me hear a 'Hell, yeah!'"

She picks up a Three Stooges VHS box and goes out onto the steps, leaving the door open. The rain is easing a bit. Out across the black, flat yard, near the far end now, she can see the TV man Jack still struggling with the camera guy over his shoulder. They aren't getting anywhere fast. Serves them right!

Jenkie lights a match, leans over it to keep the rain off, and catches the corner of the video box on fire. She flips the box through the doorway then she skips off the steps and moves out into the yard. She shoulders the camera and tries to figure out how to turn it on. There is a button, but it doesn't do anything. There is another button. That doesn't do anything, either. She shakes the camera; still won't work. Clearly, it was broken when the cameraman dropped it in the hallway. He was only pretending it worked for her benefit.

"Shit!" She hurls the camera toward the trailer. "Piece of

broken trash! Thanks for nothing TV men! I hate you all!"

And then the living room end of the trailer goes up in a roaring ball of fire.

Jenkie is blown back off her feet, her face singed instantly with crackling heat. Flames shoot skyward through the roof and out the doorway and the shattered living room window, red and white and golden, like autumn banshees reaching for heaven. The walls squeal as the metal and wood is incinerated.

"Wow!" Jenkie yells, scrambling back on her ass another few feet. "Woo hoo, baby!"

The trailer rocks on its foundation. The fire bellows and crackles, drowning out any sound the hollows might be making. "Ha, so there! Don't have to listen to you assholes anymore! Don't have to feed your sorry corpses!"

Then one of the front walls expands and bursts, slammed outward by the heat, and hangs down in the grass like a huge, panting dog's tongue.

Jenkie can see the fire dancing in the hallway now, licking and groping in the direction of the gated bedrooms.

"Bye, bye hollows!"

There is a moment of strange, hissing silence, and then a portion of the front bedroom wall bursts out, throwing glass and wood into the air, bending the siding back and down. The room is opened like a can of sardines.

Jenkie grins, until she sees what this has done.

Bobby Boo and Stead lumber out through the hole in the wall. Bobby Boo's shoulders are alight; Stead's hair is on fire, a hellish, flickering halo.

They lurch over the lip of the floor and fall onto the ground then immediately get back up. Growling, snarling, staring at Jenkie. The red of their eyes make it appear as if she is seeing through their heads to the fire behind them.

"Holy shit!"

The rain douses their fires, bringing sizzling, ash-colored smoke up off their bodies. Neither the fire nor the rain will deter them.

They come for her over the grass and weeds and rocks, arms outstretched, fingers clutching.

23
Kathy Shaw

Kathy hikes the final stretch from the road, over the wire fence, across the wet, upward-sloping, rock-strewn yard, waving the flashlight from her glove box ahead of her. She stops, stares.

The cabin is as ominous as she had dreaded. It sits at the highest point of Moon Peak, blackened with the night rain, dim lantern light glowing inside the single window. The roof is angled unusually steep, and the stone chimney is slanted peculiarly like something out of a disturbed children's book. Animal skulls line the porch flooring and sit along the porch railing. They gaze out with dead, coal-black sockets. A cluster of dried gourds dangles from the corner of the porch ceiling, and it bangs together in the wind, making a sound like that of men with no tongues—soft, guttural, hopeless.

Calling her.

Daring her.

Challenging her.

She'd had to park a quarter mile back; she knew there was no road that reached all the way to Granny's house, but in the rain the trek was excruciating. Slipping, sliding in the mud and on the wet leaves and weeds even with the help of Hank's hiking stick, catching thorny branches that she couldn't tell were thorny because of the darkness, cutting her hands, scraping her face. The bottoms of her jeans' legs are soaked. The poncho hood has blown back numerous times, leaving her hair drenched with shorter strands flattened against her face.

She knows that Calhoun or Burley or both are at the cabin;

they're the only family members who would be up there with a lantern lit. They would be the leaders of the family now that Granny was dead. Yet they might not be alone. The two men she saw at the Exxon station in Beaver Dam would be there, too. She'd hiked past their empty SUV soon after getting out of her own car. It was parked as up against the road's dead end where the footpath to Granny's cabin began. Maybe they were buying moonshine from Burley and Calhoun. That would make her unannounced visit all the more dicey.

All the way up she's imagined different scenarios:

She calls out from the yard, demanding to know what they know, standing strong and insistent and righteous.

She knocks on the door, reminding them that she is the preacher's daughter, and asks politely to know what they know.

She stops on the porch steps, telling them she will pay them if they will tell her what they know. There are sixty-three dollars in her wallet.

Halfway up the yard, she knows how best to handle it. She stops, turns off the flashlight, and cups her mouth. "Burley! Calhoun! This is Kathy Shaw! I have a question for you!" The words are out before she can decide if this is really the way to do it. Her voice bears little confidence.

Her cold hands shake madly.

She looks behind her. She's far enough away from the cabin to run if she has to. It's dark so they probably couldn't shoot her.

"Burley! Calhoun! This is Hank Shaw's daughter! I have an important question for you!"

There is movement inside the cabin; a lantern flickers then is gone, taken from one place to another.

"I'm not here to disturb you. I just need to know something. I can pay you for your trouble. Please open the door!"

A gust of wind blows rain up her face, into her nose. She coughs, rubs her nose with her wet wool sleeve. Why didn't she bring a freakin' umbrella? She waits, listens, shivers. *If you're coming out, come out! Damn!*

"I talked to Penny. She said it was okay for me to come up here. She gave me permission, so I hope you don't see this as an intrusion. Talk to me, please!"

The cabin door is yanked open. Two men step out onto the porch.

They wear wide-brimmed hats, and she can't see their faces, but she knows Burley and Calhoun's physiques well enough.

"What you doin' up here in the rain?" calls Calhoun. "Dumbest thing I ever saw."

"I need to talk to you two."

"Who told you you could come?" This is Burley.

"Penny. She said you were here. I just have a couple questions, then I'll be gone."

"Couldn't wait 'til mornin'?" asks Calhoun. "Couldn't wait 'til sunrise? Had to come up here to Granny Mustard's in the goddamned rain?"

Burley kicks the heel of his boot against the porch floor. "Who you again?" Of course, he knows. He's just playing with Kathy.

Kathy will have none of it. "My father is… sick. Really sick. I'm just trying to help him. Burley, I understand he had some dealings with Granny a while ago, back before Suze burned Beaver Dam. Will you talk to me?"

"Well," says Burley. "Nothin' more important than family, we know that for a fact."

"But we don't know nothin' about your daddy, Kathy," says Calhoun.

"Maybe," she begins. "But maybe you do and just don't know you do. It's nothing to harm Granny's memory, nothing to soil her legacy."

"Soil her legacy!" chortles Burley. "Granny's legacy ain't nothin' but soil! Big ol' muddy mess, just like that yard out there. You know that, Kathy Shaw. You lived around here your whole life."

"Will you hear me out?"

Calhoun raises his hand, waves her forward. "Why not? Ain't got nothin' else goin' on tonight. Might as well chew some fat with you. Share a glass o' shine, too, if you've a mind."

Kathy's as terrified now as if she'd been if they'd fired a shotgun at her. But she makes her way across the yard with Hank's hiking stick, head high, rain smacking her forehead, blurring her vision.

"Don' worry," says Calhoun as she steps onto the porch and then moves into the cabin. "You the preacher's girl. We respect that. Don' we, Burley?"

"Sure do," says Burley, but Kathy can't see his face to know if it is said with a look of respect, or with a wink.

24
Jack Carroll

"Hang on, Sam! Please, just hold on, I'm with you, you'll be okay!"

But Sam won't be okay. Jack knows he won't be okay because his arm is bleeding out through the shirt bandages and his face is slack and pale. Yet he still breathes. Still, he breathes. And because of that, Jack must continue to lie to himself.

Sam will make it. I'll save him.

Jack carries Sam across the stretch of grass in front of the trailer, heading for the sloping path that will take them out of Desper Hollow. He hears Jenkie behind him, shouting, "Piece of broken trash! Thanks for nothing, TV men!"

A few more stumbling steps, a silent scream toward a deity to which he feels no connection, and then there is a hot, powerful, whooshing sound and Jenkie cries, "Wooo hoo!" The ground in front of him and the trees before him suddenly reflect a wet, bright orange.

Jenkie has set the trailer on fire.

He wants to look back but remembers some story about a woman who looked back at a burning city and turned into a pillar of salt. Shit on that!

Jack's toe strikes something solid in the weeds and he goes down, dropping Sam over onto his back. Sam coughs once but makes no other sound.

He hears a crashing rush of wood and metal giving way, and another shout of crazed victory from Jenkie.

"Sam, I'm so sorry," Jack whispers. "Hold on, man." He braces himself on his knees, scoops Sam up and over his shoulder again, tries to stand. He can't. At that moment he realizes he is sobbing. It's hard to speak, to breathe. His body shudders with the force of his anger and fear.

Then he hears another blast and thunderous crack, and he cannot help himself. He looks back, half-hoping to be altered into that salt column so he can be free of this nightmare.

There is Jenkie, sitting on her ass in the grass, staring at the trailer, which is now split into several sections, massive flames dancing within and without, reaching as far up as the tallest tree limbs, sizzling against the wet needles branch tips.

And then they come out.

The two zombies.

Bobby Boo, who had eaten away most of Sam's arm.

Stead, the strange one who had let Jack close the bedroom door.

Bobby Boo's shoulders are burning and so is Stead's hair, but once free of the trailer the rain snubs out their fires. Bobby Boo snarls, licks his skeletal chin, reaches out with eager arms. Stead is a foot behind Bobby Boo, lips in a sneer, hair smoking, hands slashing at the air. They stumble through the weeds, moving toward Jenkie.

Jenkie scrambles backward on her butt for several yards, screams a piteous scream.

Around the side of the trailer come two more zombies—one an old man, the other an old woman. Both are on fire, more intently than Stead or Bobby Boo had been, with flames engulfing their shoulders, arms, faces. They move much more slowly that Bobby Boo and Stead. They jabber and squeal, their ancient, shredded hands groping. They head toward Jenkie, who is rolling on the ground, trying to regain her footing. Then a streaking fireball races around the trailer, past the two old zombies, a growling, four-footed torch, teeth exposed and glinting.

"Dan, no!" cries Jenkie. "Stay! Stop! Sit!"

The rain cannot put out this galloping conflagration; the fire is too intense, too deep. The creature—a dog, or what had once been a dog— lunges at Jenkie, flames and smoke trailing. It howls again; Jenkie screams again. She rolls out of the way as it crashes head first into the ground where she'd been a moment earlier. It rights itself, shakes its burning head, and then lunges for Jenkie once more.

Jack puts Sam down, grasps a thick, gnarled stick from the ground, and races toward the burning zombie dog just as it sinks its teeth into Jenkie's hip. She wails in agony and slaps at the dog.

Jack whacks Dan on the back, sending out sparks, then clobbers the fiery head. Dan lets go of Jenkie and turns its dreadful, fire-red eyes up to consider its attacker. Jenkie pulls out from under the dog with a strangled cry of horror. Jack stares back at the dog, and then slams the branch into it again with all his might. It totters on its burning legs then collapses on its side. The fire consumes the body, cooking away the remaining flesh, the skull, the ribs and tail and hipbones. It shudders then goes still.

Jenkie is crying and pointing. Jack looks up to see Bobby Boo and Stead now just five yards from them, shambling, moving forward. Jack grabs Jenkie's arm and jerks her to her feet.

With Jenkie screaming in pain, they race toward Sam, who lies motionless, one arm over his head, eyes still closed. Jenkie cries, "I can't run!"

Jack yells, "Shut the fuck up, Jenkie!" and she does.

Jack hauls Sam up over his shoulder, his strength, through heightened even greater terror, renewed. He thinks he feels Sam moan softly against his chest.

"Where's the nearest house, Jenkie?!"

Stead and Bobby Boo are closing the distance, their stench preceding them. Far behind them, the two old zombies slam into each other over and over like bumper cars at a carnival.

"*Jenkie!*"

"Granny Mustard's cabin!" she screams. "That way!" She points up the mountainside, the steep, densely forested mountainside.

Jack spins on his heels and heads for the slope. Sam's legs and arms flop crazily. Jack's teeth are clenched, his heart thundering. Behind him, he hears Jenkie shout, "Help me!"

Jack can't help her any more. Now she has to help herself.

He reaches the trees, struggles up the steep incline, makes the first couple of yards then slides on the sodden leaves. *Oh, God...!*

Sam takes a shuddering, whistling breath. That is either good news or bad. Either he's coming around or that is a death rattle.

But Jack can't think about that. He has to find shelter. He has to get himself and Sam away from the zombies. He has to move. His clenches his teeth, his shoulders, his entire body tightens with adrenalin. He pushes forward again, upward into the trees, fighting the wet ground, moving against the callousness of nature even as his body tries to resist.

Don't think! Just fucking go!

Then he hears Jenkie right behind him, wheezing, whining "Wait for me! Oh, shit, Dan bit me! Oh, shit! My hip hurts so bad! They're going to catch us! They're going to eat us!"

Jack doesn't have the energy or desire to answer her, and so he doesn't.

He pushes on. Upward.

25
Armistead

The two men and the One With No Eyes move up into the trees and Armistead can no longer see them.

But he can hear them. He can smell and sense them. Their warm blood and living flesh, the sparkling bright currents of their brains. The pounding of their hearts and the panting of their lungs. The sweat mingling with the smell of hard rain, earthworms, and dread mingling with desperate hope.

The other he'd shared the room with is ahead of him, huffing, grunting, heading for the slope in pursuit of the living ones. There are other creatures nearby, furred, feathered, hiding behind logs, within brush, beneath piles of leaves, but the allure of their small, warm bodies is nothing compared to the draw of the humans. Nothing compels Armistead forward, nor promises the dissolution of the pain of the Hunger like the promise of human flesh. Human brain.

He catches up to the other. They stagger up the slippery slope side-by-side, driven, hungry, hungry, following the trail of the living. Armistead looks back for a moment to see the two smaller, older ones back near the trailer. They are lying on the ground, completely swallowed up by flames they could not outpace. This is good, then. They are out of their misery. And now there are just two after the men and the One With No Eyes. There are just two to fight for the right to them as food.

The One With No Eyes cries aloud, and the sounds of her defenselessness and desperation are delicious. She cannot last long. He thinks she is wounded. He thinks something has hurt her, though he can't remember what happened. It doesn't matter. She will fall behind, and she will be the first he will eat.

The other loses his footing, slides back a bit in the leaves, growls, digs his way back up again. The eye which had been loose on his cheek is caught on a prickly juniper and ripped free. Now it dangles from the branch like a fleshy red pinecone. Armistead passes him, pressing through pines and vines and dead ferns that curl like brittle, bony fingers.

Soon the Hunger will be over. Soon he will eat!

No. You will not eat.

The powerful voice causes him to stop, to look around, though he knows he will see no one. The voice is within him; the voice is beyond him. It is everywhere, huge, formless. The Hunger eases with the sound of the voice but remains a dull ache.

Follow them. Only follow.

The other slams into a tree, moves around it, slides, gets up again.

Armistead at least knows how to lean forward and reduce the slipping. He will get to the One With No Eyes first.

"But I must feed," Armistead says.

Follow them. Only follow.

"I must feed!"

Follow them and do them no harm. Your task lies ahead.

Armistead does not know why he is being tormented and taunted and forced onward to some unknown fate. He hates the voice that speaks to him, he hates the Hunger, he hates the other, the One With No Eyes, and this living death.

"I must feed!" he snarls.

The other's head turns toward him, hearing but unknowing, mindless, and gazes briefly at him with his empty, red eye. Then he moves on, up the mountainside.

Your pain will end soon, with lesson learned and task completed.

"When?"

Follow them.

"Why am I?"

Follow them.

"Who am I?"

Trust me.

26
Kathy Shaw

"You have company?" she asks as she steps into the front room of Granny Mustard's cabin, turning around to take it in, to see if there is an escape route other than the front door. The room is small, with one window facing the porch. The curtains are made of little skulls strung on strings, and they clack together gently—*pock, pock, pock*. There is minimal furniture—a cot, a chair, a washbasin on a stand, a small table by the door.

A shotgun leans against the fireplace. A machete sits in the oak split basket next to the coal tongs.

Both men keep on their wide-brimmed hats, obscuring their eyes, but Kathy sees that Burley is clean-shaven and Calhoun has a poor attempt at a mustache. Burley stands with his arms crossed. Calhoun moves around behind her and closes the door. She turns as slowly and subtly as she can, trying her best to appear confident, unfazed, unafraid.

"Company?" asks Burley. "Who'd be company but you?"

"I… I saw a new car down on the road. I think it belonged to some men that were at the Exxon in Beaver Dam earlier this morning. I dunno, I could be wrong. It's dark out there."

"A car belonging to outsiders? Really? Now, outsiders don't make us very happy, do they, Calhoun?"

Shit shit shit. Kathy takes a sharp but silent breath. Maybe the two men did come up here for some shine and it went bad. Maybe Burley and Calhoun hurt them, stole their car keys, sent them off into the woods on foot. Or maybe Burley and Calhoun killed them. She's heard rumors that they've killed on Granny's behalf before, dispatched moonshiner rivals, claimed they'd just left the area. Not even the sheriff cared to dig too much into the stories, preferring to let it be. Talk was the sheriff was fond of Granny's shine and had no desire to tangle with the Mustard men.

Kathy shrugs, clicks off her flashlight, and puts it in her poncho pouch. "Like I said. It's dark out. My light's pretty dim."

"Well, could of been them men," says Calhoun. "We might of chatted with them around lunch time or so. Friendly enough fellows. Said they were filming a movie about chestnuts and peckers. Maybe they decided to look for peckers at night, sneak around in the dark and catch 'em by surprise."

Burley chuckles.

"You go lookin' for nuts and peckers at night, Kathy?" The sound of Calhoun's voice is low, oily.

Okay, no, this was an insane idea, Kathy. Get out of here now!

"Listen, fellas," she says. "I just wanted to ask you if Granny ever said anything to you about my dad. If she knew him. If they ever talked. Do you know if that's the case?"

"Granny and Hank Shaw?" says Burley, rubbing his chin.

"Now hold on," says Calhoun. "Granny, Granny. Lemme think. She mighta said something. Why don't you sit down there on Granny's old cot and slip out them wet clothes. And I'll see if I can remember what she might have said."

Burley's brows furrow. "No, Kathy, can't say we know nothin' 'bout Granny ever spending time or talkin' with your daddy. Calhoun, I say we let her go on home. It's way late, nearly midnight, and I'm sure her daddy will worry 'bout where she is."

Kathy nods, steps toward the door but Calhoun puts his foot up against the base. "Oh, no, we won't be no good hosts should we send you out in the cold and rain without warmin' you up a bit. What you say, Burley? Some shine? And then some good ole skin to skin friction? Rub some things together to get a fire goin'?"

Oh God, oh shit, this is bad!

Kathy keeps her voice as even as possible. "My car's not far. I'll be there in a matter of minutes. But thanks for the offer of shine, anyway."

Calhoun touches Kathy's hair, runs his hand down and pulls her ponytail out from the back of her poncho. He has a bristly lip and breath that smells like old tobacco and rotten teeth. "I can keep you warm, little girl."

Burley says, "Calhoun, back off."

Calhoun blows air through thin lips. "Why, Burley, you want first go? You don't want my sloppy seconds?"

Burley stalks over to Calhoun, grabs him by the wrist, spins him around and away from the door, keeps hold of his brother. "No, you fucker! Listen to me. She's hot, yeah. And I'd have that in a second if she weren't a PK."

Calhoun works his shoulders threateningly. "Who gives a shit she's a PK? Damn, she's probably even a virgin! You ever had virgin pussy, Burley? Nothin' like it!"

Kathy keeps her eyes on the brothers and slowly reaches for the door handle, but Calhoun immediately sees. He pulls free of Burley's grip and slams himself against the door. He's in no mood now. "Fuck you, Burley. You ain't my boss. You just get on back to the kitchen now and fix us a little after-fuck snack." He licks his lips at Kathy, puts his hand on her breast. She instantly slaps him off, her fists coming up before her.

"Damn you, Calhoun!" she says. "Don't you touch me again!"

"Or what?" chides Calhoun. "Or you'll melt into a puddle of virgin joy? Huh? That's what you'll do. It's how girls take to me."

Burley's furious. "Calhoun, you messin' with stuff you should best leave alone. You want to piss off God?"

"Ha! You think we ain't already done that somewhere along the line?"

"Her dad's a preacher. We ain't never harmed no one in a preacher's family. I don't aim to start now."

"You's a fucking pussy!"

"You's a fucking asshole!"

Burley comes at Calhoun again, swinging. He catches his brother in the jaw with a solid blow. Calhoun sputters and growls, pushes Kathy out of the way. She falls against the table, the edge catching her in the stomach, knocking her breath out.

She drops to her knees, sparks spinning across her line of vision, trying to gulp air.

Calhoun throws his weight into Burley, sending Burley flailing, arms spinning. He crashes against the shotgun, which clatters to the floor. He regains his feet in a moment, coughing, spitting, and dives at Calhoun again, driving his head into his brother's chest. Calhoun grunts, stumbles back, then catches Burley's elbow and twists it behind his brother's back. Burley squeals. Calhoun twists harder, harder, until the arm snaps with a dull crack.

"Fucking shit oh shit what did you do you fucking piece of shit!" screams Burley. He wriggles and wails as Calhoun lets him go. He bends into his chest, clutching his arm, crying, cursing Calhoun at the top of his lungs.

Then Calhoun reaches down for Kathy.

"C'mon, little girl. Time you had you some meat. Some fine Mustard-flavored meat." He takes her hand. His grip is cold, hard, ragged.

And for the first time in her life and feeling at once grateful and peculiar when she recognizes the darkness that is folding over her, she faints.

27

Jenkie Mustard

She hurts, she hurts, she *HURTS!* When that sorry-ass dead piece of crap dog, Dan, bit her on her thigh he broke the skin. She's bleeding through her jeans, though not as badly as the cameraman when he had his arm eaten up. Her thigh throbs and her chest aches and her legs burn and her heart is tight as a rubber band around a sheep's tail. She knows she can't go much farther. But she also knows two hollows are after them.

And she keeps remembering, over and over, Bobby Boo yanking the cameraman up short, eating slabs out of his arms, licking his lips, going in for more.

That could be her if she doesn't keep moving. That could be her if she doesn't get her ass up the mountain. Her arm. Her thigh. Her ass. Her whole damned body.

"Wait for me!" she cries, but Jack the fucking TV man is breathin' hard like a coal train engine, thinking he can save his friend by getting to Granny Mustard's cabin before the hollows catch them. She shouldn't have told him where it was! She should have let him and his friend become hollow food! Ha ha! Then she could have escaped to Granny's on her own while the hollows ate their fill.

She hates them both. And she feels like an idiot.

Another step, then another.

She thinks about how Bobby Boo Anderson bit Dan but how he didn't eat Dan. But then Dan died of the bite and came back to life just like Bobby Boo, all red-eyes and growly, trying to eat both her and Bink. Now Jenkie's been bit by Dan. If she dies...

Just shut up now, ain't gonna die! It ain't that bad.

But it hurts that bad!

She whimpers, wipes her snot-covered nose.

There is no moon out, and even though the rain has stopped the land is dark as the inside of a possum. She trips over briars and logs and is slapped in the face by branches that Jack pushes out of the way for himself but not for her. Her throat is ragged and raw from breathing through her mouth. Her legs rubber out beneath her, and she stops, leans against the trunk of a tulip tree, grits her teeth, spits out onto the ground. Jack keeps on going.

"Wait, Jack!" she whines. "I can't go any farther. I gotta rest! Don't leave me back here."

But Jack leaves her back there. He continues, stumbling but making ground, now vanished beyond the trees.

Jenkie looks down the mountain slope. She listens. The hollows are back there, not far, she's sure. She hears their echoes as they crash through the brush, growling, clawing at the steep earth, sending rocks bouncing down behind them.

Shit shit shit! Got to move, I got to get up and out of here!

She pushes away from the tree, takes three steps, but her legs give out again. The pain in her thigh locks her down and she can't move.

Not another step.

She kneels on the soaked ground like a Pentecostal awaiting a blessing. Or like one of those English queens awaiting the sword.

Oh, God, I'm dead! Get up!

She tries to stand but her legs collapse yet again. She begins to sob, straining back over her shoulder to see if they are close now, and how close.

"No no no no no!"

She puts her hand to her stomach and feels Granny's leather-bound book there, held in place by the tucked hem of her sweatshirt. If only there was a chant on one of the pages that would send them away from her. If she could read and understand the power in the pages.

But she doesn't. She is a moron. She was never even half as smart as Granny Mustard.

I don't want to die I don't want to hurt I don't want to be eaten!

The sound of the hollows is closer now. Twigs breaking, leaves crunching, teeth clacking. Jenkie pushes herself up yet again, only to fall back again and slide down the slope several feet. She catches hold of the tulip tree trunk. She drags herself around behind it, and tries to breathe small, tries to become small.

Maybe they can't see me. Maybe they'll pass on by.

She puts her forehead against the bark.

Shhhh, shhhh! Please don't hear me!

She shuts her eyes. Over the jackhammer of her heart and the hitching of her breaths, she thinks herself small. Small like a chipmunk. Small like a turtle. They won't see her; she is way too small now.

Shuffling, grunting, snarling, closer, so close.

I'm small I'm tiny oh please help me I'm tiny!

She hears a hollow just on the other side of the tulip tree.

Go away, move on! Oh, please don't see me! Oh shit oh shit oh shit!

A cold hand clutches her shoulder. She opens her eyes. Stead is peering around the tree trunk at her, his torch-lit eyes burning into her brain, ripping apart her fragile smallness. Jenkie wails and tries to wrench herself free, but Stead drags her around the tree and holds her up so that her toes barely touch the ground.

She's stunned at his power, his strength. But then the amazement is gone and is replaced with I'm going to die now, he's going to eat me!

Over Stead's shoulder, Jenkie sees Bobby Boo down a bit, bashing his way through a thatch of pine saplings, his head waggling, his tongue slopping, licking, drooling. He considers Jenkie with his dead gaze and clacks together what teeth he has left.

Jenkie twists and kicks but Stead does not let go. *What will it feel like to be eaten alive? How long will it hurt? How long will I scream?*

But then Stead hoists her up as high as his shoulders, gives her a push, and boosts her up into the branches of the tulip tree. She catches the branches and pulls herself up one more layer of limbs, a good ten feet off the ground.

Stead turns to look at Bobby Boo and then moves on up the mountain.

What the hell? He saved me! He saved me? Why would he save me?

Bobby Boo thrashes through the dead grasses, coming closer, his arms swinging like an ape's. He reaches the tulip tree and looks up.

I'm safe! Oh, my God! I'm safe! Bobby Boo can't get me! Yeah, baby!

Bobby Boo reaches up, clumsily swiping his arms, his fingers coming a good two feet short of Jenkie's shoes.

"Ha, you fucker!" she laughs. The sound is shrill and insane on the air, and she doesn't care. "You motherfucker! You think you can get me, well you can't! So suck on that, asshole! I'll stay up here until you starve to death or decide to go eat something else!"

Bobby Boo growls, wanders around the tree three times, slapping at the trunk, clutching up toward Jenkie's foot.

"Thanks, Stead!" Jenkie yells. "Why ever the hell you did that, thanks! Hope you catch and eat those damn TV men!" She steps down one branch lower to tease Bobby Boo, to taunt him. He swings his arms up but still can't reach her.

Jenkie throws back her head and howls. "Ha, dead shit can't catch me! I'm safe, baby, oh yeah!"

Then she looks down at Bobby Boo again. And the smile on her face freezes. Dies.

Bobby Boo has grasped the end of the branch where her feet rest.

And with one loud grunt, he pulls on the branch so hard that she bounces once, loses her balance, and slams to the earth.

And it is only a matter of seconds before she knows what it feels like to be eaten alive. How long it hurts. And how long she screams.

28
Jack Carroll

He hears Jenkie down the mountain, somewhere beyond the trees and boulders and ravines, and she is screaming.

"Oh, God," he says softly, not wanting to startle Sam. "That's it for her, she's done with."

One of the zombies, or both of them, have gotten her and now they are tearing her apart and eating her.

Dreadful… oh, my God.

But it gives him a moment to stop. He eases Sam onto the ground beside a large, moss-covered log.

Then he sits on the sodden log, leans over, and tries to pull his mind back into his head.

He is stunned that he has been able to move Sam this far up the mountain, but he knows if he actually thinks about it, it will jinx him, and he won't be able to get the rest of the way. His feet are blistered to shit, torn up and stinging as if they've been flayed. His shoulder and back are cramped. His heart pounds so hard he can't hear anything but its beats… and Jenkie's screams.

Then her screams cut off.

She's dead.

Jack listens. His heart beats. Wind creaking the trees overhead. An owl or some other night bird screeching.

Nothing else. No footsteps down the slope. At least not yet.

Jack licks his cracked lips. He shifts his aching body so he can look up the mountain. He knows they've gone close to a mile, if not that. It seems that the land levels off somewhat not too far ahead beyond a rocky outcropping. If that's Moon Peak, and if Jenkie was telling the truth, there is a cabin there. Granny

Mustard's cabin. And Granny Mustard is dead. So he and Sam will have the place to themselves. Maybe there is water there, maybe there are blankets and medical supplies. Certainly, the door will have locks or bolts. If the old woman lived way up here in the middle of nowhere, she would have done something to make her home safe from unexpected intruders, human or not. Sam's bleeding has stopped but he is still unconscious. He is still breathing.

"Not much farther now, dude," says Jack. He stands up on his torn feet and grimaces against the pain. "Just hang in there a little longer."

He tries to pick Sam up but can't. He steps back a bit and tries to work his shoulders beneath his friend's torso, but he is too exhausted. His burning muscles refuse to cooperate.

"Oh, come on. I didn't come this far to leave you behind!"

He takes Sam's hands and begins to drag him upward. Up, over the vines and stumps and leaves and thistles, willing his friend to hold on, to live, to just stay with him. He totters backward a step, but then leans over against the angle of the land. Very close now, the lay is easing up and he can see a stretch of grass ahead. At the tallest point past the grass, a cabin with faint light within.

They reach the grass, move out from the trees. It is then Jack realizes how cold Sam's hands have become. It is then he realizes that Sam is dead.

It is then he lets go of the cameraman, sits beside him, buries his face in his hands, and cries.

29
Kathy Shaw

She tumbles into awareness, her body jerking as if trying to stop itself from falling. There is something over her and she kicks at it, but it doesn't go away. Her eyes try to open and fail at first, but then they do open, blink hard, and open again.

She is in a small room. A room in a cabin.

Fuck. Granny's cabin.

She hears voices in the next room. Burley and Calhoun. They are arguing.

A lantern sits on the small table beneath the window, sputtering, burning low, casting a sheen of tainted yellow across the floor, the bed, the walls.

"I swear to God, Burley, you make me sick!"

"Me? You fucking broke my arm! Damn you!"

"Just sit still, it's almost set. Shit. You're such a baby."

Kathy lies still, glances around. The something over her is a wool blanket. For some reason, one of them decided a fainted woman should be kept warm.

"Damn it, Calhoun! You ain't no doctor, you're making it worse!"

"I said quit bitchin'! I'm almost done."

Kathy eases herself up and sits on the edge of the cot. If she can tip-toe, she can possibly get out the front door while the nursing is going on next door. She's gotten nothing out of this trip but trouble, just like Penny warned her.

Then she spies something on the far wall.

It's a small, unframed piece of old cloth, an embroidered sampler.

Even in the dim light she recognizes the thread-stitched graphic. It is a shield—a coat of arms.

She gets up carefully, silently, and moves slowly across the floor, stopping short of the doorway to the other room. On the shield she can see a knight's helmet. A hand holding a sword. Three winged birds flying upward.

The flickering light reveals the quote beneath the crest, made of tiny stitches in red thread.

Fide et Fortitudine.

Wait... no... what is this?

"My, my, look who's awake."

Calhoun is leaning against the doorframe between the two rooms, wiping his hands on a ratty dishtowel. One side of his mouth is hitched and the bristles on his lip stand out like stubby porcupine quills. His hat is gone now, and she can see his eyes... tiny, deep-set, cold. Burley stands behind him, his broken arm caught up in a dishtowel sling. His hat is also gone; his eyes are likewise tiny and deep-set. But at the moment they don't seem as cold as Calhoun's, though Kathy knows all too well that in a second they can be.

"Feelin' better?" Calhoun steps into the front room, throws the towel over his shoulder. "I'd never want to enjoy a little pecker time with a gal who'd passed out on me. You might call me a gentleman."

Kathy points at the sampler on the wall. Desperate. Seeking to grab a moment, just a moment.

"Tel me about that first," she manages. "Then I'm all yours, Calhoun."

Calhoun raises a brow, nods in surprise and pleasure. "Well, now you're talkin'."

"Calhoun," warns Burley.

"Shut up Burley. You got one more arm I ain't got to yet."

Burley steps up to look at the sampler. "What you want to know? It's just a piece o' crap Granny had hangin' up there ever since I can remember."

"I came up here to ask if you knew what connection my father had to Granny. That is the Shaw family coat of arms."

"What the hell's a coat of arms?" Burley comes out of the

kitchen, favoring his arm. "I got a coat with arms. Never seen a coat without arms." He chortles, as if he thinks he's made a good joke, but the jostling seems to hurt his arm, so he shuts up.

"It represents a family," says Kathy. She backs a step toward the front door. Her stomach clenches, sending bile into her mouth. She swallows it back, steels herself for the worst, hopes for the best. "We have the same emblem on our wall, down at my house."

"No shit?" Calhoun steps closer to the sampler on the wall. "What's that mean, then, that Granny liked the Shaws so much that she put that up so she could think about ya'll? That don't make no sense."

Burley scratches his chin with his free hand. "Or does it mean we're… related?"

Related? That's impossible!

Another small sliding step. If she can get within reach of the door, she'll dash out. Calhoun might catch her, throw her back, and rape her.

But how could it be any worse than what will certainly happen if she stays?

If she stays, the rape might be less violent.

If she runs, he will probably beat the crap out of her then rape her.

But she will at least know she tried.

"Maybe we're cousins," says Calhoun. "Fuck, can you imagine that? Related to the Shaws? To that preacher man and…" He turns to Kathy and sees what she's doing. He grabs her by the hair and yanks her back.

She screams.

And a second scream, from out behind the cabin matches her own.

Burley lets go of Kathy's hair and Kathy stumbles and catches herself against the wall. Burley and Calhoun turn toward the sound.

"Who the hell's that?"

"Get your gun, Calhoun. We got company!"

30
Jack Carroll

Jack cries in the wet grass, shivering in the cold, his friend dead beside him in the wee hours of a November morning. On some god-forsaken mountaintop. With zombies on his trail.

"I fucking tried, Sam," he whispers. "I tried, I swear I tried. I'm sorry I couldn't get you to help. I'm sorry I thought this would be a good idea. I'm sorry I talked Nate into it!"

A wind blows, catches his hair and the grasses around him. He swallows, wipes his eyes, but the tears continue. He looks at the cabin, at the faint light, and knows he must go there. He can't stay here and let Jenkie's hollows catch up to him. He must move.

But the thought of leaving Sam here is just wrong. So very wrong.

He touches Sam's face. "Hey man, I got to go. I promise to come back for you if I can. Rest well, wherever you are. Rest well and..."

Sam's eyes snap open, wide. They burn with a bright red fire.

Jack leaps to his feet, and he screams.

31

Jenkie Mustard

There is wetness. There is darkness. And there is Hunger. Jenkie tries to sit up, but she has no legs, no hips. She tries to pull herself forward but all she has is one flesh-stripped arm with two fingers at the end.

She tries to turn her head, but it won't roll because it is flat, eaten mostly away, leaving only a portion of jaw, one cheekbone, and half a brain.

But she is hungry. So hungry…

There is something over her, chewing on a foot. It looks like her foot, but she's not sure and doesn't care because the only thing she knows now is the Hunger.

But then the thing that ate her foot throws the empty shoe aside and dives back down, scooping out the rest of her brain and that's all there is.

Jenkie is gone.

As the thing pushes itself upward and shambles away, a small furry creature scuttles over to what had been Jenkie's body, finds a leather-bound book torn and lying on the leaves, and decides the paper would make nice nesting material. It chews away bits of a page, stuffs it into its mouth, and runs off. Other creatures get the same idea, gathering fragments and taking them off in differing directions in the dark of night.

Then a fox finds the leather, gnaws it a bit, and then drags it home to its lair.

32
Armistead

He is near the crest of the mountain now. He feels strangely better, strangely stronger. The Hunger, while there, clings less ferociously.

It is as if he is walking up and away from it, though toward what he can't know.

Follow, Armistead. You have a task to accomplish.

He pushes around a thorny ash tree, up over a ragged boulder. Overhead, rain clouds part, revealing a silver moon. He knows it is a moon now. There is no doubt.

The sense of moving upward is familiar and comforting, even in the dreadful world in which he finds himself.

"Dreadful world," he whispers. "Why am I here, in this dreadful world? This dreadful, dreamful place?"

You wanted to know.

"Know what?"

The voice doesn't answer.

Armistead climbs over the boulder, steps off onto an even steeper section of slope. He smells warm-blooded animals nearby, but he moves on.

Then he remembers. Blue warmth surrounding him. Light encircling him. Peace. Weightless.

Home?

Home.

"I want to come home."

You wanted to know. And you have a task ahead.

"But what is the task?"

You'll know. Follow.

He follows the scent of the two men, though he can tell they are no longer moving. They've stopped. He will encounter them soon.

Then he hears one of them scream.

"He is in anguish. What now? What do I do now?"

Follow. When the time comes you'll know.

33
Kathy Shaw

Burley steps out of the way as Calhoun grabs up the shotgun and races back into the kitchen. Burley then fumbles for the machete—clearly his dominant hand is the one at the end of the fractured arm—and he follows after. Kathy didn't recognize the voice that screamed, but she has no desire to wait and find out who it was. She throws back the front door latch and races out to the porch, jumps off into the grass.

And her ankle twists painfully beneath her. She goes down with a thud, bright shards of pain coursing up her leg.

"Damn!" she wails, then gets up and runs, hobbles, across the yard.

She can hear the screaming from the other side of the cabin. She hears Burley and Calhoun's shouts.

"Get back in the cabin!" cries an unfamiliar male voice. "They're after us! My God, don't stand there, get back inside!"

A shot is fired, the sound reverberating the air, the ground.

Burley shouts, "Fuck, Calhoun, you got that fella in the gut and he's still comin'! Look-a that hole in him! Shoot the other one!"

"Don't shoot me, please! We got to get inside, hurry!"

Then Calhoun, "The one I shot got red eyes! Now that ain't right!"

"Get inside! Please! Go!"

Red eyes?

"Oh, shit, oh no!"

Annie had red eyes.

"My mother had red eyes!"

Hank said there was evil set free on the mountains.

She hears the back cabin door slam shut. She hears men inside, yelling at each other.

She hears a faint growling sound on the cold air. A sound so much like the one Annie made when she tried to kill Kathy in the creek.

Against the pain in her ankle, she limps to the fence, climbs over, and struggles through the underbrush toward the road, toward her car.

34
Jack Carroll

The two large men in the cabin's kitchen alternately stare at Jack and then out the small window that faces the rear yard. He has recognized them as the Mustards who stole his rental car and money. Clearly, they are too discombobulated to have realized yet who he is. He's all too happy to have it stay that way.

"What the hell is that thing out there?" asks Burley. His arm is in a sling, and he winces as he speaks.

Jack can see Sam out the window, more than halfway across the yard now, arms outstretched, red eyes like clinkers, body shaking side to side. "It was my friend, Sam," he says. "He's... he's a zombie."

Calhoun turns to Jack. "A zombie? A fuckin' zombie? Don't pull our dicks, man, we ain't partial to... Wait, I know who you is. That dude on the road who's makin' a nature film!"

"Okay, yes. And that's my partner outside, my cameraman Sam. He died a few minutes ago. Now he's..."

Calhoun's face screws up. "A fuckin' zombie? Ha! Now don't this beat all? Hey, PK, you hear that?" He looks through an open doorway to the room at the front of the cabin. It's empty.

"Ah, shit, she's done run out," says Calhoun.

"Guess the zombie'll get her?" asks Burley.

"Zombie? You fall for this outsider's lies?"

Jack's heart skips several beats.

"He's workin' us, he's tryin' to see how far we'll follow him down his rabbit hole!"

"But..." Burley points out the window. "That guy out there

got a shotgun hole in his gut! He got red eyes, Calhoun!"

Calhoun shakes his head, clutches his gun. "Fuck that. I can't believe we came in here with this asshole, hidin' from what? A sick, wounded dude with red eyes? Well, I'm goin' out to take care of him once and for all. Then I'm comin' back in to take care of Mr. California here."

"Calhoun, don't..." says Burley, but Calhoun is already yanking the door open and moving out into the darkness, his shotgun at his hip. Jack and Burley crowd at the window.

"Zombie?" asks Burley. "Really?"

Jack nods. "Wouldn't have believed it myself, if I wasn't down at Jenkie Mustard's trailer in Desper Hollow just a few hours ago."

"Jenkie? Damn!"

"She had zombies in the trailer. One of them ate part of Sam's arm..." Jack tightens against a surge of grief that threatens to weaken him. He can't be weak now. "She set the trailer on fire and I think some died but I know a couple are after us. I had Sam, carried him, dragged him, but he died. And now he's out there. He's one of them."

Across the grassy, weedy yard, peering from behind the black, bony branches of the peak-top trees, there is a faint glow. Sunrise, a teasing of morning yet to come. The yard fades from pewter grey to blood orange.

"Hey, there, Hollywood!" shouts Calhoun. Jack's attention turns from the expanding light to Sam, who is closing in on the mountain man. "I see my shotgun didn't quite do the trick on you. Lemme give it another go."

He raises the gun to his shoulder, leans his head into it, and puts his finger on the trigger. Sam's arms—one whole, one chewed down to bone and random, bulging hunks of flesh— stretch forward, fingers scrabbling. Sam moans and clacks his teeth. His red eyes do not blink.

"Get in here, Calhoun!" shouts Burley. "You idiot!"

But Calhoun just laughs out loud and pulls the trigger. A shot cuts through Sam's chest and Sam shudders, pauses, bits of ribs and shoulder blades and heart spattering his face and flying out into the air.

"What the…?" Calhoun is clearly stunned, suddenly afraid. He skips back, breaks open the gun barrel, and jams another cartridge in as Sam lashes out with his arms.

"Get the fuck in here!" Burley slams his fist against the wavery window glass, but Calhoun will have none of it. He is determined to win against the red-eyed dead man.

Jack is horrified, mesmerized. He stares at the confrontation, which now seems to be slowing down to a surreal pace. The monster and the mountain man, seconds from contact, the orange glow of the tangled wet grasses, and now, on the far side of the yard, emerging from the trees, Stead, the smaller zombie from Jenkie's trailer, shuffling forward. Heading for the cabin.

Shit! He would have shouted it, but the shout is locked in his throat as he watches Calhoun lifts the shotgun to aim it again, but it's too late now, Sam lunges forward and knocks Calhoun off his feet. The gun bounces on its butt and flips away. Calhoun backs up onto the weather-worn kitchen stoop with Sam over him, matching him move for move. Drool oozes from his mouth and spatters on Calhoun's upturned face.

Then Burley slams the kitchen door and bolts it.

Calhoun screams. "Let me in!"

But Burley shakes his head. "Can't let that thing in here! It'd have gotten in here!"

Jack can't speak. He can only watch between Burley, his broken arm, and his tiny terrified eyes, cowering beside him, and the sight out the window of Stead, and now the one-eyed Bobby Boo close behind, coming across the yard. He can no longer see Calhoun but can hear him against the other side of the door, slamming against the wood, wailing, shrieking in exquisite pain as Sam does his thing.

Then Calhoun goes quiet. The slamming continues. The sounds of eating are loud now, slobbering, wet ripping sounds. Choking, swallowing.

"Oh God oh God!" says Burley. He steps back farther into the kitchen. "It's 'cause of that PK! God's getting back at Calhoun for trying to have it with Kathy Shaw!"

The name sounds familiar to Jack, but he doesn't have time or focus to think about it. Stead and Bobby Boo are getting closer. "You got any more guns?" he asks, grabbing Burley by the shirt collar. "You got to have more guns around here!"

Burley looks back and forth, frantic. "I got my machete," he says. "But I ain't no good with my left hand. Fuck Calhoun for breaking my arm! Wait, you got a gun in your pocket, I see the grip stickin' out there!"

Jack pulls it out. "No bullets. You two stole my car with the bullets in it!"

"Oh, oh, oh!" Burley goes into the front room and paces back and forth.

Jack, slowly, presses his face to the kitchen window, angles his head to see what's going on by the door, not wanting to see but needing to see...

And Sam is suddenly at the window, an inch and small pane of glass separating their faces, Sam's red eyes impossibly large and deep and scarlet, his tongue lolling, licking the glass, teeth chattering.

Jack shrieks and falls away from the window as Sam begins to pound on it. Jack runs into the front room where Burley stands, now reduced from haughty moonshine grandson to a trembling, stammering child.

"What are we gonna do? They's more comin' this way! They wanna eat us!"

"As long as the windows and doors hold we should be all right..."

"For how long? We can't stay in here, they either break in or we'll starve to death. Ain't no food up here but some jerky and two old potatoes!"

Jack bursts out laughing. The insanity is perfect. The craziness is excellent! If only he had Sam's camera! If only he could film this, what a killing he'd make in Hollywood! What a hit Madness in the Mountain would be!

Oh, my God, but the money would come rolling in! He'd be hailed as the most daring reality show creator in the whole fucking business! He laughs so hard it hurts deep down inside.

Then Burley smacks him upside the head and brings him out of it.

"Your car's down the road not far. You got bullets in there?

We make a run for it!"

"I..." Jack looks back into the kitchen, at the fingers clawing at the glass. *Shit... we have to. There are three now. Together, they'll find a way in. If we get to the Tribute we can drive out. And there is the box of ammunition.*

"You can run okay with that arm?"

Burley scowls. "I could run with a fuckin' broken leg to get away from those things!"

They move to the door. Jack takes the latch. He throws it up and they run out into the wakening nightmare.

35
Kathy Shaw

Skidding, sliding, her ankle cut through the pain, Kathy makes it to her car.

"Thank you, Hank's God!" she cries. Fumbling with hands as cold as a stream in February, she opens the door and falls into the driver's seat.

Keys, keys, shit, where are the keys?

In her jeans' pocket, there! She picks them out, drops them on the floor, grabs them up, jams them into the ignition.

Okay, good, now drive back down the mountain, back to my house. Wake up Hank. Talk to him. And make him talk. Then warn the authorities, Sheriff Mullins, Deputy Floyd! Tell them that something horrific is spreading and they have to stop it!

Safe in the car now, she turns the key. The car grumbles, then kicks into life.

Yes!

She steers it around on the narrow road, carefully, avoiding the sharp drop on the east. Around now, and…

The wheels start to spin helplessly, stuck in deep mud.

No, no, this is not possible. This isn't happening!

She presses her foot on the accelerator again, and again the tires spin, throwing clots of mud out behind. She cries out, pounds on the steering wheel, rocks her own body back and forth, hoping her weight will be enough to kick it out of the deepening rut.

The car won't budge.

"No!"

The only options now are to try to find enough branches to

put under the tires for traction, or to get out and run.

Neither is good. Neither is safe.

She pounds the steering wheel. She screams. She stomps on the gas.

And the wheels spin round and round.

36

Armistead

The men have run out of the cabin. He can't see them, but he knows. The sun—yes, it is the sun! —has begun to appear between the trees down the slope to the east. On the stoop of the cabin, against the door, lies the body of one who had recently been alive.

Now, there is little left but spattered blood, a bit of hair, some clothing. The one that had his arm eaten back at the trailer stands over him, sucking marrow from a leg bone that has been stripped fairly clean of its flesh. The one Armistead had shared a room with is next to him now, his longer legs carrying him forward more quickly, heading around the side of the cabin, following the scents of the living.

Bobby Boo. That is the other's name. Armistead remembers it now.

He has heard it over and over, called down from the hole in the ceiling, spat out down at the other end of the trailer as the two had wandered back and forth in their room. Why is Bobby Boo as he is? Dead but living? What happened?

Why is he?

Who is he?

The one whose arm was eaten stumbles from the back door, trips over a hidden piece of metal farm equipment in the grass, then pulls himself up and continues forward, picking up his pace, almost jogging.

Who is this one, the one whose arm was eaten?

Why is he like this?

Armistead does not get an answer, but he knows what would be said if he did. It would say "Follow."

Follow.

37
Kathy Shaw

She looks in the rearview. No one is coming down the road, though the shadows are deep and wide, with only a fraction of the morning sunlight leaking through to this side of Moon Peak. She can get out, walk down to Penny's, though it is more than a mile and her ankle is swelling.

Does swelling mean it's a fracture, or does it mean it's only a sprain? She can't remember. All she can think is:

There is another one like Mom. There is another red-eyed, living dead person, and he is outside Granny's cabin. He might have broken in already. He might have killed Burley and Calhoun.

Or he might have been unable to get in and is now coming in her direction.

She pants, her hands flexing open and shut, her foot rapidly tapping the floor.

Then, "Okay, one more time. Please!"

She turns the key, presses the gas pedal again, this time more easily to keep from chewing deeper into the ground. The tires squeal. Mud flies out behind.

"Oh, damn! I'm dead!"

She opens the door and pulls herself out. The weight on her ankle is red-hot. She hops to the front of the car, then stops.

"I can't make it. I'll be safer in the car."

Then she hears wet, heavy footsteps behind her, pounding on the road, coming downward, just beyond the curve that leads to Granny's wire fence. The footsteps are running.

She jumps into the car, locks the door, curls up on the seat, and buries her face in her hands.

Go on by, pass by, please just keep going!

They're closer now, heavier, louder. Something slams into the back of her car, something grabs the door handle and pulls.

No!

"Kathy Shaw!"

She looks up to see Burley Mustard at the window, his face contorted in terror, his greasy fingers streaking the already muddy glass. Beside him, watching up the road, is the man she saw at the Exxon station in Beaver Dam, years ago. This morning. Either one.

"Let us in!" says Burley. "Please!"

Please? How strange, coming from one of the Mustard grandsons!

"Kathy, Calhoun's dead! Eaten up! Let us in!"

She shakes her head. "I'm stuck, stuck deep! This car isn't going anywhere!"

"Shit, well, come on, then," he says, waving his hand and glancing back up the road. "I got the keys to the other thing. It's not far. But we got to move, girl!"

Kathy gets out of the car again. Burley and the other man trot down past her car, heading to the curve around which the new car is parked. She stumbles, limps after them, teeth clenched, refusing to complain. Calhoun is eaten up! That is what Annie would have done to Kathy had Hank not come to her defense. If Hank had not saved her.

The man she does not know looks back, sees her struggling. "I'm coming," she says.

"Not fast enough," he says. He returns, reaches for her but she pushes him away. "No, don't."

She hobbles painfully, her shoes sucking mud, her lungs sucking air at the sharp spears that drive up into her with each step.

He watches her then repeats, "No, not fast enough!" With that he grabs her up and carries her, running— thump, thump, thump—following Burley down to the good car. His feet slip every so often, but he remains up right. Kathy is at once relieved and mortified… someone is holding her. Someone is helping her, holding her, carrying her, when she cannot help or carry herself. The vulnerability that surges through her is heart-breaking and astounding. Her heart clenches. She begins to cry.

And she is surprised to hear him whisper into her ear, "It'll be okay, just hold on. We'll be all right. Don't worry. We'll be okay."

38

Jack Carroll

Burley has the keys and insists on driving. He shoulders Jack out of the way. "I know the road better than you, so shut the fuck up and get in the other side."

"You got a damn broken arm."

"So what?" Burley growled. "I can do anything with one arm, so get out of my fuckin' way!"

"Yeah, I bet there's a lot you do with your one hand," Jack mutters, and Burley says, "What was that?" and Jack replies, "Nothing."

Jack doesn't push the driving issue, no time. He carries Kathy to the other side of the Tribute, eases her down by the back door, pulls it open then turns to help her in.

"I'm Jack Carroll," he says. "From California. Just visiting. Nice place you got here."

She is crying, or has been, and her eyes are swollen, her lips trembling.

But she tries to steady her voice. "Kathy Shaw. Saw you earlier today at the store. Yesterday. Whatever the hell it is right now."

He smiles. "I think that was only yesterday. Time flies when you're having fun, right?"

She doesn't laugh. She looks away from him, and he doesn't blame her. Who wants jokes when there are zombies up the road, seeking you out to eat you?

He reaches out to give her a hand, but she avoids it and pulls herself into the back seat, dragging her foot. Jack gets into the front, slams the door.

"Okay, get this vehicle out of here," he says.

With his broken right arm, Burley clumsily guides the key toward the ignition, but it falls to the floor mat. He curses, scratches his left fingers around and comes up with them. Both hands shake crazily; he tries again with the right hand, missing the ignition. The keys take another tumble.

"Damn, you said you could do this!" shouts Jack.

"Gotta get the keys in first!" says Burley. "Can't do that with my left. When they're in we'll be good to go!"

"Hurry the fuck up!" This is Kathy in the back seat. Jack glances back at her, glad she is coming around.

Jack gropes for the keys under Burley's leg, comes up with them, gets them into the ignition on the first try.

"Don't say nothin' bad to me!" says Burley. "I never had to run from monsters before!" He guns the gas, and the SUV roars to life.

At that moment three zombies round the corner on the dark road, stumbling and running down the incline faster than Jack could have imagined even in his most dreadful of nightmares.

39
Kathy Shaw

"Turn the car around!" Kathy screams.

Burley yanks on the steering wheel with his good hand, and the Tribute jerks, moves forward toward the red-eyed creatures then arcs to the left, coming up against the steep wall of stone and clay and vines on the west side of the road. Kathy stares out her window, slack-jawed, heart crashing against her ribs, her breaths deep, ragged. One of the monsters looks like Bobby Boo Anderson with many body parts dangling or missing. One looks like the guy she saw in Beaver Dam, sitting in a passenger's seat... the passenger's seat of this car, she realizes... this morning. Jack's friend? Oh, no... The other, she has no idea.

Burley backs the SUV several feet, coming close to the sharp drop on the other side of the road. "Careful!" Kathy says.

"Shut up, PK!" Burley shouts.

He cuts the wheel hard again and the Tribute lurches forward, nearly clearing the wall of earth but not quite.

"One more time!"

The Tribute rolls backward. Kathy glances behind them, half-expecting the rear tires to drop off the edge, but Burley slams the breaks in time.

The creatures are approaching, legs wobbling, hands outstretched, mouths snapping open and closed, red eyes glowing. Closer now, almost to the vehicle.

"Where're the damn bullets?" This is Jack, digging in the glove box. "I thought they were in here!"

Burley presses the gas pedal, wrenches the steering wheel,

and the Tribute jumps forward, circling past the wall of earth, missing it by inches.

But the creatures don't miss the Tribute. They fall against it, their bodies heavy and sloppy. The Bobby Boo-monster heaves himself across the hood. The Jack's-friend-monster clutches the passenger's side mirror. The third, which appears less damaged than the other two, reaches up and grabs the edge of the luggage rack. His face is not as tattered as the others, yet it is dreadful with its bright red eyes. He considers Kathy through the window, angles briefly as if studying her, and then the eyes blink and he looks away.

"Where's the damn box of bullets, Burley?" Jack slugs Burley in the arm.

"Fuck, arm's broken, I'll kill you!"

"They'll kill us! Where's the bullets?"

"I don't know!"

Bobby-Boo-monster clings to the hood, staring in through the windshield, and Burley can't turn the Tribute side to side sharply enough or drive fast enough on this precarious mountain road to knock him off. It seems as if his oozing, sticky flesh is helping him cling to the metal. The others hold the mirror and the luggage rack, their bodies dragging and thumping the car and the ground.

"Shake them off, Burley!" cried Kathy. "Run them over!"

"I'm trying!"

Jack looks over the seat at Kathy. "See if you can find the ammunition for my gun!" He holds up a pistol, waves it.

Kathy glances around, spots a squashed cardboard box on the floor.

She snatches it up, passes it over. "This it?"

"Shit, yes!" He grabs it, dumps it open, grabs several from the seat beside him.

Burley takes a sharp turn on the road, but the creatures continue to cling, continue to growl and slobber and stare. The one on the mirror pounds a pulpy flesh against Jack's window. Jack looks over, shudders, and turns back to the gun.

"You know how to use a gun?" asks Burley.

"I think so!" Jack tries to open the pistol but can't. Kathy reaches across, snatches it, pops open the chamber, hands it back.

"Put them in now!" she yells. "And shoot! Shoot them in the eye. Shoot them in the head. I think that's what kills them!"

"How the hell do you know?" says Burley through clenched jaws.

"That's how Hank killed Annie..."

"What?" This is Jack.

Dad couldn't kill her until he drove the hiking stick into her eye, into her brain!

"It's... it's how my father killed my mother! She was like that, like them! Red eyes, falling apart, trying to kill me!"

"Oh, God, I'm sorry!" says Jack.

"Don't be sorry. Shoot!"

Jack aims the gun at the window where the man who might have been his friend lolls and screeches and clings to the rearview. "Forgive me, Sam. I tried to save you, I really did!" Jack pulls the trigger. The Tribute bumps in a pothole. The bullet pierces the glass, sending spider-cracks radiating outward. Only the creature's cheek is grazed, stripping off bits of skin and muscle. The creature snarls, tries to force his free fingers in through the bullet hole.

"Shoot again!" says Burley.

"The window'll be gone then, and he'll reach in and grab me!"

The Tribute lunges down a straightaway, picking up speed, creatures still clinging and clutching. The sun is slightly higher now, flushing the earth with washes of white and gold. Trees fight back, slashing the land with shadows that seem to want to rip everything to shreds.

Up ahead, beyond a small field and dilapidated barn is the small, brush-shrouded intersection that connects this road to the one along which Kathy's house stands.

"He can't reach you if you kill him!" says Kathy.

Jack's hand trembles, he aims at the red-eyed creature at his window.

He fires. Another hole appears and the creature squeals and his red eyes spin. There is a blackened, smoking hole in his forehead. He gulps, shudders, then lets go of the mirror and is left behind on the road.

"Sam...!" Jack cries.

"He was your friend."

"Yes," Jack manages.

Then Kathy pounds on Burley's back. "Here! Turn! Get to my house! We'll get inside, call the authorities!"

"How we gonna get...?"

"Just turn!"

Burley nods, steers sharply to the right, almost missing the road, the end of the vehicle swinging wide and whacking the stop sign, the creature on the hood still clinging, the one on the luggage rack still dangling.

Jack aims the gun at the windshield and pulls the trigger. A blast of glass, but the bullet misses as the Tribute hits another pothole and his head snaps out of the way.

"You can't shoot worth shit!" says Burley.

"You can't drive worth shit!" says Jack.

Down the road now, bouncing, swirling, past broken fences and sheds and trailers. Past Penny Mustard's tar-shack house, where Yard Putcher is just now leaving, standing outside on the little cement walkway, adjusting his ball cap. He stares up as the Tribute drives past, removes his hat, scratches his head.

"Again!" says Kathy.

Jack aims the gun again, shoots, but hits it in the shoulder. The creature slams his forehead against the windshield as if taunting.

And there is Kathy's house, up on the right, the double-wide at the end of the long, rutted driveway.

"Here!" Kathy shouts.

Burley forces the Tribute off the road and onto the driveway, the car skidding, bouncing hard then harder in the ruts as it roars toward the house —thud, thud, THUD. The creature on the luggage rack is knocked loose. He rolls away behind the car. The one on the hood bounces, too, but remains stuck in place, foul facial fluids leaking, gumming up the glass like the remains of countless insects.

The Tribute rounds Hank's rusted truck, reaches the house,

and crashes into the deck, cracking a support beam. Burley slams it into reverse then stomps the breaks. This dislodges the creature, who slides off and strikes the ground on his back.

"Out!" orders Jack.

Kathy jams the box of bullets into her poncho pouch and heaves open her door as Jack opens his. They race out and up the deck steps to the sliding door. Her ankle screams but she tightens her jaw against the pain. She tugs the door, giving Puffster a swift kick to keep her from trotting out.

"Dad!" she shouts. There is no answer.

"Oh, damn!" says Jack.

Kathy looks across the deck to see what Jack is seeing.

Burley is still in the Tribute. The Bobby Boo creature is blocking Burley's door so the big man can't get out, scratching with ragged hands at the window, his one hideous eye blinking. Burley leans away, trying to slide his bulk over the seat to the open door but unable. His broken arm flops in its sling, and he weeps.

"Oh, fuck it, Burley!" Kathy says. "Jack, shoot the thing!"

Jack aims across the deck and fires, but the bullet strikes the deck flooring and misses the creature, who is now moving around the back of the car to the open passenger's side. Burley cries more loudly.

"Here, let me!" Kathy grabs the gun, which is heavier than she expected. She aims, fires, and the bullet strikes the car roof. She can see the other creature now, the smaller one with dark hair, up now and approaching on the driveway. He doesn't wobble as much as the other one. His dark hair catches the early morning sunlight, shattering the light into little bright fragments. He does not growl.

"We got to get closer to shoot them," says Jack.

"Then you do it!"

"I'm no good with a gun!"

"Neither am I!"

"You knew how to load it!"

"Haven't you ever watched TV? Shit, Jack!"

"How many bullets left?"

"I don't know. Two? One? Oh, screw this!" She darts out

onto the deck and props the gun on top of the railing. The creature has leaned into the car, grabbed Burley's broken arm, and is biting down through the sling. Burley kicks, struggles. His scream is so strained and high-pitched it is almost silent. Then the creature lets go of Burley's arm, moves his mouth as if to kiss the man, then takes a chunk from the side of Burley's thick neck.

"Aim for the head!" she tells herself, and points the gun, directing it at the creature's temple. She pulls the trigger. There is a soft click. The gun is empty.

"No!" she cries, and just at that moment Burley kicks the creature hard enough to send it shuffling back out of the car. Burley forces himself across the seat pulls the door shut with his good hand. Then he throws his head back and wails in terror and agony, his chewed, broken arm bleeding and trembling against his chest, his neck glistening red like the inside of a freshly filleted trout.

The Bobby Boo creature slaps at the car, and then notices Kathy on the deck. He angles his head. The shadows across his face make it look as if he is smiling.

Kathy scoots across the deck and stops in the doorway. She fumbles the box of bullets from her poncho pouch, but the box falls and the bullets clatter away across the deck. Most drop through the cracks and disappear into the grass below. She manages to hold on to one, which she punches into the chamber.

Bobby Boo starts up the deck steps.

"Shoot him!" cries Jack. Kathy aims. Puffster thumps up against Kathy's leg and the shot goes wild, striking the railing, chewing the wood.

Kathy curses, pushes the cat back inside the house, and slams the sliding door. She latches it and draws the vertical blinds just as the monster reaches it. She shrugs out of the poncho and throws it to the floor.

"Dad! Dad!"

No answer.

As Puffster stands meowing beside the door, Kathy and Jack shove the sofa and chairs against it then upend the heavy bookshelf, dumping years' worth of books onto the floor.

"He can't get in now, right?" Kathy asks Jack.

"I have no idea. I've never dealt with zombies before!"

Zombies? That's what they are? That's what Mom was? No! No fucking way!

Then Kathy glances over at the closed door off the living room—

Hank's bedroom. She takes a breath, steels herself, limps over, shuts her eyes.

If he's dead, I can't bear it. If he's gone, I can't bear it. Whatever reason he has not answered me, I can't bear it.

She reaches for the knob, turns it, pushes the door open.

Hank isn't there. The bed is unmade, but his boots are gone. So is his coat, which he usually hangs over the bedpost.

A note is on the nightstand, written on the back of the one she'd left earlier. She reads it with trembling hands.

"Dear Kathy,

Thank you for your note. I do worry about you, but I know you are strong, and you are smart. I know you will be all right. Do not stay here any longer. Go back to the beach and don't return to Beaver Dam or Black Rock Ridge. Maybe what happened will die out. Maybe not. But I want you safe. Please trust what I say. Please don't be hardheaded this time. Please.

I have loved you and will always love you. Know that, if you believe nothing else.

Dad."

Kathy goes back to the door and leans against the jamb, pressing her face to the sharp edge, feeling the sting, crushing the note in her hand. She hears Jack says, "You okay?" He's close behind.

"Okay?" she says into the wood. "Zombies are trying to kill us. My father's gone off to kill himself and probably already has. I can't get to him to find out either way. So am I okay? Oh, fuck, yeah."

Jack touches her shoulder, and she flinches, feels faint.

"Where do you think your father went?"

"To his church."

"Where is the church?"

"Half-mile from here, on the road to Beaver Dam."

"If we can get to it, and you have the keys, we can take that old truck out there."

"That old truck hasn't worked in years!"

"Can we make it if we run, then? If we wrap your ankle?"

"Maybe, I don't know! Oh!" She spins around, stares at the litter of books and papers on the living room floor. "We got to call the sheriff's office! They can get to the church before us! They can send help for us!"

"Will they believe...?"

"Shut up! What else are we supposed to do?" Tears spring, hot and unbidden and she digs them away.

"Of course, call," says Jack. "Sorry. I'm as scared as you are."

Kathy paws through the litter on the floor and finds the phone. She pushes the button for the dial tone. There is none.

"What the hell?"

The Bobby Boo zombie slams against the sliding door. Kathy drops the phone, snatches it back up again. Puffster arches her back at the commotion, then stares at Kathy, pissed she isn't getting let out when she wants to be let out.

"Damn it! He let the battery run down!"

"Isn't there another phone? Do you have a cell?"

"No!"

The zombie slams, pounds the glass on the door.

"Is there a keypad on the base unit?"

"No! We have cheap shit, okay? We're fucking poor, not like you guys out in California!"

"Okay, okay, let's think." Jack puts his hand on her shoulder. She twists out of his grasp.

"Stop touching me! I can't stand it!"

Jack blinks, shocked, then nods. "Fine, then. All right. I'm getting something for you to secure your ankle. Then, you can run, or hobble really fast, we can go out your back door, cut around the side and into the trees. I think we have a better chance of running from the zombies in the woods, since we have a better sense to watch the lay of the land. I've gotten away from them before. I can do it again."

Kathy nods, the sense of fear going soft now as numbness sets in.

Jack is gone and a moment later is back with an ace bandage from the bathroom. She winds it around her ankle and secures it with the clip.

Then the glass on the sliding door cracks. The vertical blinds shudder.

Puffster runs out of the living room and into Hank's bedroom. The Bobby Boo creature howls as if in victory and continues to pound. The glass cracks again, louder.

Kathy's hands go to her heart. "He's coming in!"

"Then let's move!"

They cross the living room and into the small laundry porch, which is piled high with clothes in plastic baskets and others on the floor and piled atop the washing machine. The box of detergent was on its side, with sparkling blue crystals spilled across the top of the dryer. The faucet over the laundry sink drips.

Hank's depression got the best of him. He never let things go like this! He can't be dead! Please, God, if you're God, don't let him be dead!

Jack turns the faucet, dips his head beneath the flow, and sucks in long gulps. He lifts his head. "Okay, now!"

Kathy grabs the door handle, throws her hip into it, and turns the deadbolt. She pulls the door open, which squeals loudly.

"He'll hear us! He'll come around back!" she says.

"No, he's coming through!" Jack hitches his finger back toward the living room, where the glass of the door is caving in now with a bright, tinkling sound and the zombie is shoving against the pile of furniture. His hands and arms are visible through the vertical blinds, groping, pushing.

The sofa scrapes on the living room floor as the zombie makes his way in.

Kathy and Jack hurry out through the rear door.

40

Armistead

He is even stronger now, in the light, away from Desper Hollow. His mind is clearer. He has followed the others and senses that soon he will know who he is.

Why he is.

He reaches the vehicle smashed against the deck of the house and he peers in. The one who had been driving sits on the front seat, his head hanging back, blood no longer flowing from the vicious wounds in his neck and arm, his eyes open but glazed over. Armistead opens the door, reaches in, and touches the man carefully. Yes, he is dead. Armistead hopes his death will be death, will remain death, but he suspects that isn't the way it will be. Because this man died by Bobby Boo's hands, or rather his bites, he will live again as Bobby Boo did. As the others at the trailer in Desper Hollow did, killed then living again because of bites.

As Armistead, himself, had died and then lived again.

He remembers now how that had happened. He'd gone to borrow a ladder and had stopped to help a wounded, distressed creature by the road. Why had he gone for a ladder? Who had asked him to do that? He cannot remember that. But he recalls the creature. Not big but wild-eyed, red-eyed. The creature had caught him on the wrist as he'd picked it up, chewed, bit deep before Armistead could knock it off against a tree, smashing its head and killing it. Then he'd stumbled, wandered dazed and lost, then faded.

I lost a lot of blood and I died.

Then I came awake again and I wandered and ended up in Desper Hollow.

Up on the deck, Bobby Boo smashes the glass of a sliding door, then shoves his way in. Bits of glass, still clinging to the frame, slash him as he goes, nearly severing his right hand. But still he goes.

The living ones are in the house.

They are in danger.

Armistead turns from the vehicle, starts for the steps.

The voice surrounds him, enfolds him, and stops him in his tracks.

Follow.

"Follow what?" He is surprised to realize that even his voice is stronger now, no longer a whisper, no longer raspy. "Follow who?"

Then he sees the couple dashing across the side yard, past a corral of squealing pigs and a pen of fluttering chickens, and into the shadows of the trees.

"But what of Bobby Boo? And what of the one in the car?"

Follow. You wanted to learn. You wanted to experience, to understand. Your task is at hand.

"Then I will come home?"

Yes. Then you will come home.

41

Jack Carroll

She limps visibly and sucks air through her teeth, but she is moving at a respectable clip, dodging low branches and hoisting herself over rocks and downed trees. He wants to reach out for her, to help her, but she is one of those damned determined people who must do it all on their own.

Like himself, to a degree.

He grins a small grin, and then is surprised he can grin. There are zombies behind them. They have nearly a half-mile to make off the road. How the hell can he smile?

She sees him grin.

She scoffs, pushes low branches aside, moves ahead of him. "So you came to Virginia for what, a vacation?" Her voice is edged with pain and fear.

"Something like that."

"You came to seek your fortune?"

"What?"

"Like Jack in the folktales. Jacks are always seeking their fortunes and end up in trouble."

"No shit."

He can see the road off to the left. A car passes by, rattling, belching exhaust. How much easier to be on the road. But if the zombies smell them, come after them, how much easier to beat them in a foot race through the woods.

Kathy's foot catches a vine, and she goes down on her face. She tries to push herself up, but the vine is thorny and has caught the leg of her jeans. Her hands are bleeding now. He reaches out his hand to her, she takes it, and he hauls her up. She immediately lets go.

"Let me carry you."

"No," she says. "Just run!"

They run. His heart thunders in his neck, his head, like a bass drum inside a tunnel. Loud, so loud.

So loud he doesn't at first hear the footsteps crashing through the brush behind them. Kathy hears them first.

"They're coming!"

He looks back but sees nothing, yet he recognizes the growlings, the awkward thrashings.

And it sounds like more than one.

This time, it sounds like three.

42
Kathy Shaw

She hears them only a second before Jack does, and they glance at each other with expressions of dread that comes with an expected terror. She knows she has slowed the two of them down, she can barely breathe with the pain in her ankle, and now the zombie—*zombies!*—are coming again.

Faster! You've got to move your ass!

But she can't move faster. She is sweating and aches, she is dizzy and terrified.

There is snarling, growling, howling back in the trees. There is stumbling, too, but they are keeping up. The zombies can smell them, clearly. Can hear them. Want them.

Then a squealing mingling with the snarls, not a human sound nor a dead-human sound, but animal. One of them snatched up a pig. One of the Shaw piglets, clearly snatched up by one of the zombies, making it a handy snack on-the-go.

Run! Move!

Jack hunches over as he moves, his face tight, his eyes trained ahead, the pulse in his neck visible. His features catch her by surprise.

They are handsome, stripped of anything but determination, fear, and compassion. She doesn't want to need him, but she does. She doesn't want him to carry her, to pick her up and take her to the church, but she does want it.

She shields a pine branch from her eyes, pushes through, her hair catching, yanking, tearing strands from her scalp. And there is the church yard, the rear of it with the graveyard and its granite and marble stones protruding like fingers of the dead reaching up toward the sun and the living.

"The church!" She looks at Jack and he nods. He holds out his hand.

She hesitates, takes it, and he runs with her through the dead and around to the front of the church where the arched red doors wait, closed against the cold fall air.

43
Armistead

He follows Bobby Boo and Burley, close on their heels, wanting with every fiber of his being to grab them and bring them down but still not quite fast enough, not quite strong enough.

Though his strength grows with each step, his speed increases.

Back at the house, Burley had pushed his way out of the car with unexpected power, knocking Armistead aside. Armistead had grabbed for him, but his grasp fell short, and Burley kicked him with a surprisingly well-aimed foot, driving Armistead down against the muddy driveway. Burley headed for the pen filled with pigs and piglets, licking his lips, the tendons flexing and shining through the hole in his neck, his broken arm swinging at an unnatural angle, free of the sling.

Bobby Boo emerged from the house, bits of glass embedded in his sides, moving out onto the deck, aware in his own dead way that the living had escaped. His head tipped backward to catch their scents and then quickly detecting them, he headed off into the woods, passing Burley who had snatched up a squirming brown pig and had taken a bite out of its buttocks. Bobby Boo snatched up a piglet that had squeezed through the pen fence and was running in mad circles, and he immediately bit off one of the animal's front legs.. Then the two carried their squealing food into the trees.

Armistead regained his footing, took a deep breath, and then realized that he was breathing. Breathing. That was what the living did. What a strange sensation. Was he reverting to a living thing? A living creature no longer like those he followed?

"Am I going to live, then?"

You are going to follow. You wanted to learn. You wanted to know. Your task awaits you.

"What is my task? What is my lesson?"

The voice said nothing.

Armistead followed the others into the trees.

And he follows now, determined, breathing hard, his body seeming more alive with each step. Certain that soon, he will indeed know all he wants to know.

44

Kathy Shaw

"**D**ad!"
Kathy stumbles to the red church doors, pounds on them with trembling, bleeding fists. She tries the handle, but the doors are locked. It feels as if even her heart pounds on the door, pleading, begging.

"Dad! Please! Open the doors!"

She presses her ear to the wood, listens, hoping to hear his voice, or at least movement within. But there is only silence.

"Jack!" She turns to him, grabs his coat. She knows he can't open the door, he isn't magic, but he is a friend, he cares. The vulnerability in her soul is almost as terrifying as the zombies who stalk them, but maybe there is something in caring, in needing and sharing that holds a power she's never fully understood. "Jack!"

Jack grabs the back of her hand, presses it to his chest, and nods.

"We'll get in. It will be all right. Is there another door?"

"No!"

"And the windows are too high to crawl through."

"Yes!"

"You stay here by the door. I'll get us in somehow!"

"But!"

"Don't walk any more. I'll get us in!"

And he leaves her on her knees, leaning against the arched red doors.

He disappears around the far side of the church.

She can hear the zombies coming from back behind the

church, sloshing into the grass of the graveyard. Snarls, growls, the sounds of wet jabbering. No more pig squeals. It is dead now. Consumed.

A Beaver Dam truck rumbles past on the road, heading toward town.

Kathy waves her arms as best she can, and she cries out for help, but exhaustion has stolen most of her voice. The men in the truck merely wave back and honk the horn.

"Dad, Dad." She covered her eyes. "Dad, what did you have to do with this? How could anything you have done have brought something like this to life?"

45
Jack Carroll

The only windows in the church are on the two sides and the rear, all three of them a good seven feet off the ground.

Jack has to get inside; he has to get Kathy inside. Perhaps her father is dead, perhaps he has killed himself, perhaps he is swinging from a rafter or lying with a bullet in his head, but if so then at least he is dead and not a living dead. That is better. That would be easier for Kathy to handle than him as a zombie.

Though her mother was living dead. She saw that. How dreadful. More dreadful, perhaps, than your friend coming back to life with red eyes and teeth hungry for living flesh, and then having to kill him all over again.

Or maybe not.

He sees the zombies at the rear of the churchyard. Bobby Boo, Burley, who was able to get from the car and join the hunt. Stead behind them, moving almost like a ghastly shepherd driving his evil, soulless sheep forward.

Then Jack spies a wrought iron bench at the edge of the graveyard. It would give him the height he needs to break through a window into the church. He rushes over and tugs on it, but it is brutally heavy. He has very little strength left, but what is there must suffice. What is there has to be enough. He tugs again, keeping his eye trained on the zombies, who have seen him and are coming through the gravestones.

Digging in with his heels and leaning back with all his weight, he frees the bench from years' worth of settling, then drags it, thumping and resisting, to the side of the church.

He works it flush against the siding as the zombies approach, twenty feet now, fifteen feet. Sunlight flashes off the window glass. Sparrows, nesting in the eaves over the window, startle away in a burst of feathers and cries.

Bobby Boo shuffles up first. He is in worse shape than even fifteen minutes ago. Great gouges are in his body from his trip through the sliding glass door. Glass is embedded in his flesh. Most of the skin of his face is rubbed away, revealing the skull beneath. He reaches out for Jack's leg as Jack tries to jump up onto the bench.

Jack leaps down and away, turns, faces the zombie.

You have to kill them in the head, Kathy had said. But he has no gun, no weapon. He steps back again, again, and then sees, leaning against a small, barren brush near the church—a scythe. Long handle. Sharp, curved blade.

Yes!

Jack darts to the brush, gathers up the scythe. It is awkward in his hands, but he'll work with awkward. This is one kick-ass weapon, and he has some killing to do!

Bobby Boo turns on his heel, following Jack. Right behind him is Burley, his mouth covered in sticky blood and hair and a curly tail and bits of brain matter. What had been a pig.

"Nothing personal!" says Jack as he lifts the scythe over his shoulder, hunches into it, and arcs it out and around. The blade catches Bobby Boo in the side of the head and pierces it with a satisfying crunch. Bobby Boo gurgles, drops to his knees, and then flops over on his face.

"Yee-hah!" cries Jack. He slams his foot against Bobby Boo's head, wrenches the scythe free just in time to swing it up and around at Burley's face, but it comes short and whistles past, throwing Jack off balance with its weight and he hits the ground.

Burley leans down and lashes out, his hand grabbing hold of Jack's foot. Jack yanks it free, rolls over and up onto his feet, pulling the scythe with him.

"This is for Sam!" he cries. "This is for Kathy's mother!"

He swings the scythe, his shoulders on fire with exhaustion and rage, and the tip of the blade crashes into Burley's face, right above his nose.

Burley shudders, looks at Jack then tries to claw the metal out of his head.

But his slashing fingers weaken. He sputters foul spittle from his mouth and through the hole in his neck.

He falls backward, crossing over the body of Bobby Boo, which is already attracting insects.

"One more!" snarls Jack as Stead approaches. The zombie's hands reach out, and as strange as it is, they seem less mangled in the daylight.

His flesh more appears more whole, though his eyes stare with the same hot red as the others. Jack remembers Desper Hollow, the trailer, the metal gate in front of the bedroom door. Stead pulling Bobby Boo away, Stead reaching out through the bars. Seeking something? But what?

It doesn't matter, he's a zombie!

Jack tugs on the scythe, but it's stuck tight in the bone. He screams, and pulls, but it does not come free. Stead steps closer, and says, "No, you do not need to do this."

"The fuck I don't!"

There is a large rock beside his foot. With a shout of triumph, he scoops it up, raises it, and brings it down with all possible force against Stead's skull. Stead's red eyes snap shut. He stumbles, collapses, groans into the ground. One arm, still outstretched, twitches in the dead grass.

Then it stops. There is silence. Except for the distant sound of frustrated sparrows, waiting in the trees to return to their nests in the eaves.

"Yes! Oh, God, yes!" cries Jack, his body shot through with more jagged energy than he's ever felt in his life. Renewed! Rejuvenated! A conqueror! He jumps on the bench, clutching the stone, and smashes it into the window glass. He knocks bits from around the sill, and then climbs into the church. He lowers himself down to the floor, looks around.

He licks his dry lips.

"Mr. Shaw?"

No answer.

He steps along one of the benches, watching the floor.

"Mr. Shaw?"

No answer.

Jack goes to the front door, unlocks it, and pulls Kathy inside.

46
Kathy Shaw

Jack pulls her into the church by her hands, and eases the door shut behind her. Then he sits on the floor and gathers her up in his arms and holds her. Holds her without a word.

She tenses at first, and then lets the warmth of his arms move around her, enfold her. She is beyond crying now. There are no tears left. There is only weariness. Only numbness.

"They're dead," Jack says into her hair. "I got them all. Like Jack and the Three Giants. Remember that story?"

She shakes her head. She really doesn't. All she remembers is Jack and the Beanstalk.

"You got them?" she whispers.

"Yes. In the heads."

"Dead?"

"All three."

Then Kathy shudders, and she sits up and looks down the length of the church. "My father?"

"I don't know. He might not be here, I didn't…"

Kathy forces herself up, holding to the nearest bench.

"Dad? Is he dead, Jack?

"I don't know, I honestly don't."

"Tell me the truth!"

"I don't know!"

"Dad?" Kathy moves up the aisle on her swollen ankle, only vaguely aware of the pain now. Before her is the altar where her father preaches each Sunday, telling his congregation about love and compassion and self-sacrifice and trust and faith. "Dad! You better be in here! I'm tired of looking! You better not be dead!"

There is no answer.

"I'm tired of being scared! I can't be scared anymore! Do you hear me? Do you hear me?"

There is a rustling behind the altar. A barely audible sigh.

"Dad!"

Kathy pushes her way forward, and then Jack is beside her, helping her, moving her toward the altar. They circle around it, look down.

On the floor is Hank Shaw. He sits cross-legged, staring at a knife in his hand. A knife he'd found under Kathy's bed. He looks dreadful, like the living dead. Like a zombie. Only when he turns his face up to look at Kathy, his eyes aren't red.

He speaks slowly. "Kathy, I couldn't do it. What can I do to make right what I've done? I thought this would be it. But what sin, to take a life when I'm not the one who created it?"

"Dad."

"So I'm boxed in. I can't make it right, I can't make it better, and there is nothing I can offer that will pay the debt."

"Dad, it's all done. It's taken care of."

Hank frowns, looks at Jack. "Who are you?"

"Jack the Zombie Killer."

Hank's lip hitches. He looks back at the knife. "I prayed for help to come. None came."

"Dad, get up. Talk to me face to face. Tell me about Granny Mustard. Tell me what you did. I know we're related in some way. But you have to tell me everything. I'm your daughter. I deserve at least that."

Hank shakes his head but gets up and walks to the front row bench, where he sits heavily, still holding the knife.

"Let me have that," says Kathy.

Hank passes it over and she puts it into her coat pocket. She sits beside her father, and Jack beside her. Jack puts his hand on hers and she doesn't shrug it off. This time, it feels right.

"Tell me, Dad, please?" she says. "What is there to lose now?"

And so he does.

"The Mustards and Shaws are both from Scotland," he says, looking at his hands, then at the floor, then at his daughter.

"The Mustard family was small and fell under the protection of the Shaw clan. There was trouble with the Mustards from way back. As well as the Shaws treated them—like their own, as if they were brothers and sisters—there were several Mustards in each generation that resented the fact that they were indebted to the Shaws. It's easy to understand. No one wants to feel he is controlled by another, even if it's an illusion."

"No," says Kathy.

"There was a large volume in our family. A book of chants, of spells that had been passed down orally for thousands of years in a language long dead, and then at last put down on paper, bound together, and hidden away so no one would ever have to speak them again."

"What kind of spells?"

"A variety. Spells against enemies. Spells to curse with illness or death. Spells for immortality. Such a cold book, Kathy. So cold to the touch. Like ice."

Kathy glances at Jack. She knows he must be thinking her father is insane, but nothing can match insane compared to the past twenty-four hours. Jack nods encouragingly and gives her hand a squeeze.

"There were potions in the back, recipes meant to accompany some of the spells," says Hank. "Liquids, potions meant to be consumed or in an anointing, a baptism of sorts."

"Like... moonshine?" asks Kathy.

Hank chuckles without humor. "Some distilled liquids, yes." He rubs his chin, shakes his head. His dark eyes darken even more. "Liam Shaw and his family came to Virginia in 1703. Settled on Black Rock Ridge, farmed the stony soil. He was the only one of our clan to leave the homeland, but he had a good reason. He'd been entrusted to bring the book with him, to never let it fall into the hands of the angry, disgruntled Mustards who knew about it and wanted it. Young Mustard sons who wanted the power it promised. There'd been fights in which members of both families were killed. It was best to get the book away, so it could no longer be a temptation. For either side."

"Oh."

"Joseph Mustard was a trusted friend who considered the

Shaws family as much as his own. He brought his wife and son to Virginia on the same ship as Liam. He set up his homestead next to Liam's. But Joseph didn't realize that his teenaged son, always a quiet boy, had found out that the book of spells had come to America. He secretly begged Liam's son to let him have a look and tore part of a page from the back and sneaked it home. It was part of a recipe for a distilled liquid that would give immortality to anyone anointed with it."

"Part of a recipe?"

Hank nods. "Clearly that paper was passed down through the Mustard family. Most probably had no concern about it, too busy or too doubtful. Until Granny Mustard got hold of us. She believed it. And she knew the book was in our family. She knew that I had it."

Kathy draws back. "You've had that all this time? In our house? That… that evil book? Why didn't you just burn it?"

"It was said that burning it would release all the evil within at once. And it was safe, Kathy. Your mother never knew about it. But then…"

Hank clenches one fist inside the other and now he speaks through his teeth. "But then one morning, when Annie was pregnant with you, she went on a walk. She wasn't paying attention and ended up on Mustard land. Granny's son, Pauly, caught her and took her to Granny's cabin. Granny sent a note to me… It said…" Hank looks at the ceiling, at the altar, then back at the floor. "The note said that if I wanted my wife and unborn child back alive, I would give her the book."

"Damn. That's some kind of fucked-up fairy tale," says Jack.

"It's some kind of terrible truth," says Hank. "I could protect the world from the scourges in the book and lose my family or offer the book into the hands of an old woman who wanted to live forever and have my family back. I chose to have you back."

"Of course. Thank you for saving us." Kathy swallows hard, and she reaches up to touch her father's face. It is fevered with guilt.

"Granny Mustard didn't have the entire recipe, so for years she's been experimenting. Seems she finally found a combination of ingredients that brought a kind of immortality.

But it was a twisted one. A living death. When I saw the horrific red-eyed dog that killed Annie and then saw Annie herself with red eyes, hungry for flesh, dead but alive, I knew that Granny had accomplished something. Not what she'd wanted, exactly, but something. The evil was released, set out in the world."

She lowers her hand. "Dad, it's not your fault."

"I gave her the book."

"It's Granny's fault. It's the fault of whoever made the chants in the first place, way back when."

"It's my family's fault for ever writing them down."

"So where does blame really begin, Dad? And now it's done and over, so why does it even matter?"

"It matters because Annie is dead. And others may well be dead, too."

"We got the others," says Jack.

Hank stands, walks to the altar, picks up the purple cloth. "God never sent help. I was never forgiven. I pleaded, I begged. He heard nothing."

He tears the cloth apart and throws the pieces to the floor.

And then the front door opens, and a zombie walks in.

47

Armistead

He awakens in a daze, staring up at the peaceful blue sky and the white clouds that drift across it like threads of unspoiled cotton. Sparrows flit past, moving from trees to the eaves of the church beside which he lies. Bits of feathery seeds and crumbs of colorful leaves spin by in a breeze. He stares, confused but untroubled, until the voice says, *The time has come.*

The voice is peaceful, certain, and comforting.

Armistead pushes himself to his feet, staggers a moment, and then looks at the ground. There are two bodies there. Dead and empty. Wholly empty.

And he remembers them. Bobby Boo. Burley. Dead then living dead now dead again. Gone from this earth at last.

Armistead takes a powerful, invigorating breath. "Where do I go?"

Follow inside. There you will complete your task. And you will learn what you wanted to know.

Armistead moves around the church to the front doors. They are painted red like a sunset, like a cardinal, like an apple red on a tree branch.

Follow.

He opens the door and steps inside.

There are three people at the front of the church. Two men and one woman. They stand immediately from the bench on which they sit and turn to stare at him. He knows the young man and woman. They are the ones he has been following ever since Desper Hollow. But the older man... he is familiar, but he isn't sure why. Then he recalls. The preacher.

The man Armistead had come to help long ago. Back in the summer.

The man Armistead had been sent to help.

Do you remember now, Armistead?

Armistead whispers, "Yes. I do. I helped him clean the churchyard, fix the roof, paint the sign. I talked with him and became his friend, but my task wasn't completed."

Do you know now? Do you recall the reason you came here?

"Yes."

Then the young man shouts, "No! That's wrong! I killed you! I bashed your brain in! You can't be alive!" He grabs for a large stone on the floor, the one he'd struck Armistead with outside.

The young woman screams, "You didn't hit him hard enough, Jack! You have to hit him harder!"

The older man stares, his arms to his side, as if thinking Armistead is there to destroy him, to eat him. Awaiting his fate.

The young man rushes down the aisle with the stone, but Armistead holds up his hands and says, "Sanctuary."

The older man breaks out of his trance and cries, "No! Stop! Don't kill him!"

The young man says, "Oh, fuck yeah, I will!" He reaches Armistead.

Armistead steps out of the way, clearly more quickly than the young man expected, for he gasps and then curses.

The older man runs to them, stopping short, grabbing the young man's arm and shaking the stone out of it. "I said no! This is a place of sanctuary. Anyone who comes in this place shall not be harmed. It's been that way since I built the church. I must stay true to its purpose!"

"He's a fucking zombie, Hank! Look at those red eyes! Tell me they don't look like your wife's!"

The young woman is hurrying to catch up now, and she stares at Armistead, her eyes narrowed, her mouth open in shock, terror, and wonder.

"Not anymore, Jack," she says, pointing. "Look now."

"What?" Jack looks at Armistead. "What the hell is this? His eyes are green."

Tell them, Armistead. Tell them why you've come.

"I was sent," Armistead says simply, quietly. "I was sent because Hank prayed for help. For forgiveness. I was sent to tell him, to tell you, Hank, that you are certainly forgiven."

Hank puts his hands to his heart. "No, that is impossible. Who are you?"

"A messenger."

"Oh, my God." Hank slides down onto the edge of a bench, staring.

The young woman and young man look at Hank, at each other, and then at Armistead.

"I came here to visit with you, to get to know you, but my task was delayed, sidetracked. I was caught up in the evil that had been set loose. But I'm here once more, Hank. Your prayers are answered. You are, indeed, forgiven."

"Why..." begins the young woman. "If you are... that... what you say you are, why didn't you stop the bad things from happening?"

"That wasn't my task. Such things are for you to stop, to change, to alter. You set things in motion and must deal with them. But you have the power for good or evil. You have all you need to make things right. Forgiveness is a good place to begin."

Hank smiles a sudden astonished, broken, grateful smile. Then he bows his head over his knees. His hands tremble. The young woman and man reach for each other, watching Armistead, amazement reflected in their faces.

Armistead feels his body altering even more now, his strength growing, his breathing easing, the sense of being weighted down lightening. Warmth surrounds him like great arms. Before his eyes the church and those within it begin to shimmer.

The voice speaks gently. *You have done your task well.*

Armistead whispers, "Thank you."

You learned what you wanted to learn. You learned of human suffering. You learned of the depths of human pain and fear. You witnessed human resolve and courage and sacrifice.

"Yes."

Are you satisfied?

"Yes."

Come home, Armistead.

"Thank you."

Come home.

He closes his eyes, and the earth falls away and the blue and the warm enfolds him.

48
Kathy Shaw

She stands with her arm linked in Jack's watching as the zombie... the man... the messenger shifts, morphs into something beautiful, bright, and intangible, then fades away to nothing.

She gazes at the empty space where he had been, feeling her heart pounding, but this time from awe and not fear, from amazement and not terror. She doesn't know what to say. She knows no one else in the church knows what to say. They wait silently, wondering in their own minds, listening, watching to see if there is more.

But it is done. It is over.

Kathy slides her arm from Jack's and goes to her father. She puts her hand on his shoulder and he reaches for it, holds it. "I love you, Kathy," he says without looking up.

"I love you, Dad," she says.

"So we start over, now."

"So we do."

Jack watches, then says, "There are bodies in the church yard. There is one back on the road. What should do about that? How can we explain to the authorities what happened?"

"We'll tell them the truth," says Hank.

"They'll lock us up for being crazy."

"Maybe. I hope not."

"Or they'll lock us—me—up for murder. I can't face that. I have to get home to California. I have to be back where I can think things through, decide what really happened here."

"You know what really happened," says Kathy.

Jack sighs. "Okay, I guess I do. But that won't play out in the real world. I'm going out to at least cover the bodies until we decide our next move. Hank, you got any tarps? Cloth?"

"Just the altar cloth."

They take the two halves of the cloth out to the side yard, to find that the bodies of Burley and Bobby Boo are already degraded to a near unrecognizable state. The bones and flesh are drying, flaking, powdering into the soil. The hair is blowing away to mingle with the dead grasses over in the graveyard.

"Guess it won't be long before they're gone completely," says Kathy.

"Looks like we won't have to explain anything after all." She unbuttons her coat and opens it. The day is warming more than she would have guessed this late in the year. "I feel sorry in a way for Granny Mustard. Such hopes. Such desperate hopes."

Jack shakes his head. "No sorrow from this man." Then he shrugs. "Okay, if you want me to, I'll feel a little sorry. Though it's damn hard."

Kathy smiles. "I know it is." She puts her head against Jack's chest and she feels him smile back.

"I'll pray for her soul," says Hank.

"Thanks, Dad."

"I'll pray for all of us."

"Thank you."

They draw together, creating a circle in the dead grasses outside the New Light Church of the Creator.

A circle of three, three small giants who withstood terror, three souls who united in need, three hearts drawn close now in love.

49
Randy

Randy sniffs the ground, picking up scents of squirrels, chipmunks, and skunks, bright, fascinating scents that get his nostrils quivering and his tail wagging. His mistress has let him out of the house to go take a dump, pee, stretch his legs, bark and get it out of his system.

He isn't a hunting dog like most in and around Black Rock Ridge.

He's part hound but mostly setter. He's old, but of course doesn't know how old. His legs ache sometimes but not enough to keep him from investigating any and every wriggling, squiggling, crawling thing in the trees around his home.

There is something odd there, lying in the leaves. It is a small creature with a rounded body, little hair, folded ears and a curled tail.

It is missing all its legs, though, and half of its back is shredded away.

The intestines hang out in slick, ropy coils. It has bright red eyes and it stares at Randy as he comes up to have a closer sniff.

Randy nudges the thing, then tries to pick it up, but the thing twists its head and bites deep into Randy's throat. Randy howls and tries to shake the thing free, but it holds on tightly, the little razor-sharp teeth puncturing the throat. At last, it is thrown free. It strikes the ground and lies there, unable to move, but watching Randy its piggish red eyes.

Slowly, stumbling, Randy makes his way back to the tar-shack house, knowing he is dying but wanting to do so in the warmth of home. Wanting to be with his mistress, Penny, when his life bleeds out.

She hears him paw weakly on the door, and she opens it to find him trembling, on the verge of collapsing. She takes him up in her arms, carries him to the fireplace, holds him until he dies. Until he goes still.

Until he opens his bright red eyes.

About the Author

Elizabeth Massie is a Scribe- and Bram Stoker Award-winning author of numerous novels and short stories, primarily in the horror and historical genres. She writes for adults as well as young adults and middle grade readers. Her novels, novelizations, and collections include *Sineater, Desper Hollow, Homeplace, Wire Mesh Mothers, Hell Gate, Madame Cruller's Couch and Other Dark and Bizarre Tales, It Watching, Sundown, Afraid, The Tudors: King Takes Queen, Versailles, Buffy the Vampire Slayer: Power of Persuasion*, the Young Founders series, the Ameri-Scares series – which was optioned by Warner Horizon – and more.

A former middle school science teacher, she now presents creative writing workshops to students in grades 3-12 as well as at the college level. She lives in the beautiful Shenandoah Valley with her mega-talented illustrator husband, Cortney Skinner. In her spare time, she likes to geocache, travel, knit, read, and sip a chai at Starbucks.

Curious about other Crossroad Press books?
Stop by our site:
http://store.crossroadpress.com
We offer quality writing
in digital, audio, and print formats.

www.ingramcontent.com/pod-product-compliance
Lightning Source LLC
Chambersburg PA
CBHW030250200626
46816CB00002BA/590